Kelly Elliott is a *New York Times* and *USA Today* bestselling contemporary romance author. Since finishing her bestselling Wanted series, Kelly continues to spread her wings while remaining true to her roots and giving readers stories rich with hot protective men, strong women and beautiful surroundings.

Kelly has been passionate about writing since she was fifteen. After years of filling journals with stories, she finally followed her dream and published her first novel, *Wanted*, in November of 2012.

Kelly lives in central Texas with her husband, daughter, and two pups. When she's not writing, Kelly enjoys reading and spending time with her family. She is down to earth and very in touch with her readers, both on social media and at signings.

Visit Kelly Elliott online:

www.kellyelliottauthor.com
www.twitter.com/author_kelly
www.facebook.com/KellyElliottAuthor/

LONDON

D0620638

THE LOVE WANTED IN TEXAS SERIES

Without You
Saving You
Holding You
Finding You
Chasing You
Loving You

Chasing You

Love Wanted in Texas
Book Five

Kelly Elliott

piatkus

PIATKUS

First published in Great Britain in 2016 by Piatkus
This paperback edition published in 2016 by Piatkus

1 3 5 7 9 10 8 6 4 2

Copyright © Kelly Elliott 2016

The moral right of the author has been asserted.

*All characters and events in this publication, other than those
clearly in the public domain, are fictitious and any resemblance
to real persons, living or dead, is purely coincidental.*

All rights reserved.
No part of this publication may be reproduced, stored in a
retrieval system, or transmitted in any form or by any means, without
the prior permission in writing of the publisher, nor be otherwise circulated
in any form of binding or cover other than that in which it is published
and without a similar condition including this condition
being imposed on the subsequent purchaser.

A CIP catalogue record for this book
is available from the British Library.

ISBN 978-0-349-41350-1

Printed and bound in Great Britain by
Clays Ltd, St Ives plc

Papers used by Piatkus are from well-managed forests
and other responsible sources.

MIX
Paper from
responsible sources
FSC® C104740

Piatkus
An imprint of
Little, Brown Book Group
Carmelite House
50 Victoria Embankment
London EC4Y 0DZ

An Hachette UK Company
www.hachette.co.uk

www.piatkus.co.uk

WANTED
family tree

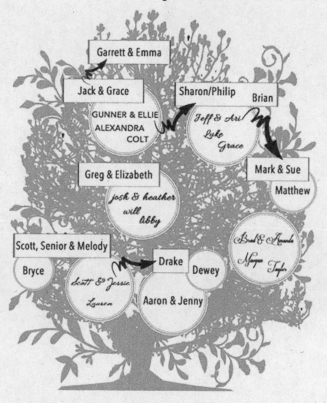

PROLOGUE

Meagan

IT HAPPENED AGAIN yesterday evening. Another knock on my dorm room door. Another guy asking about a blowjob. *What in the fuck is going on?*

Ever since James asked me to the frat party, things had been different. I couldn't put my finger on it, but even he was acting strange.

As I made my way to class, I tried to work it out in my head. Three girls approached me with smiles on their faces. I'd recognized the one girl from the party the other night. James told me it was his ex, Claire.

All three girls stopped and waited for me to get closer. "If it isn't the blowjob queen herself," Claire said with an evil grin.

I stopped directly in front of them. "Excuse me?"

With a smirk, Claire slowly shook her head as she looked me over. "Please, like you really think someone like *you* could catch James' attention."

So this is about James? With a smile, I tilted my head and said, "I see what's going on here. The jealous ex doesn't like the guy she can't get over showing up with another girl on his arm?" This wasn't the first time I'd dealt with jealous bitches. Although, I had hoped all this shit would stop when we graduated high school.

An evil look spread across Claire's face as she took a step closer to me. "You don't want to fuck with me, sweetheart. I will make your life a living hell."

Little did I know my next words would cause four years of relentless bullying and endless rumors.

With a wink, I laughed and said, "Bring it on."

Chapter
ONE

Meagan

GRAYSON RUBBED HIS thumb across my hand while we drove in silence. *What am I doing?*

I turned and looked out the window as I slowly took in a deep breath before exhaling it ever so slowly. I loved spending time with Grayson. Even when we weren't between the sheets, I had fun with him.

"What are you thinking about, Meg?" Grayson asked as he squeezed my hand gently.

With a turn of my head, I took in Grayson's features. His strong jaw, beautiful face, and hair that I wanted to just run my fingers through. Never mind his rock-solid body. It never bothered me that Grayson worked as a stripper to make his way through college. I even fantasized about him doing a little strip show for me, not that I would ever admit that to him. I loved giving him hell about his stint as a male dancer.

Clearing my thoughts, I forced a smile. "Nothing."

"Liar. Have you forgotten I'm trained to be able to tell when someone is lying?"

With a chuckle, I shook my head and stared out the front window. "What are we doing, Gray?"

Lifting my hand to his lips, he kissed the back of it as my stomach clenched. Ugh. Why did he have to do little things like that? It made me feel all silly inside.

"We're going back to my hotel to fuck like rabbits."

Ah. There is the Grayson I know.

My eyes closed and I turned my head.

"Hey, Meg, I'm kidding. I wouldn't care if you wanted to sit and talk all night. I just want to be with you."

Anger built up inside as I thought about overhearing him earlier today talking to his cousin Noah about Claire.

My head snapped back to him. "What about the new girl at work?"

Grayson turned and looked at me with a shocked expression. "What?"

"Listen, I've changed my mind. Let's just drop you off at your hotel and then I'm headed to my parents'."

Grayson immediately pulled the car over and put it in park. "Meg, what just happened here?"

With a halfhearted laugh, I shook my head. *I can't believe this. I cannot believe that Claire Watkins is coming back into my world and turning it upside down again.*

"I overheard you talking to Noah." I glanced over to Grayson and smirked. "Seems to me you have a date waiting back in Durango for you."

Grayson's mouth dropped open as his eyes searched my face. "Claire?"

Her name off his lips caused my skin to crawl as memory after memory of guys walking up to me in college, asking me to give them the Meagan Special, hit me full force.

Swallowing hard, I pushed the car door open and got

out. My hands went to my knees as I dragged air in.

Damn it! This hadn't happened to me in a few months. *Breathe in, Meg.* Dragging a deep breath of air through my nose, I slowly blew it out.

I jumped when Grayson's hands grabbed my shoulders. "Baby, talk to me. What's going on?"

Tears built in my eyes as I quickly got my emotions under control. I loved when he called me baby or babe. It did crazy things to me.

With a quick spin around to face him, I tried to plaster on a smile. The moment his concerned eyes met mine, something in me broke. The shock of seeing him with Claire that day and the idea of my past coming back to haunt me hit me like a brick wall. My smile faded and I lost the battle I had been fighting. Tears pooled in my eyes as I felt the first one fall.

I'd never in my life cried in front of a guy, anyone for that matter. I'd gotten so good at hiding my emotions; I was a pro at keeping myself strong.

Grayson's eyes widened in disbelief as he watched the tear slowly move down my face.

"Meg," he whispered as his thumb wiped the tear away.

I quickly snapped out of it and pushed him away. Wiping my tears away, I let out a curt laugh. "Listen, if you're dating this girl Claire, fine. Just don't think I'm going to be your little side hook-up, asshole."

Grayson's eyes pinched together. "You really think of me like that? That's what you think we have here, Meg?"

Now I felt the anger coming back. *Yes. This is the emotion I need.*

My hands folded across my chest. "You tell me, Gray. One minute you're talking to Noah about a date you've got with the new girl at work you're attracted to, and then next you're bringing me to your hotel to, what was it you said?" I lifted my eyes up like I was thinking. With a snap

5

of my fingers, I pointed to him. "That's right. We were going to fuck like rabbits."

Grayson slowly shook his head. "I was kidding."

My head tilted as I stared at him. "About what, Gray? Fucking like rabbits or the new hot girl at work you're taking out to celebrate the new year?"

Grayson closed his eyes and pushed out a frustrated breath as his hands combed through his hair. "Fucking hell, Meg. I don't understand you. What is it you want from me? I've tried like hell to have some sort of relationship with you and you push me away. I've been chasing after you for months, only to get mixed signals. So you tell me, what is it you want out of this?"

I swallowed hard and looked away. A part of me desperately wanted to open my heart fully to Grayson. Could I risk being hurt by him if things didn't work out? Between my father's expectations of me and the fact that Grayson could easily rip my heart out, I wasn't sure I was willing to take the chance. "You wouldn't understand if I told you."

Grayson grabbed onto my shoulders again and gave me a slight shake. "Talk to me, Meg. How do you know I wouldn't understand? I want to understand. I *want* to be with you. Stop pushing me away."

Grayson's phone rang. *Who in the hell would be calling him this late?*

Without taking his eyes off of me, he reached into his pocket and pulled out his phone. "This is Gray."

His face drained and my heart dropped. With Grayson being a detective now, I couldn't imagine the phone calls he got.

"Oh hey. Um, yeah, happy New Year to you too."

Grayson turned away from me and walked back toward my rental car. "Yeah, no I was still up."

Seriously? He's going to chat with someone now?

When he lowered his voice, curiosity got the best of me and I moved closer to him.

"Listen, Claire, I'm in the middle of talking with a friend, can I call you back tomorrow afternoon?"

I stopped walking the moment I heard her name.

Friend? So I'm a friend now?

My hands balled up into fists as I watched Grayson walk a little ways away from me.

Fuck. This.

Heading around the front of the car, I got into the driver's seat, put it in drive and took off. Never once looking back at the asshole on the side of the road.

~ ❦ ~

Two weeks had passed since New Year's Eve. Grayson had called me almost every single day. The first week he left messages, now he just hung up.

I took a sip of my coffee and glanced around. My favorite spot to be on Saturdays was Durango Coffee Company on Main. I'd sit outside if the weather was nice and read while eating an omelet and sipping on my favorite coffee . . . Nitro Cold Coffee.

With a smile, I settled back into my story. Two minutes later, my phone buzzed. With a quick glance down, I saw Grayson's name flash across. My stomach dropped as I sat up straighter.

I swiped my finger across the screen and pulled up his message.

> *Gray: Why won't you return my calls? I should be pissed that you left me on the side of the road in the middle of the night.*

I rolled my eyes and set my phone down. I tried to get back into my story when it pinged again.

> *Gray: Are you not even going to say you're sorry?*

My mouth dropped open. *How dare he!*

Me: Fuck you, Gray. You took a fucking phone call from that bitch while pretending to care about what was going on in my world. So imagine me giving you the finger right now asshole. That is your apology.

I set my phone down and gave it the finger as I whispered, "Asshole."

Gray: That mouth. What would the kids you work with think of that mouth of yours? I'm disappointed.

I'm pretty sure my eyes popped out of my head.
What.
A.
Jerk.

Me: You know NOTHING about what I do or me for that matter! I hate you.

Tears filled my eyes as I dropped my phone on the table and started giving it the double finger. My perfect morning just went south.

Chapter
TWO

Grayson

WITH MY LIPS pressed together, I held back my smile as I watched Meagan shoot her phone the finger. She looked pissed.

Good.

I was still a little butt hurt from her pulling off and leaving me on the side of the road stranded, although I deserved it. The moment I realized it was Claire, I should have ended the call. Total dick move on my part that I owned up to and called Meagan and left a message to apologize.

I had been racking my brain for the last two weeks trying to figure out how in the hell Meagan even knew about Claire. I didn't tell Noah what her name was, so how did Meagan know?

Once Meagan settled down and buried her nose in her Kindle again, I headed her way. Kam glanced up and saw me walking toward the coffee shop. I held up my hand and gave her a thumbs-up as I pointed to Meagan's table. I'd been here enough times for her to know what my regular drink was.

With a quick turn, Kam walked back into the coffee shop as I stopped and stared down at Meagan.

"How was the omelet?"

Meagan's head snapped up as she glared at me. I placed my hand on the back of the chair and stood there while her eyes quickly did a once over. I didn't normally work on Saturdays, but I'd been working all night with Derrick on a case. I knew with the weather being unseasonably warm, Meagan would be here this morning, so I decided to end this silent treatment of hers once and for all.

She swallowed hard and then straightened her shoulders as she narrowed her eyes at me. "How did you know I was here?"

I pulled the chair out and sat down as I loosened my tie. Meagan's eyes flickered for one moment as I pictured her dirty little mind going into a fantasy.

"I'm a detective, Meg. It's my job to know things."

She let out a curt laugh and rolled her eyes. "I'd hope you were tracking down the bad people and not what I've had for breakfast." Her mouth dropped open and she tapped her finger on the side of her mouth. "Oh wait. You're sleeping with one of them, so . . ."

Her voice cut off as she looked away. *What in the fuck did that mean?*

"Excuse me?" I asked as I leaned closer to her.

"Never mind."

Kam walked up and set a black coffee down in front of me along with a piece of banana nut bread. "There ya go, Gray." Turning to Meagan, she smiled. "Do you need anything else, sweetie?"

Meagan flashed her that beautiful smile of hers and

shook her head. "Oh wait! The check please. I'm being chased away."

"Put it on my tab, Kam," I said as I continued to watch Meagan.

She flashed me a dirty look and gathered up her things. I knew from following her, she normally sat here for a few hours and read as she people-watched. She'd leave Kam a more than generous tip for taking up a table all morning, and then she headed to her office.

"I can buy my own breakfast."

With a nod, I said, "I know that."

Meagan grunted as she stood. Her next stop would be her office. She worked for a non-profit organization called Helping Hands. Meagan worked as a counselor to middle and high school kids dealing with issues like bullying. I'd never seen anyone so passionate about their job. From the little I gathered from Grace, Meagan had a hell of a time in college dealing with bullying of her own.

"Why don't you spend the day with me, Meg?"

With raised eyebrows, she smirked. "What's wrong, Claire busy today so you're going for your backup?"

My body jerked as if someone had slapped me. "I'm sorry for taking that call. I didn't know it was her."

Something passed over Meagan's face. "It doesn't matter. It's over and done with."

I stood and reached for her arm. "Spend the day with me . . . as friends."

Meagan lifted her eyebrow. "Friends?"

"Yes."

"What are you playing at, Gray?"

With a puzzled look, I flashed her the smile I knew she loved. Her breath would hitch every time.

Meagan sucked in a breath as she quickly licked her lips. *Bingo.*

"Why do you think I'm up to something? You think all I care about is fucking you; I want to show you that's not true. I want to show you how much I enjoy just hanging out with you."

Meagan glanced around, worried someone had heard what I said. Turning her head back to me, she narrowed her eyes.

"What did you have in mind?"

I could see her holding back her smile. We may do some magical shit in bed, but we had just as much fun hanging out with each other. Standing, I remarked, "I plan on showing you what real fun is."

Meagan laughed as she shook her head. "Oh really? Would that consist of dancing on a stage?"

I placed my hand over my heart like she mortally wounded me. With a crooked grin, I said, "I could add that to the list of things to do today if you'd like."

Meagan's smile faded as she bit down on her lip and looked away. "Um, I have to stop by my office. Maybe another day?"

I had no idea why she kept me at arm's length all the time, but today I was bound and determined to show her exactly how I felt about her. After all, the chase would be worth it in the end.

"I'll swing you by work. Do what you have to do and then you're mine for the rest of the day."

With a smirk, Meagan asked, "As friends?"

I held up my hands and nodded. "Friends."

Meagan stood there and watched me intently before sighing. "Fine. I'll spend the day with you, but I seriously doubt you can stay in the friend zone."

"Is that a challenge, Ms. Atwood?"

With a nonchalant shrug of her shoulders, Meagan gathered up her things and looked at me. "I call it like I see it, Mr. Bennett."

Ah hell. This is going to be a fun day.

Chapter
THREE

Meagan

GRAYSON GAVE ME that damn sexy smile of his as he motioned for me to start walking across the street. "I'm parked in the lot around the corner."

My heart fluttered at the revelation he knew exactly where I would be this morning. Then again, he was a cop. Finding people was his job.

Risking a peek over my shoulder, I took him in again. Good lord.

No one should look that good in a pair of damn khaki pants. Of course, with the blue button down shirt tucked into his pants it really showed how fit he was. Then there was the badge hanging from his belt.

Did the Earth just spin faster or something? Fuck.

Grayson walked to the passenger side of his silver Toyota Tundra. Opening the door, he motioned for me to get in. Normally he would take my hand or my elbow and help me in. I looked at him for a second before realizing what he was doing. With a smile, I handed him my stuff. "Will you hold this please?" I asked as I climbed up into the truck. The black leather seats were cold, even through my jeans. I sucked in a breath. The weather outside was beautiful for it being the middle of January, but it was still pretty chilly. This winter had been mild with hardly any snow so far.

"Here's your stuff," Gray said as he plopped it down on my lap. Okay, so he was totally taking this whole friends thing seriously. As he shut the door, I smiled and decided if he even tried to make a play on me I would totally cut it off.

Oh yeah. I have this one in the bag.

Grayson headed toward where I worked as he made small talk.

"So how are things going with work?"

"Good I guess. I have one kid who I'm really worried about."

Even I could hear the worry in my voice. Mitchell was a smart kid and had everything going for him. Unfortunately, he had become the subject of bullying. It was tearing him apart.

"What's going on with him?"

With a frustrated sigh, I shook my head. "He's had some bullying going on. They don't do it to him at school very often, mostly online."

"Really? Who's doing it?"

"Another teammate. He plays football and just got accepted to Stanford to play."

I could see Grayson look over at me. "That's amazing. Why in the hell is someone bullying him?"

With a shrug, I looked at him while he was sitting at a red light. "Why does anyone bully?"

A look of compassion moved across Grayson's face. My heart melted a bit with that small gesture from him.

"That's true. Hurt people tend to hurt other people."

"Yeah," I barely said as I looked away.

Grayson pulled into the parking lot of Helping Hands and parked as I quickly opened the truck door and jumped out. Rounding the front of his truck, Grayson winked and laughed. "I promise not to treat any part of today like a date, but I am still a gentleman, Meg. Getting the door for you doesn't mean I want in your panties."

With a tilt of my head, I decided to test Mr. Bennett. "You don't want in my panties, Gray?"

Without so much as a flinch, Grayson shook his head. "Nope."

Huh. He's holding out strong. Impressive.

Grayson pulled the door open and motioned for me to lead the way. Jennifer, the receptionist, was sitting at the desk with a bright smile. The moment she saw Grayson her mouth dropped open.

"Hey . . . um . . . Meg."

Jennifer worked part time for us. Three days a week and Saturdays. She brought such a lightness to the office with her amazing sense of humor. Something we needed now and then with the type of work we did. "Hey, Jennifer. This is my *friend,* Grayson."

I couldn't believe how fast she jumped up and reached her hand out for Grayson's. "Hi there," she said with a purr.

Turning back to me, she asked, "Friend?"

My eyes darted between Grayson and Jennifer. "Yep. Just friends."

That was her signal to flirt mindlessly with him. "Well hello there, handsome. Please tell me you're single."

Grayson laughed as he took Jennifer in. She was about five-six with flaming red hair. She gave me hell for two weeks when I dyed my auburn hair brown, along with my father who questioned why I wasn't happy with my original color. I loved my new color though and planned on keeping it.

"I am single. Yes."

The growl that came from Jennifer caused me to look back at her as I made my way to my office. "The things I could do to you."

With a chuckle, Grayson headed down the hall. "Behave, Jennifer, or I'll have to put the handcuffs on you."

I rolled my eyes and made a gagging face as I unlocked the door to my office and headed in. Grayson followed me in and sat in a chair as I fumbled with my jacket. I looked through a few files, looking for Mitchell's, as Grayson sat there watching my every move.

Finding the file, I sighed as I sat down and opened it. I flipped through the paperwork as I read over my notes from yesterday when I met with Mitchell.

"Grayson, would you mind if I made a phone call? I won't be long."

With a slap of his hands on his legs, Grayson stood up. "Sure. I'll go flirt with Jennifer."

He was out the door before I even had a chance to protest.

With a shake of my head, I typed in Mitchell's number.

"Hey, it's my shrink!"

I smiled as I pulled up Facebook. "How are you doing today?"

"Personal phone calls, wow, Ms. A, do you have a thing for me?"

This kid reminded me of someone.

Jennifer laughed as my eyes traveled to my office door.

"Very funny, Mitchell. Did you still want to meet today?"

"Nah, I think I'm good. I think we can wait and meet this Wednesday."

I heard a lightness in his voice. "Did you ask her out?"

I asked, hoping he would say yes.

"I did. She said yes."

With a smile, I did a fist pump. Mitchell had been a star quarterback at his previous high school. He moved to Durango a few months back and obviously his instant popularity threw a few of his teammates off. What started off as innocent teasing by other players was slowly becoming something more. An observant teacher was the one who notified Mitchell's mom which led to our weekly meetings.

"Good. Take her somewhere nice. I'll see you Wednesday."

"Thanks, Ms. A. Later!"

I made a quick note in Mitchell's file, closed it and then grabbed my jacket and slipped it on before heading out of my office. As I locked the door I could hear Jennifer giggling. My stomach turned at the idea of Grayson flirting with her.

I rounded the corner and saw not only Jennifer standing in the main lobby, but my boss, Melissa was also standing there. Both were staring at Grayson with puppy dog eyes. He had them eating out of his hands.

Gag me.

"Gray, are you done here?"

Grayson looked up and smiled. "Yeah, I was showing them a video."

I lifted my eyebrow and gave him a quizzical look. With a smirk, he shook his head. "It was a kitten we got out of a tree yesterday."

My eyes widened. Here I imagined him to have this badass job where he hunted down bad guys and he was saving kittens from trees.

"Wow, your job isn't boring," I said.

Jennifer snapped her head up and glared at me. "I think it is sweet that they saved this kitten."

I forced a smile. "Oh, I do too, Jennifer. Far cry from

his last job."

Grayson cleared his throat and took a step away from both women.

"Well ladies, it was nice chatting with you."

"Bye, Detective Bennett. Be safe!" Jennifer called out as Grayson held the door open for me.

"Bye, Grayson! Come back and visit anytime!" Melissa called out.

As we walked over to his truck, Grayson stopped and opened the door for me. "They were nice."

I didn't say a word as I climbed into the truck. By the time he walked around the front, Melissa had run back out and handed him something. My mouth dropped open when I saw him kiss her on the cheek.

"What the fuck?" I whispered as Melissa glanced into the truck and gave me a quick wave. Somehow my hand lifted as I waved back with a stunned smile.

Grayson jumped into the truck and started it up. "What in the hell was that all about?"

Grayson shot me a confused look. "What do you mean?"

"Seriously? You're showing them kitten videos and kissing my boss on the cheek?"

Grayson threw his head back and laughed. "She gave me a brownie. It was nice of her. Besides, she's like the age of my grandmother. I was being polite."

I rolled my eyes and sighed in disgust. "Whatever. And she isn't that much older than us you jackass."

"Are you jealous, Meg? Do you want a kiss on the cheek?"

I shot him a smirk. "Friends, remember?"

Grayson's head pulled back. "Isn't that where you kiss friends, on the cheek? I mean I wasn't about to lay one on Melissa's lips."

"Whatever, Gray. What are we doing today anyway?"

With a chuckle, he reached down and turned the radio

on. "I need to change so first stop is my place."

My heartbeat sped up. Oh shit, alone at Grayson's place. The things we've done at Grayson's apartment. My face blushed as I thought about all the places we've had sex in that place. The feel of his hands moving up my skirt as we rode up the elevator after a night on the town. Grayson pushing me up against the wall in the entrance hall as he ripped my panties off because he couldn't wait a second longer to be inside of me. Grayson slipping a condom on and—

"You okay over there?"

My head snapped over to look at him. His blue eyes commanded mine. It's almost like he knew what I was thinking about. "Yeah, why?"

"Your face is flush."

My eyes darted to the heater as I pointed to it. "I guess I'm just hot."

Grayson reached over and turned the heat off. Good thing I had a light jacket on since it was still rather chilly outside and with the truck heater off now, I was surely going to get cold.

"So, where are we going after your place?" I asked, trying to change the subject quickly.

An evil smile spread across Grayson's face. "You'll see."

I rolled my eyes and crossed my arms over my chest as I let out an annoyed sigh.

Grayson tittered as he placed his hand on my leg and gave it a quick squeeze before pulling it back away. My body instantly came to life. It's getting hot in here again.

"Don't be a baby, Meg."

With a pout, I said, "I'm not being a baby."

Grayson's smile caused my heart to skip a beat. I wanted to dream of a future with him, but who was I kidding. The moment I open my heart he'll stomp on it and move on to Claire.

19

I decided to stop talking as I pulled out my phone and began checking emails.

"It's Saturday. Put your phone away."

"I'm just checking my email."

"Not today. It's a technology-free zone today."

My laugh was somewhere between a *yeah right* and a *hell no* as I continued to look at my phone.

Grayson pulled into the parking garage and whipped into his spot. He had two reserved spots for his unit. I couldn't help but notice the light-blue BMW parked in the other spot. My heart raced as a memory popped up in my head.

I wiped the tears from my face as I quickly walked away from the two guys who had followed me out of my class. Each one had asked me to meet them later this evening. I wasn't sure how much longer I'd be able to take this. "Come on, Meg. We heard you were the girl to go to for a good sucking."

Glancing over my shoulder, I yelled, "Fuck you, assholes."

"I'll take that as you're booked up!"

I walked as fast as I could back to my dorm as I fought like hell to keep my emotions in check. Stepping off the curb, a silver BMW pulled in front of me causing me to stop. The tinted window rolled down and Claire Watkins smiled at me.

"Having a bad day, Meg?"

"What in the hell did I ever do to you, Claire?"

Her smile dropped and was replaced with a pure evil look. "You took something that was mine. I don't play nice when sluts take what is mine."

My mouth dropped open as I stared at her. "You're sick. You have a serious problem."

"Rumor is so do you." Her tongue pushed against her cheek as her two flunky friends laughed.

I took another step closer and leaned over, causing her to pull back from me. "Some day, Claire, karma is going to come around and I pray like hell I'm there to see it when it happens. Meanwhile, you can spread all the rumors you want, you will never break me, bitch."

With a raised eyebrow, Claire glared at me. "We'll see about that."

"Meg? Earth to Meagan. What's wrong?"

I swallowed hard as I slipped out of the door Grayson was holding open for me. "Whose car is that?"

Please don't say Claire. Please.

"Derrick's. He bought it for his wife for their ten-year anniversary. He's keeping it here for a couple of days."

Feeling silly for where my mind had taken me, I grinned. "That's sweet of him."

Grayson reached for my hand and laced his fingers through mine. I knew it wasn't a second thought on his part and a part of me wanted to point out our friend status. Instead, I let the warmth from his touch move across my body.

"Yeah, he's a good guy. They've been trying for a baby for a few years. He's taking her on a ski trip in a few weeks to some romantic cabin or something. He's hoping this will be it."

I didn't even know this couple and my heart broke for them. "Wow. Is everything okay with both of them?"

"Yeah, he's thinking it's the stress of her job and trying for a baby."

We stopped outside the elevator as a cold breeze blew through, causing me to shudder. Grayson must have realized he was holding my hand because he dropped it. "Sorry," he said with a wink.

Missing his touch, I gave him a silly grin. "Friends hold hands."

The elevator opened as Grayson guided me in. I backed

up against the wall as he leaned ever so close to me. My breathing began to increase as his eyes searched my face. He was going to say something when he quickly stepped back and practically stood on the other side of the elevator. Letting out the breath I didn't even know I was holding, I wrapped my arms around my body.

This was going to be one hell of a long day.

Chapter
FOUR

Grayson

FOCUS. FOCUS ON anything but her.

Meg wrapped her arms around her body and I knew she was trying to push away the same feelings I was. I needed to prove to Meg I thought of her as more than just a fuck buddy, and I couldn't do that if I told her how much her touch drove me crazy.

The door opened and Meagan practically raced out of the elevator. She walked quickly to my door and plastered on a fake smile.

Pushing the door open, I motioned for her to go in first.

"It's freezing in here, Gray!"

"Damn. The heater must have quit working again."

Tossing my wallet and keys on the coffee table, I pulled my phone out and called the manager of the building. After telling her the heater was out again, I set my phone next to my keys. "I'm going to get out of these clothes I've been in for two days and take a quick shower if you don't mind."

Meagan looked at me with a confused look. "You didn't come home last night?"

I could see the panic in her eyes. She probably thought I spent the evening with some girl.

I began unbuttoning my shirt as I made my way into the kitchen. "Derrick and I worked all night on a case."

"What? Gray, you must be exhausted. Why in the world do you want to spend the day with me if you've been up all night?"

I shrugged my shoulders as I took a drink of water. "I got a few minutes of shut eye last night. Besides, I want to spend the day with you."

The look of happiness that passed over Meagan's face made me smile. I knew I was going to be exhausted later, but that one smile was worth the misery I would go through later this evening.

"Help yourself to anything. I'm going to jump in the shower."

Before I walked into my bedroom, I saw a sweatshirt sitting on the sofa. I picked it up and tossed it over to Meagan. "In case you get cold."

With a laugh, Meagan took her light jacket off and slipped the oversized sweatshirt on. My dick jumped seeing her swallowed up in it as she pulled her brown hair up and twisted it in a bun.

Turning before I jumped her, I headed to take a cold shower.

～✖～

"It's snowing!" Meagan said as we pulled out of the parking garage of my apartment building. I'd showered and quickly got ready for our day.

Perfect. I knew a cold front was blowing through and there was a chance for some snow. It's about damn time. The last week was mild for January in Colorado.

"Well this makes the first thing on our list even better."

Meagan glanced over and I could practically see the smile beaming off her face. If there was one thing I knew about this little Texas beauty, is that she loved snow.

"Please tell me, Gray! Where are we going?"

The excitement in her voice had me excited. I should have been exhausted but how could I, hearing how thrilled she was.

"First up is ice skating."

With a fist pump and a small shriek, Meagan bounced around in the seat as I attempted not to think of her doing that while sitting on my face.

Shit. Focus on anything other than sex. Or her lips. Wrapped around my dick. No . . . stop this. Damn it.

"Gray, are you okay? You look pale."

With a quick glance over to her, I smiled and said, "What? No yeah, I'm totally fine."

"Are you sure you're not too tired?"

I reached for her hand, which I knew was not part of the friend-only zone, and placed my lips softly on her skin. "I'm positive. Today is all about spending it with my best friend."

Meagan's eyes lit up. "Best friend, huh?"

I hadn't meant to say it, but it was true. If there was anyone I wanted to do stuff like this with, it was Meagan. Now that it was out in the open, I was going to run with it.

"Yeah. I mean I think we have fun together. Don't you?"

"Are you talking fun sex, or fun hanging out?"

My stomach flipped at the mention of sex.

Focus, Gray.

Focus.

"Fun hanging out. Don't get me wrong, sex with you is

fucking amazing, but since we're now in the friends zone, yeah . . . you're my best friend."

I stopped at a red light and looked her way. Meagan was staring at me while chewing on the corner of her lip. With the cutest damn smile I'd ever seen, she scrunched up her nose and said, "You're my best friend too. Well I mean, after Grace, and Taylor. Oh and Alex and Libby."

My smile dropped. "I'm at the fucking bottom of the best friend list."

"Not really. You're my first guy best friend. Well . . . there's Luke, Colt, and Will."

"Stop." I rolled my eyes and hit the gas when the light turned green. "You're making it worse."

Meagan let out a chuckle as she squeezed my hand. I wasn't about to let go if she wasn't. We drove in silence as I made my way to the outdoor skating rink. I was glad she still had my sweatshirt on, but I knew she would still be cold.

I parked my truck and quickly reached into the backseat and grabbed the bag from yesterday's little shopping trip.

I set the bag in Meagan's lap as I reached back for my jacket.

"What's this?" Meagan asked.

With a quick wink, I motioned for her to look. Meagan pulled out a pair of gloves and matching hat. She smiled and glanced back over to me. "So are you buying yourself girl stuff now?"

I laughed and shook my head. "No, I bought them for you. I saw them yesterday and that's when I got the idea for today."

Meagan raised her eyebrow. "What made you think I'd agree to spend the day with you?"

Shrugging, I took the gloves and removed the tags, followed by the hat. "I didn't, but a guy can hope. You're not going to be too cold in just my sweatshirt, are you?"

The look in Meagan's eyes told me she was beyond thrilled I had already been thinking about today. Clearing her throat, Meagan put the hat and gloves on. Damn it . . . she looked adorable. "If I get cold, I'll find a hot guy to snuggle up with."

Narrowing my eyes at her, I shook my head and opened my door. "Let's go get our skating on."

Thirty minutes later and my ass was killing me. Who thought ice skating would be so damn hard. Meagan glided across the ice like she had been doing this for years.

"Tell me you've had lessons!" I called out as she zipped by me and then did a little circle thing.

With a naughty smile, Meagan stopped right in front of me as I grabbed onto her hips for balance. "I may have taken a few lessons."

"Define few, Meg. You're fucking spinning around like an ice princess."

Her smile grew wider across her face as my stomach dropped from her beauty. "Six years of lessons."

My mouth dropped to the ice as I stared at her with a stunned expression. "Six. Years?"

"Yep. I thought I wanted to be one of the Disney ice-princess girls who go on tour and skate for the Disney shows."

"Somehow I totally see that."

With a wiggle of her eyebrows, she took off skating backwards. Before I could say anything, she ran right into another guy.

"Shit!" Meagan said as she landed right on the guy. Trying to make my way over to them, I couldn't help but notice the asshole holding onto Meagan as she lay across him.

"You okay?" he asked as they both managed to get up as I slowly made my way over to them.

"I'm so sorry about that. I shouldn't have been skating backwards. That was totally my fault."

The fucker's eyes lit up as he took Meagan in. "No problem at all." Reaching his hand out he winked. "I'm Dex."

"Oh. My. Gawd! Dex Brewer! The baseball player?"

I stopped skating. "Holy shit," I mumbled as I stared at the starting first baseman for the Colorado Rockies while he made a play for my girl. This was not happening.

His eyes widened as he nodded. "I'm impressed, you're a baseball fan? What was your name?"

"Yes! Oh, it's Meagan. Meagan Atwood," Meagan said as she shook the guy's hand and finally turned to see me struggling to make my way over to them.

"Oh, Gray! Sorry!" She held her hands out and pulled me closer to her. I wrapped my arm around her waist and looked this asshole straight in the eyes. Never mind the fact that he was looking at me like some kind of bug he needed to stomp right away. His eyes moved down to my arm around Meagan's waist.

That's right, dickhead. She's mine. Take your baseball and shove it up your ass.

Meagan looked between us and surely had to have noticed the testosterone stare going on between us. "Sorry! Um . . . Dex, this is my friend, Grayson."

And there went the knife in my heart.

Dex reached his hand out for mine. "Friend huh?"

Pretending I didn't hear either of them utter the word friend, I smiled big. "Colorado Rockies. I'm really looking forward to the season."

Dex smiled and I was pretty sure he puffed his damn chest out some. "A fan huh?"

"Fan? Oh my gosh! I love baseball," Meagan said as I turned and glared at her. That smile of hers was pulling this guy in deeper and deeper. *I wonder if I made her fall, if she would stop smiling?*

"Really? Well, I have to say I don't normally run into such beautiful fans."

Holy shit. Is her face blushing? Seriously, is this happening right now?

"Well, my dad is a huge baseball junkie. I pretty much have grown up watching it."

Why didn't I know this? Why have I never taken her to a game? I'd like to punch myself in the face.

Before I could even get a word in, I watched as Dex the Great pulled out his phone. "It's not broken."

"Oh thank goodness," Meagan purred as I stared at her with a dumbfounded look on my face.

"What's your cell number, Meagan? I'll be sure to arrange for some tickets for you and—"

Dex glanced over to me and looked me over as he smiled that smile dudes do when they think they've just won the girl. "Your friend Grayson here."

"Seriously? I can't wait to tell my father!" Meagan spit her cell phone number out as the asshole sent her a text.

"You've got mine now."

Meagan stood there staring at this guy until I cleared my throat and said, "Um, we probably should be heading out before my ass goes permanently numb."

Meagan gave me a once over and nodded. "Right." Turning back to the dickhead pro baseball player, Meagan reached her hand out again. "It was a pleasure meeting you, Dex."

Dex flashed Meagan a *fuck me fast and hard* smile. "The pleasure was all mine." With a quick look my way, he nodded. "Nice meeting you, Grayson."

And just like that, the bastard skated off.

"Wow. I can't believe I have Dex Brewer's cell phone number! Wait until I tell Taylor!"

I rolled my eyes and made my way to the wall. I needed to get the hell out of there, and fast.

After making my way off the ice, I headed down the stairs and to the benches where I promptly took the skates off and replaced them with my comfortable sneakers.

Never once uttering a word to Meagan.

I returned the skates and headed to the parking lot. Meagan grabbed my arm and pulled me to a stop. "Hey, what's wrong?"

Never mind the fact she was totally clueless that Dex Brewer, her hero, wanted to fuck her and she gladly handed him her phone number, but she was also clueless how jealous I was of that whole little exchange. Stopping, I turned and looked at her. "You really don't get it?"

"Get what?"

"That guy wants in your pants, Meagan. You just gave your phone number to a complete stranger and practically told him you'd fuck him."

Her mouth dropped open as her hands went to her hips. "Excuse me? He's Dex Brewer! And he said he wanted to give us tickets."

My head dropped back as I laughed. "Oh yeah, he wants to give *us* tickets. No sweetheart, he wants to give *you* a ticket, and in turn he wants your mouth around his cock."

I didn't expect her hand to slap me, but the moment it hit my face the sting caught me off guard as I took a few steps back. For a brief second I was too stunned to notice the hurt in her eyes.

"You can take me home now, Grayson. I don't much feel like hanging out with someone who is going to call me a whore."

My eyes widened in surprise. "What the hell, Meg? I didn't call you that. Look at it from my point of view. What would you have said if I had handed over my number to some hot tennis star? Sure, I just met you two seconds ago pretty little thing, but let me give you my number so you can send me tickets to Wimbledon, oh and one for my little friend here too."

Meagan looked away. "Meg, I care about you and yes, I was extremely jealous watching you drool all over that asshole, but baby, you handed him your number like you'd known him for years."

Peeking at me through her eyelashes, Meagan forced her smile back. "You were jealous?"

I draped my arm over her shoulders and guided her to my truck. "Hell yeah. We may be best friends, but I'm still a guy and I didn't like the way he was looking at you."

Lightly tapping my stomach, Meagan chuckled. "Stop it. I promise if he happens to call or text I'll let you know right away."

"Hell yeah you will, I want tickets to a Rockies game, bitch."

Chapter

FIVE

Meagan

I HAD TO admit, I kind of liked knowing Grayson was jealous of Dex. I may have gotten a little star struck when I noticed who I had plowed into. Baseball was a huge part of my life though and the moment Dex Brewer mentioned tickets, all reason went out the door. My father would have been just as pissed off as Grayson was by me handing over my phone number. His comment about the blowjob instantly brought back memories from college I had tried so hard to bury. My knee-jerk response to slap him caught me off guard as much as it did Grayson.

"So, that was fun," I said with a giggle as I watched Grayson trying to find a comfortable way to sit.

"Fun? No, that was far from fun. What was I thinking with the whole ice skating thing?"

Pressing my lips together to keep from laughing, I looked out the passenger window. "So where to now?"

"It's a surprise."

I couldn't hold the smile back as I continued to look out the window. Grayson and I had hung out together before, but there was always so much sexual tension around us, we usually ended up sneaking away to his truck or my car or back to one of our apartments to release the build-up. This whole friend zone thing was kind of fun.

We ended up hitting up a bowling alley, then a laser tag place and finally an indoor paintball place where Grayson got way too into the whole thing. I was positive I was going to be bruised from head to toe tomorrow.

Climbing up into his truck, I let out a moan. "Holy fuck, Gray. Was the paintball your payback for the ice skating?"

With an evil smile, he shut the door and headed around the front of his truck. Jumping in, he started up the truck and headed out toward the San Juan Mountains.

"Doesn't your mom live out this way?" I asked as I glanced back over to him.

"Yep."

My heart started beating harder in my chest. I had yet to meet his mother. Grayson had met my parents, but as far as they knew he was just Noah's cousin who happened to live in the same town as me.

"Um . . . are we . . . ah . . . are you going . . . to um . . . well . . ." Jesus H. Christ, I can't even talk.

"Spit it out, Meg."

"Are we going to your mother's house?" My words were laced with fear. Meeting Grayson's mom would be taking a major step. Why was he bringing me to meet her? Today we were in the friend zone for Pete's sake!

With a smile that melted my panties, Grayson looked at me and then back to the road. "With the storm coming in tonight, I want to make sure she has everything. I'm not sure I'll be able to make it up tomorrow. You don't mind, do you?"

I breathed a sigh of relief. Thank goodness was only making a quick run to check on her. This was no big deal. He wouldn't think twice bringing me. *I'm his best friend after all.*

With a smile I found I had to force, I said, "No, of course I don't mind." Sadness filled my chest as I realized I might have actually wanted Grayson to bring me home to meet his mother . . . and not as his friend.

⚬✖⚬

Snow was beginning to fall harder as we drove down a street filled with simple homes. They weren't very big, yet you could tell it was a nice neighborhood. Each house looked like it sat on at least half an acre of land.

"I made pretty good money in my stripping days. I bought my mom this house a few years back."

My stomach clenched at the idea of seeing Grayson dancing. There were plenty of times I wanted to ask him to give me a private show. I was certain he did very well in his last career. Not only was he beyond handsome, he knew how to dance. My mind drifted back to the first time I had ever seen Grayson.

I couldn't pull my eyes off the guy Lauren had talk-ed into jumping up on the bar and dancing. The way he moved was almost sinful. Grace yelled out for him to take his pants off as I quickly joined in on the fun.

Oh yes . . . I wouldn't mind a little private show of my own.

"It's a cute neighborhood," I said as I forced all images of Grayson stripping far from my mind.

Grayson swung his truck down a driveway that wind-ed back just a bit from the road. "My mother loves nature, so I bought the lot at the very end of the road. It's two acres of land."

As he pulled down the drive, I took in the site of the cabin sitting in front of me as I smiled. "It's a cabin!"

The truck came to a stop as I looked over at Grayson. He was smiling a wide smile. "Yeah, she always used to talk about owning a cabin in the mountains. This is the best I could do for now."

My heart melted at the idea of Grayson doing all he could to make his mother's dream come true. "I'm sure she loves it."

Giving me a quick wink, Grayson jumped out of his truck and ran around to get my door. The snow was coming down even harder now as he grabbed my hand and pulled me toward the front door as we both ran.

The door opened right as we got on the porch. Grayson's mom stood in front of me and she was beyond beautiful. She couldn't have been but in her early forties. Her light brown hair was pulled into pig-tails and she had a smudge of green paint on her cheek. Her blue eyes lit up the moment she saw Grayson.

"Baby! I told you not to drive up here!"

My chest tightened as I watched the two of them exchange hugs. You could see how much Grayson loved his mother, and that did crazy things to my guarded heart.

"Why, who is this gorgeous girl standing on my porch?"

Grayson laughed as he reached his hand out for mine and pulled me closer to him. My heart was beating so loudly in my chest, I was sure it would eventually beat right on out.

"Mom, this is Meagan. She's a good friend of mine, my best friend as a matter of fact."

My smile faltered one quick second. I wasn't prepared for that to hurt as much as it did. Praying like hell neither Grayson nor his mother caught my reaction, I held my hand out and said, "Ms. Bennett, it's a pleasure meeting you."

Her eyes sparkled as she quickly looked me over. "Oh, call me Ashley, Meagan. My mother-in-law was Ms. Bennett."

With a polite chuckle, I nodded. "Ashley it is."

"Well get in here kids, it's getting colder by the second."

Grayson motioned for me to go first as I followed Ashley back into the house. With a quick glance around, I noticed Grayson's mother was a simple woman. Everything was neatly in place and hardly anything was on the walls. A few pictures of Grayson were spread throughout the house, along with pictures of the two of them together.

"I'm not much of a decorator. The simpler the better!" Ashley said as I followed her into a huge kitchen.

"Wow! I love this kitchen. It reminds me of my parents' kitchen back in Texas."

Ashley beamed as she looked over at Grayson. "Well, Grayson knows how much I love to cook. This kitchen is my dream kitchen. I've cooked plenty of pies and cakes for him and his friends over the last few years."

With a smile and wink toward Grayson, I sat on one of the stools at the kitchen island. "Would you like something to drink, Meagan?"

"Water is fine, thank you."

Ashley reached for a glass as she filled it with ice and then purified water from the refrigerator.

Setting the glass down, Ashley looked between us before she took a seat opposite of me and grinned. Oh shit. I had a feeling the grilling was about to take place.

"So what do you do for a living, Meagan?"

Grayson moaned. "Mom, really? You're going to start grilling her?"

"No! I'm just curious."

With a giggle, I looked at Grayson and shook my head. "It's fine. I don't mind at all." Turning back to Ashley, I took a sip of my water and set it down in front of me. "I have a masters degree in social work. My specialty is clinical therapeutic services. I work for a non-profit company that deals a lot with schools. I mainly focus on middle school and high school kids with bullying."

Ashley's eyes rose. "Really? I think that's amazing. Grayson helped start a program for young boys from troubled homes."

With a smile, I turned to Grayson as his face blushed. "Yes, I know. I've worked with them a lot."

"What made you decide that was the field you wanted?"

I moved about nervously in my seat. I rarely talked about what had happened to me when I was at Baylor. "Well, unfortunately, I had my fair share of bullying in college."

Ashley's eyes pinched together as she reached across the table and took my hand in hers. I was touched by the action more than I wanted to admit. "I'm so sorry, sweetheart. Was it bad?"

The lump in my throat formed as I tried like hell to push it down. With a fake smile, I nodded. "At times, but it made me a better counselor, so I'd like to think it was all worth it."

I stole a peek over to Grayson who was watching me intently.

"What made you decide to move to Durango?"

"Mom, I think you've grilled Meg enough today."

With a chuckle, I waved Grayson off. "It's totally fine. I'm an open book."

Grayson lifted his eyebrows and smiled. Turning away from him, I focused back on his mother. "My sister and a few friends of mine came up for a girls trip the summer before my senior year. I fell in love with it and knew I had to move here."

"Meg and I actually kind of met during that trip."

"Kind of?" Ashley asked with a confused face.

Grayson's eyes burned with desire as our stare locked. I was instantly taken back again for the second time to him up on that damn bar dancing. Looking away, I cleared my throat. "He actually met one of my best friends, Lauren. Then come to find out Noah was dating my other best friend, Grace."

Ashley leaned back in her chair. "I wish I could have made it to Texas for Noah's wedding. Crazy small world isn't it?"

"Totally," Grayson and I said together.

Grayson pushed off the counter and clapped his hands together. "Okay, Mom I'm going to go cut up some of that firewood and bring it in here. They're calling for a lot of snow up here in the next few days."

"You're too good to me, Grayson."

I watched as Grayson kissed his mother on the forehead and smiled. "Nonsense, there isn't anything I wouldn't do for you, Mom."

Died. I just died.

There was something utterly romantic about a man who isn't afraid to show his love like that.

Ugh. Friends, Meg. You're just friends today. Wait. How long did we decide to do this friends thing? Shit! Was it just for today? I think so. Damn it. Why didn't I put down better rules?

Not being able to pull my eyes from Grayson, I watched as he made his way out back.

"He's something else," Ashley said.

"He certainly is," I barely said.

"Friends huh?"

My eyes snapped over to Ashley. "Excuse me?"

With a tilt of her head, Ashley crossed her arms over her chest and gave me a smile that said, *you're not fooling me.*

"Grayson has brought plenty of *friends* home before."

My heart felt as if it physically ached from that statement.

"And none of them have been girls."

The smiled that spread across my face was involuntary.

Shit. That last statement made me much happier than I should be.

With a nervous laugh, I opened my mouth to talk as I stole a look at Grayson through the huge bay windows in the eating nook.

"Well, I won't lie to you and tell you we're just friends. I mean, we are friends. Just friends with ben . . . um . . . I um."

Oh Jesus H Christ. Was I really about to say that?

Shaking my head to clear my thoughts, I wished I could dig a hole and crawl into it. "Oh gosh, I can't even believe I was about to say that. What I mean is . . . ahh."

Ashley laughed as she stood up. "Let me put you out of your misery, Meagan. You can think all you like that my son only sees you as a friend with benefits, but I know Grayson. I've never seen him look at anyone the way he looks at you. I would dare say you are much more than what you think you are in his eyes."

I swallowed hard as I looked back out to Grayson. Maybe what was between us was more than just casual sex. I chewed on my lip as I let the idea of Grayson and I together settle in. Did I truly not see how he really felt about me?

"Now, let me heat up some chili for the two of you for an early dinner. I'm sure Grayson wants to beat this storm before it really blows in."

With a grin, I stood. "Would you like some help?"

"Sure! You can grate the cheese."

Ashley and I settled into an easy conversation as I helped her get the chili ready. A few times I would glance out at Grayson and she must have noticed.

"He's turned out to be such an amazing man. I was

worried how it would affect him after his father left us and it was just me raising him."

With a slight smile, I stole another look at Grayson before directing my attention back to Ashley. "You did an amazing job with him. He really is a great guy."

Ashley beamed with pride. "Thank you, Meg. That means a lot to me." Grayson was just finishing up bringing in the firewood when Ashley called him to the table. I carried over the grated cheese and crackers as Ashley set three bowls of steaming hot chili on the table.

"Damn, Mom. That smells heavenly."

Ashley's face blushed as she grabbed three beers out of the refrigerator and set them on the table.

Grayson grabbed some cheese and tossed it into his chili followed by a handful of crackers that he crumbled up and tossed in the bowl. It was clear to me that Grayson and his mother had a close relationship. I started to imagine what Grayson would be like as a full on boyfriend and that caused my lower stomach to clench. Deciding I needed to stop where my thoughts were going, I focused on the food in front of me.

Taking a bite, my eyes about rolled into the back of my head. "Oh. My. Gosh. Ashley this is amazing!" I said as I shoved another spoonful in.

"She has a secret she won't tell me. I'm convinced she keeps it a secret so I'll keep coming home."

Chuckling, I took another bite. "Well, whatever it is, it's amazing."

"Thank you, Meagan. Save room for dessert. Caramel apple pie."

Moaning, I closed my eyes and mumbled, "I just gained ten pounds."

Chapter
SIX

Grayson

"BE CAREFUL DRIVING back, kids."

With a smile, I pulled my mother in for a hug. "We'll be fine, Mom. Thank you for the chili and apple pie."

"Anytime, Grayson." Giving her a quick kiss on the cheek, I took a step back.

"Love you, Mom. I'll see you soon."

I watched as Meagan walked up to my mother with a huge grin across her face. I knew instantly my mother loved Meagan. "Thank you so much for the amazing food. I'll have to try to convince you to share your secret ingredient."

With a chuckle, my mother gave Meagan a hug. "We might be able to make some kind of arrangement."

My mother shot a look at me and winked before turning back to Meagan. I'd never before brought a girl home and I knew my mother's mind was going into overdrive right now.

"We better get going, Meg. The snow is really coming down now and sticking pretty good to the ground."

Meagan hugged my mother one more time before jumping into the truck.

I lifted my hand and waved goodbye as my mother gave me that all-knowing look. "I'll be sure to call you tomorrow, Grayson."

Oh hell.

With another quick kiss on her forehead, I whispered, "Don't start planning a wedding, Mom. We're just hanging out."

"Uh-huh. Sure you are."

Running around the front of the truck, I called out, "Later, Mom!"

I jumped into the truck and glanced over to Meagan. She only had my sweatshirt on still as she wrapped her arms around her. I cranked up the heat and headed back to Durango.

We drove a good part of the ride back in silence before Meagan broke it. "Your mom is so sweet."

With a smile, I said, "Yeah, she's the most amazing woman I've ever known. I'm not really sure how she did it all those years on her own."

I could feel Meagan's eyes pinning me with a stare but I chose to keep looking straight ahead. "What was it like? Growing up without a father and your mom having to work so hard to provide for you?"

My hand pushed through my hair as memories flooded my mind. "We had good times and bad. I can remember breaking down at the table one day and crying because my mother put a plate of scrambled eggs in front of me with toast."

"Why did that make you cry?" Meagan asked as I turned to look at her.

"Because it was the tenth night of eating the same

thing. Eggs and bread were cheap."

Meagan's eyes widened, and I saw pity in them. I couldn't stand when people felt sorry for me.

"My friends gave me hell when I became a stripper, but they quickly shut their mouths when I was bringing in more cash in one night than they made in three months working at Home Depot."

Meagan cleared her throat as she asked, "Does your mom know you were a stripper?"

"She didn't at first, but I finally told her. The only reason I did was because she thought I was dealing drugs."

With a chuckle, Meagan looked straight ahead as I pulled into the parking garage of my apartment. "Did you um . . . you know . . . ever get offered to do other things for women?"

My head snapped over to look at her, but she was still looking straight ahead. "All the time," I said as I whipped into my space.

Now it was Meagan's turn to snap her head over to me. I couldn't tell if she was angry or scared by what I had said. Something about that small look of jealousy in her eyes had my heart beating just a little faster.

"Like . . . what?" Meagan asked.

Putting the truck in park, I opened my door and got out as Meagan did the same. As I walked around the back of my truck, I met up with her. "Do you really want to know?"

She swallowed hard. "I guess that depends on what it was and if you did it."

"Why do you care if we're just friends, Meg?"

With a shrug, she acted unaffected. "I don't and you don't have to even tell me if you don't want to."

I grabbed her hand and led her to the elevator. I liked the fact that she didn't try to pull her hand away. "I had an older woman, maybe forty-six, ask if I wanted to come home with her and have a threesome with her husband.

She offered me six thousand dollars to come and spend the weekend with them."

"Holy shit! You didn't, did you?"

With a laugh, I shook my head. "Fuck no I didn't. There was another lady, probably around twenty-eight. She offered to pay me two thousand for a threesome with her and her best friend. They were on a girls' weekend and both wanted some action with one guy. Both were married and they wanted some fucked up fantasy of watching each other get fucked by a younger guy."

"Wow. That's messed up."

"Yeah it is."

Stepping into the elevator, I hit the floor my apartment was on. The lack of sleep was kicking in.

"So did you?"

The doors opened and I looked at Meagan. "Did I what?"

"Hook up with the two girls?"

My stomach felt like it was twisting in knots. I didn't want to be talking about my past with Meagan.

"My mother was about to have her car taken away from her for late payments. It would have been easy money, but I turned her down. Told her I wasn't into that kind of thing. The girl offered me fifteen hundred to fuck her alone, but she still wanted the friend to watch."

For once in my life, I felt ashamed for some of my actions when I was younger. "I figured it would be an easy way to make some quick cash."

Meagan's eyes widened as she searched my face before she looked away. "Did you um . . . did you use protection?"

I closed my eyes and stopped walking. When I opened them, Meagan was staring at me. "I've always used protection, Meg. I've fucked around with my fair share of women. I regret almost all of it, but none of them meant anything to me. I was younger, and it was money. Money I used to buy my mother that house."

Her eyes softened as she took a step closer to me and placed her hands on my chest. The air in my lungs felt like it was sucked out the moment she touched me. "Gray, I'm not judging you. Besides, it's not like I'm a sweet innocent girl. I've slept with my fair share of guys."

The thought of Meagan fucking another guy drove me insane. "How many guys?" I asked as I narrowed my eyes at her.

"How many girls?"

With a shrug, I said, "Probably around twenty."

Meagan took a step back and covered her mouth. "You fucking manwhore!"

My heart dropped as I looked at her. "Wait! You made it seem like you've slept with a lot of guys!"

Meagan shook her head as she dropped her hands and stared at me with a gaped mouth. "Yeah, I've slept with like six guys! Six! Jesus H. Christ, twenty? Here I thought I was a slut. Oh my God. I don't want to talk about this anymore."

Meagan turned and headed to my apartment as I closed my eyes and shook my head as I cursed myself.

Stupid! You stupid fucking idiot! Why did I tell her the truth?

Slowly making my way to the door, Meagan stepped to the side and looked down at the floor. "Meg, I don't want this—"

Her blue eyes looked up and pierced mine. "It doesn't matter, Gray. It's your past like I have my past." With a smile she winked and said, "Besides, isn't this what best friends talk about?"

I instantly felt sick. "Maybe best friends who don't have feelings for each other. I'm fucking going out of my mind trying to think of how I can track down those six guys and pound their faces in."

Meagan's eyes sparkled as a wide grin spread across her face. "You have feelings for me, Gray?"

I opened the door and pushed Meagan in as I backed her up against the wall. Keep it simple, Gray. This is not about sex.

My eyes lingered on her lips before I searched her face. Each breath looked as if it was a labored action on her part. "Really, Meg? You can't feel it when I kiss you?"

Meagan's mouth parted open as I moved closer to her. Our lips were inches apart from one another.

"Gray." She barely spoke as I placed my hand on the side of her face and gently rubbed my thumb over her soft skin. Son-of-a-bitch, touching her was one of my favorite things to do.

"It's just a kiss."

With trembling lips, Meagan said, "It's dangerous."

I lifted my eyebrow as I looked into her eyes. I'd never felt like this before with anyone. Meagan had a way of bringing out the one thing I was so afraid to let out.

Love.

"Why is it dangerous, baby?"

"This feeling . . . I've never felt it before with anyone but you and that scares me."

I held my breath as I asked, "Why does that scare you?"

Meagan closed her eyes. "I'm so scared you're going to break my heart, Gray." Her eyes opened as she chewed on the corner of her lip. "I honestly don't know if I would survive if I let you in and you left me."

My knees about buckled out from under me as I fought to keep my breathing steady.

"Meg," I whispered as I lightly brushed my lips across hers. The energy that raced between our bodies was something I'd never in my life experienced before.

Deepening the kiss, our tongues slowly danced together as I placed my other hand on her face as I kissed her with more passion. Meagan let out a small whimper as I pulled her lower lip into my mouth. Her head dropped back when I released her from the kiss. I softly spoke as I kissed along her jawline. "Don't you feel it, baby"?"

Meagan's hands grabbed onto the side of my sweatshirt as she pulled me closer to her. When our eyes met, her smile said everything my heart was feeling.

"Yes, I feel it."

My hands moved up as I took her hair out of the bun and let it fall along her shoulders. Running my fingers through her hair, I pulled her head to the side as I gently blew in her ear and spoke. "Good. Don't ever forget this feeling, Meagan." My lips moved softly across her neck. "I'm pretty sure this is what falling in love feels like."

It felt as if Meagan's legs gave out as she started to slide down the wall. Picking her up, she wrapped her legs around my waist as I brought her lips to mine and claimed her with just a kiss.

Chapter
SEVEN

Meagan

JUST A KISS, my ass. My head was reeling from that kiss and from Grayson's confession of falling in love.

Please God, *please* don't let him hurt me.

When we finally stopped kissing, I couldn't help but smile. I'd never experienced anything like that before. Being with Grayson had always been different, in a good way. I knew I had feelings for him, but I never had the courage to admit it.

Grayson looked deep in my eyes as my heartbeat pounded in my ears. Was I ready to admit to him what my heart knew the moment he first touched me? I wasn't sure, but I knew running from it was the last thing I wanted to do.

His blue eyes lit up as he took in my smile. "I'm falling in love with you too, Grayson."

The grin that spread across his face was the most

beautiful sight ever. Those dimples caused my chest to tighten as I pressed my lips together to keep from asking him to make love to me.

"Are you in the mood to go dancing?" he asked as he lifted an eyebrow.

With a giggle, I nodded and said, "Aren't you ready to pass out?"

"For some reason I got my second wind."

Wrapping my arms around his neck, I tilted my head and fought to keep my giddiness down. For Pete's sake, I wasn't Lauren. I didn't get giddy. "I'm not really dressed for dancing."

"How about we go to your place, you change and we head to Moe's."

"Moe's? They have an outside dance floor. It's snowing!"

"Nah, they have one on the inside too." Grayson set me down and quickly kissed my lips. "Let me go change and we'll head to your place."

❧

I stepped out of my bedroom dressed in tighter-than-tight jeans, high heels, and a light-blue shirt that was dressy enough, but not too dressy. Plus it really highlighted my blue eyes and showed off the right amount of cleavage.

"Ready!" I said as I reached down for my heavier coat.

"Jesus, Meg, you look hot as hell. I'm not sure I'm willing to take my best friend out to a bar looking like this."

I looked Grayson over from top to bottom. "You look pretty damn good yourself, bestie."

Placing his hands over his heart, Grayson pouted. "You're just now noticing? I'm hurt."

My eyebrows lifted as I gave him a sexy look. "Oh I noticed before, it was hard keeping my hands to myself on the way over here."

Grayson's eyes turned dark as he walked up to me. "Don't make me break my promise to you, Meg."

Heat surged between my legs as I silently begged him to kiss me again. "What promise was that?"

"No sex. Today we're friends only."

My lips slowly formed into a pout as Grayson shook his head. "Don't even look at me like that."

When I placed my hands on his chest I felt his body shudder. I loved knowing I had such an affect on him.

Grayson closed his eyes and moaned as he took my hands off of him and led us to the door. "Let's go before I lose control."

Smiling like a little girl, I quickly put on my coat as Grayson pulled me out the door.

⁓❦⁓

Moe's was packed as Grayson held onto my hand and led us over to a table. "Looks like they're having some kind of function tonight," he shouted over the music.

Glancing around, I couldn't help but notice all the women. What in the hell kind of function was this anyway?

After sitting at the table and placing our order, an older woman approached us with a wide grin on her face. "Hey, handsome! You gonna do a show for us tonight?"

Grayson pulled me closer to him as the older woman looked between Grayson and me. I couldn't help but notice he was making some sort of statement. "Not tonight, Diana."

"Oh come on, Gray. It's for a good cause."

Grayson moved about in his seat like he was uncomfortable as he glanced my way. Oh how I loved seeing him squirm around. With an evil smile, I shrugged and said, "Gray, if it's for a good cause." I looked up at Diana and asked, "What organization is it for?"

"Kids against bullying. It's a local group here in the area."

My heart stopped. "Yes I know, I'm a counselor at Helping Hands, so I know of that organization." Diana's face lit up as she looked back down at Grayson.

"Oh that's wonderful! What is your name, sweetheart?"

With a polite smile, I said, "Meagan Atwood."

Diana glanced back over to Grayson. "See, even your girlfriend wants you to do it."

A silly grin spread over my face as Grayson looked back at me. "What do you say to that?"

The fluttering in my stomach took off as his stare felt like it penetrated deep into my soul. I loved the way he was looking at me. I took a mental picture and stored it deep inside my heart. My lower stomach tightened and the need for Grayson to touch me became almost unbearable. The idea of knowing he wasn't going to make a move on me tonight had my heart racing. "At least we did it right and were friends first," I said with a wink.

I'd never seen Grayson smile at me like he was. Standing, he reached down for my hand and pulled me up. "I'll dance for you tonight, Diana, but I want my girlfriend front and center, no one else."

Wait. What?

What does front and center mean, and did Grayson just call me his girlfriend? Holy shit. He's dancing?

"All money goes to the organization?" Diana asked.

Grayson turned to Diana and smiled. "Of course. You ought to know me better than that, Di."

Diana looked at me with a pleased smile. "You're one lucky girl, darling." She turned and walked over to the bartender and then to the DJ.

Grayson took my hand and walked us over toward the stage. "Who was that?" I asked.

"My old boss."

Pinching my eyebrows together, I pulled him to a stop.

"From the strip club?"

With a chuckle, he nodded. "Yep. She likes to do little fundraisers throughout the year where she gives the ladies a taste of what they can see if they come to the club. Show them just enough to have them wanting to come back for more. It's a win-win for Diana. She's helping the community and marketing her club at the same time."

"Holy shit," I whispered as I realized what was happening. "Wait, you're not going to?"

"No, I've done these for her before. I promise, nothing will be shown and no one will touch me. Besides, my job would frown on that."

Biting down on my lip, I felt the bubble of excitement begin to build at the idea of Grayson dancing. I had no idea how I was going to keep my hands off him after this.

Diana brought over a chair and sat it down on the stage as she gave Grayson a high five and said, "Have fun, darling."

Grayson brought me over to the side of the stage. "Don't move from this spot okay?"

Nodding my head, I smiled. "I won't move, I promise."

Diana stood on the stage and called for everyone's attention.

"For those who just got here, we have a silent auction going on for a great cause against bullying. Ladies, it's time for our next dancer and boy do I have a surprise for you. Get those dollar bills out for this great cause! Our very own Grayson Bennett has agreed to come out of retirement to give us a little . . . performance . . . with all proceeds going to Kids Against Bullying here in the Durango area."

The audience erupted in cheers as I turned and looked at the women pushing closer to the stage. Jesus, what a bunch of horny bitches. It's like they'd never seen a guy dance before.

My eyes darted over to Grayson who was talking to

the DJ. I watched him as he made his way over while the crazies in the audience screamed when Grayson sat in the seat.

Maybe this wasn't such a great idea after all.

Grayson smiled as a few girls screamed out his name. *Former customers I'm guessing.*

"We have one rule tonight ladies, no touching, unless the dancer touches you first."

More screaming as I started laughing when Grayson looked at me and made a funny face. Rolling his eyes, he blew me a kiss as I chuckled and blew one back.

"Are you ready?" Diana called out as the place erupted again.

The lights went dim as the music started and my body caught on fire just from the beat. "Powerful" by Major Lazer started and Grayson's body moved with each beat. Screams from the women at the front of the stage caused me to jump and look at them before quickly looking back at Grayson.

"Oh my," I breathed out as I watched Grayson begin dancing. His hips moved in a graceful sexy way as he moved to the beat of the song. My mouth went dry as I thought of the things I wanted him to do to me. The way he moved had my heart racing as I forced myself to remember to breathe.

I couldn't pull my eyes off him as he captured his audience with his hotter-than-hot moves . . . and that smile. He quickly unbuttoned his shirt as the crowd went wild. My eyes scanned the sea of women and my heart stopped when I saw her.

Claire.

She stood right up at the front, waving a one hundred dollar bill around as Grayson slid across the floor, making some pretty erotic moves with his hips as women threw money onto the stage. Claire tried to reach over and touch Grayson but a security guy pulled her back.

"You bitch," I whispered as I balled my fists together.

I jumped when I saw Grayson in front of me. He pulled me further out onto the stage as the second chorus started. His hands moved over my body when he dropped to his knees as women screamed out louder. I quickly forgot all about Claire and looked down at the man I was falling for hard and fast while he smiled up at me. With a sexy wink, he threw my leg over his shoulder as he lifted me up and carried me over to the chair.

The words to the song rang so true at that very moment, as Grayson set me down.

"Do that to me next!" someone screamed.

My mind was running wild as Grayson sat down on me and moved his hips in the most erotic way. My eyes widened with delight. My hands went to touch him before he grabbed them and shook his head. "Friends only tonight, baby," he shouted over the music as I held my hands up like I was in a no-touch zone.

Grayson jumped back and danced around me as dollar bills flew everywhere. I took the chance at peeking over to Claire. I could practically see the steam coming from her ears as she stared me down. Pulling my eyes from her, I watched Grayson do his thing while an extended version of the song continued to play.

Grayson would get close to the crowd, but stop out of their reach to tease them before he would turn his attention back on me.

Grayson picked me up as I wrapped my legs around him while he dipped me back as we danced together in the most sensual way possible. I could feel his hard on pressing into me as he moved his body against mine. Setting me back down in the chair, he climbed on me again and pushed down as I sucked in a breath of air. Grayson laughed and then placed his hands on the sides of my face as he looked into my eyes.

Jesus these feelings . . . what is happening to me?

It was like a roller coaster of emotions that I never wanted to get off of. His lips brushed lightly across mine as he slipped his hand into my hair and deepened the kiss. I wasn't sure how long he kissed me for after the song ended, all I knew was I heard lots of women screaming and then Diana talking.

"Oh, ladies aren't we all very jealous of Grayson's girlfriend, Meagan. She got all the attention tonight, didn't she?"

Grayson and I laughed against each other's lips as he pulled back and looked at me. "I think I'm ready to get out of here."

Rolling my eyes, I nodded. "You're gonna have to sneak out the back!"

Grayson stood up as he reached down for his shirt and put it back on as I stood up. I could feel her stare as I looked down and saw Claire shooting daggers at me.

I wasn't sure why I said it, but I regretted it the moment it slipped from my lips. "Your friend Claire is here."

Grayson turned and looked directly at Claire who smiled and waved. I quickly turned and started toward the side of the stage that led to the back. Grayson was right beside me within seconds as he took my hand and led me straight toward the back door.

The moment the cold air hit my face, I sucked in a deep breath. I hated that she still had some sort of control over my actions.

"Tell me how you know Claire," he said as he looked at me with a concerned face.

Trying to get my senses straight, I stalled with a question. "What?"

"I never said what her name was. You knew back in Texas her name was Claire. How do you know her?"

Something came over me and I pulled away from him in anger. "Why haven't you asked her?"

Grayson's eyes softened as he placed his hands on my

arms. "Because I'm asking you. The first time you saw us that day, when we were at lunch, I saw your face, Meagan. Please talk to me, baby."

Swallowing hard, I looked away. Grayson placed his finger on my chin and pulled my eyes back to him. "Meg?"

"I know her from Baylor."

A look of recognition passed over Grayson's face. "Shit, that's right she mentioned graduating from there. Damn it, I didn't put two and two together."

My eyes searched his face as I took in a deep breath and slowly blew it out. "She didn't . . . um . . . she didn't say anything to you about me after that day?"

Grayson looked at me with a dumbfounded face. "No. She didn't utter a word to me."

I either kept pushing this off, or I faced it head on and told Grayson the truth. It was time to put my past in the past. There was no way in hell I was ever going to let that bitch dictate my life again.

"My freshman year of college I started dating this guy, James was his name. He took me to his frat party and Claire was there with some friends. She was his ex girlfriend, but apparently she hadn't gotten that memo. It was her and another girl who ended up making my life a living hell."

Grayson's eyes widened. "The bullying?"

Chewing on the corner of my lip, I slowly nodded. "Yeah."

"Was it bad?"

Tears built up in my eyes before I pushed them away. I'd never shed another tear because of those girls. "Bad enough that I changed my degree plan and vowed to fight against bullying."

"Baby, I'm so sorry."

With a shrug of my shoulders, I plastered on a fake smile. "It's over. I made it through and I'm a stronger person for it. I won't lie and say I don't have my moments where I get shaken, but there is so much more to life than the rumors and lies those vile girls spread about me."

Grayson placed his hand on the side of my face. "Surely Claire realizes what she did."

My stomach dropped and I instantly felt sick. "I doubt it."

"I mean, that was college."

I swallowed hard as I realized what Grayson was doing. *This is not happening.*

Chapter

EIGHT

Grayson

MEAGAN STOOD BEFORE me with a stunned expression on her face. "I'm ready to go home, Grayson. I'm sure you're exhausted."

Turning, she headed down the alley toward the parking lot. I reached out and grabbed her arm and pulled her back to me. "Wait. I'm not trying to lessen what Claire did to you, Meg. I'm just saying people change and she seems to be really nice and . . ."

"And she doesn't seem like the kind of girl who would send guys to my dorm room telling them I gave out free blowjobs. All hours of the night my freshman year of college, they were at my door. I couldn't walk to class without some asshole approaching me about sex. So, forgive me if I just don't have the heart to forgive her or think someone that vile would ever change."

With a yank of her arm, she pulled away as she started

walking.

I pushed my hands through my hair and cursed. "Fuck." *This was not the way I wanted our night to end.* It started snowing harder as I took off after her. Rounding the corner, I must have hit a patch of ice because I instantly went down and landed on my ankle wrong.

"Shit!" I called out as Meagan spun around.

"Gray! Oh my gosh are you okay?"

She was by my side in less than two seconds, helping me up. My ankle was fine, but I decided to put a plan of action into place. "I think I sprained my ankle."

"No! Oh shit! I'm so sorry."

I draped my arm around her shoulder as she helped me back to the truck. "It wasn't your fault. It was mine. I didn't mean what I said, Meagan and I would never say something if I knew it was going to hurt you."

Her eyes looked into mine as she smiled. She knew I was telling her the truth. "I have no idea what you went through and I'm sorry I tried to lessen any of it."

Meagan's smile slipped away as she looked toward my truck. "It doesn't matter. Like I said, it's in the past and Claire will never hurt me again."

Fuck no she wouldn't.

"I'm not sure I can drive," I said as I tried to hold my smile back.

"Do we need to go to the doctor?"

Panic set in. "No! Um . . . I just need to get back home."

"Okay, I'll drive," Meagan said as she opened the passenger side door. Slipping in, I couldn't believe how easy this was going to be. Meagan was so wrapped up in my ankle being hurt, she wasn't even thinking that I couldn't drive her home.

Sitting on the couch, I turned the television on and let out a deep breath. My lack of sleep was finally catching up to me and I was fighting to keep my eyes open. I could hear Meagan making something in the kitchen and I smiled at the idea of her messing around in my kitchen every day.

She walked around the corner holding a tray. "Okay, here ya go!" she said with excitement in her voice.

I sat up as I watched her put the tray down on the coffee table. My eyes widened at the sight of a bowl of noodle soup, hot chocolate, two pieces of toast with honey drizzled over the top, two chocolate cookies that I was almost positive I bought like three weeks ago, and was that a protein bar?

"Meg, baby, I hurt my ankle. I'm not starving to death."

With a giggle, Meagan flopped down on the couch next to me as she grabbed a piece of toast and the hot chocolate. "Doesn't chicken noodle soup help you with everything?"

Glancing between the soup and the beautiful girl sitting on my couch, I felt my chest tighten. I wasn't falling in love with her, I was already in love with her.

"If I had the flu, yeah. But I have a twisted ankle. Soup isn't going to make the pain go away."

Meagan looked at me through her eyelashes as her eyes danced with fire. "What would make the pain go away?"

An idea popped in my head as I leaned back and looked up toward the ceiling. "Let me think." Snapping my fingers, I pointed to Meagan as she raised her eyebrows.

"You can pay me back."

Pinching her eyes together, she asked, "Pay you back for what?"

"I think I should get a dance since you got one from me."

Meagan started laughing. "What? Are you insane? I'm not dancing for you, besides you used to do it for a living."

Reaching down, I rubbed my ankle and moaned. "The

pain. It's so bad, I don't think I'm going to be able to even sleep."

With a probing gaze, Meagan cocked her head to the side and shook her head. "You're not even hurt, are you?"

My eyes drifted over to the window. The snow was coming down so hard now I knew there was no way I'd be able to take Meagan home. My eyes were burning as I forced myself to stay awake. I didn't even know how many hours I had been up at this point, but my body was for sure beginning to feel it now that I was sitting down.

"It might be feeling a little better. The only way to know is if you shake that sweet ass of yours."

Meagan's teeth sunk down into her lip as she moved her eyes over my body. "Do I get to pick out the song?"

My dick jumped as I sat up straighter and got my sixth wind. "Yep, you've got song choice."

Stay. Cool. Grayson.

Standing, Meagan flashed me an evil smile. "Okay. Give me a second here to think."

I closed my eyes as Meagan made her way over to her phone. Please don't let me be asleep and dreaming.

My body jumped when Meagan cleared her throat. "I need to change out of these jeans."

I tried like hell to swallow the lump in my throat as I simply pointed to my room. Meagan headed toward my bedroom as I dropped my head back and stared up at the ceiling. What song would she pick? Would she really get into this? God, I hope she doesn't touch me because I don't think I can keep up with the whole goddamn best friend thing.

"Ready?"

Lifting my head, my mouth fell open as I took in the sight before me. Meagan had changed into one of my T-shirts that fell to the middle of her thighs. My eyes moved down her body as I moaned and adjusted my hardening dick.

"They're just high heel shoes, Gray."

"No. No, they are so much more than just high heels, baby."

"Should you really be looking at your best friend like that?"

Licking my lips, I nodded my head. "Just dance, Meg."

Meagan turned and walked over and plugged her phone into my speakers. The moment I heard the song, I dropped my head back and groaned.

"God, help me be strong."

Beyoncé's "Dance for You" began playing as I lifted my head and watched Meagan sit on the coffee table with her back facing toward me. If I thought I loved this girl before, I had fallen way over the edge for her with this . . . and she hadn't even started dancing.

The music started and Meagan's hands moved over her body. With the first beat, her legs spread open and she moved like I'd never seen her move before.

"Meagan," I whispered as I watched her whip her hair around as her body moved perfectly to the beat of the song. She stood and put her leg on the coffee table as I forced myself to remember to breathe.

Walking up to me, she dropped her hands to my knees and moved her hips as my mind instantly thought of all the times Meagan had been on top of me, fucking me fast and hard.

"I'm going to die. Right here. Right now."

Meagan smiled as she pushed off me and shook her ass around as she moved her hands across her body.

Taking a few steps back, she leaned over the chair and slowly lifted the T-shirt as she stared into my eyes.

I wonder if I could talk her into doing this every day for the rest of our lives?

"Is this what you wanted, Gray?" Meagan asked as she sat down on the chair and continued to torture me with the way her body was moving. Legs were spreading open . . . then closing. Hands moved over her body as she touched her breasts and I let out a deep growl from the back of my throat.

Meagan moved to the couch and kneeled next to me as she got into the beat of the song.

I swallowed hard as Meagan stood in front of me. Pushing the blanket off of me, I stood and pulled her to me as she gasped at the feel of my dick pushing against her stomach.

It didn't take long for our bodies to melt into one as we danced together. I'd never danced with anyone like that before and it felt so fucking right.

Placing my hand on her lower back, I dropped her back as my eyes took in the pulse beating in her neck.

I lifted her and pulled her closer to me as she hooked her leg around me. Meagan's chest was heaving as she looked directly into my eyes. "I take it that made your ankle feel better?"

My mind was spinning as I tried to make sense of everything. I wanted to tell Meagan exactly what I was thinking. I loved her. I wanted her and only her. Her body did things to me I'd never be able to understand. Her smile shook the very ground I stood on. Her laughter pierced through my chest and made my heart stronger.

"Gray?" Meagan whispered as she ran her finger over my lower lip. "I should go home."

I slowly nodded my head. "You can't."

With a sexy grin, Meagan asked, "Why? Cause you can't drive?"

Shaking my head, I gave her a sexy grin. "It's snowing too hard. I think you're stuck here."

When her lips parted open, I was sure the earth moved. "Huh. Then I guess I should go take a shower."

"Alone?"

Her tongue slowly danced across her lips as she nodded her head and her hands landed on my chest. Meagan slowly pushed me down on the couch as she crawled over me and pushed her pussy against my dick. "You have no idea how much I want you to fuck me."

"The fuck I don't," I said as I grabbed onto her hips and pushed up against her, causing her to moan.

Meagan began grinding her body against mine as I dropped my head back and moved my hands up to her breasts. "I want you so fucking bad."

Her lips moved softly across my neck as she whispered, "I want you too, Gray."

My body relaxed as her lips took me to a place of euphoria. Who the fuck knew simple kisses could be so damn hot.

It was getting harder to keep my eyes open as Meagan pressed against my dick and kissed along my jaw line.

"Fuck, baby. Feels. So. Good."

I felt as if I was floating on cloud nine while Meagan lightly kissed my lips.

"Gray? Baby, you're falling asleep."

As I drifted off into a deep sleep, I wrapped my arms around her as the world slipped away. Life would never be better than this.

I loved her.

I loved her so much.

Chapter
NINE

Meagan

SMILING, I WATCHED as Grayson slipped further away from me. "Gray? Baby, you're falling asleep."

Grayson wrapped his arms around me. "I love you. I love you so much."

My body froze as I stared at him. It wasn't long before he started snoring and his arms slowly fell to his side.

Holy shit.

Oh. My. God.

I slowly crawled off of Grayson and stood. *Did he just? Wait. Did I just hear?*

Turning away from him, I slammed my hands over my mouth to keep my scream in.

Grayson said he loved me.

No. He was falling asleep. That doesn't count. Does it?

I grabbed the T-shirt and my phone and quickly made my way to Grayson's bedroom where I quietly shut the door. Pulling up my contacts, I found Grace's number.

Wait. Maybe I should call Libby. She'd be more level-headed, but then she had a newborn, so she'd be tired. Speaking of, I needed to get my little nephew, Trey, a present. Damn it.

My sister. Yeah, I'll call, Taylor. Then again, Alex is the most levelheaded one.

Closing my eyes, I moved my fingers over my favorites list. When I opened my eyes, I was on Grace's name.

Shit.

I hit her number and paced back and forth until she answered.

"Bitch, you better have something good to tell me if you're calling after midnight."

"Oh shit, I'm sorry, Grace! I didn't realize it was so late."

Grace let out a long dramatic sigh. "It's okay. At least tell me you're calling because you had mind blowing sex."

"Better!"

Silence. Followed by some movement and a door quietly closing. "Better? What in the world would be better for you than mind blowing sex?"

"First. I need a second opinion from your opinion so say one of our other best friends names. First one that comes to your mind."

"Um . . . Lauren?"

"Okay, hold on!"

I clicked over and hit Lauren's number.

It sounded as if Lauren answered and then dropped her phone. "Hello! Meg? Is everything okay?"

"Yes! Sorry Lauren to call so late. Hold on, let me get Grace back on the line."

I brought Grace back on and cleared my throat. "Are you both there?"

Grace and Lauren both said yes at the same time.

"Meg, what's going on?" Lauren asked.

I drew in a deep breath and slowly blew it out. "Okay, so I had the most amazing day of my life today."

"Hot sex?" Lauren asked as I rolled my eyes.

"No! Damn it, y'all. My life is not only about sex."

There was a moment of silence before Grace and Lauren both started laughing.

"Says the girl who sucked her cucumber like a boss," Lauren said with another chuckle.

I took in a deep breath and counted to five. "Do you want to hear my news or not?"

"Yes! Of course we do, sweets. Sorry. Lauren, behave for Christ's sake."

"Me? Tell me you didn't think sex first?"

Grace laughed. "Oh, no I did."

"Ugh! Stop you two!"

"Sorry, Meg. You had the best day of your life. Why?" Lauren asked.

"Okay, so I was pissed at Grayson and then he showed up and said he wanted to spend the day together but as friends only. We went ice skating and then he brought me up to his moms and we ate lunch and—"

"What?" Lauren shouted.

"Hold the fucking phone! You met Ashley?" Grace shouted into the phone as I quickly started getting undressed for my shower. Glancing around, I saw Grayson's robe and slipped it on as I heard a door open and close through the phone.

"Noah! Wake up! Grayson took Meg to meet Aunt Ashley."

Noah mumbled something as I tip toed back out to Grayson's living room to check on him. He was out cold.

Turning, I headed back into the bathroom and shut the door. "No, I'm delirious from being pregnant," Grace said as I heard a door shut again.

"Can we move on from meeting Gray's mom?"

"No!" Grace said. "Meg, that is like huge. A guy like

Gray doesn't bring home just any girl."

"Oh my glitter! This is so romantic. You met his mom!" Lauren said as she sighed dramatically into the phone. At this rate I'm thinking I would have been better with the sleep-deprived new mother.

"Moving. On," I said as I sat down on the toilet. "So anyway, after that we went to a club and Gray danced. Jesus H. Christ, it was hot as hell."

"Gray danced? As in he stripped?" Lauren asked as concern filled her voice.

"No, not really. His old boss was there, and they had a few guys dancing, only taking off shirts and stuff, they weren't showing anything. Anyway, she asked Gray to dance and he said yes, and he put me on stage and got me all turned on and I couldn't do anything because today we were just friends." I dragged in a deep breath and kept talking.

"Then Claire was there and I got pissed and did what I always do and took off, but Gray wouldn't let me and I ended up telling him everything about Claire and what she did to me in college."

"Good!" Grace said.

"Yes, I agree with Grace. I'm glad you told him about that bitch."

I nodded my head even though they couldn't see me. "Well, then he twisted his ankle, but he really didn't—he just said he did and we came back to his place and he told me the only way he'd feel better was if I danced for him, so . . . I did."

"What song?" Grace and Lauren asked together. How in the hell they were keeping up, I'll never know.

"'Dance For You' by Beyoncé."

"Nice!" Grace said as Lauren giggled. "Then you had hot sex."

"I tried to."

"Um . . . you tried to? Meg . . . I've never known you

not to be able to have sex. Especially with Gray. I'm pretty sure his sergeant was made for your Wonder Woman."

Lauren busted out laughing as I bit down on my lip to keep from laughing.

"Shut up, Grace. Shall I get back to my story now?"

"Please do," Grace said.

"Anyway, I thought things were going to move on, but Grayson had been up for hours. He worked all through the previous night, so I honestly don't even know how long he had been up for . . . well he fell asleep as I tried to get my sex on."

"So, let me get this straight," Grace said, "you spent the day with him as friends only."

"Yes."

"Then you met his mom, as friends only."

"Uh-huh," I whispered as I chewed on my nail.

"Then he took you out, danced and put his junk all up on you, right?"

"Oh yes he did."

"Then you returned the favor after you finally told him about the whore, Claire?"

"Yes."

"And as you were getting hot and heavy, he fell asleep."

"Right."

"Okay yeah, I'm with Grace on this one, why in the hell did you call us in the middle of the night to tell us that, Meg?"

I closed my eyes and pulled in a deep breath through my nose before I pushed it slowly out between my lips. "I called y'all because as he was falling asleep he . . . he um . . . well . . . he said . . ."

"What? What did he say for the love of all things good?" Lauren said.

"He said he loved me. But earlier today he said he was falling in love with me. I forgot to tell y'all that part. It was during an amazing kiss."

"Wait a second. I need to process," Grace said slowly.

Lauren gasped. "How in the hell do you forget to tell us he told you he was falling in love with you? Oh. My. Glitter. This is huge!"

Grace cleared her throat. "What did you say to him?"

"When?"

"Jesus H. Christ, Meg. When he said he was falling in love with you."

My heart felt like it stopped beating. "I said I was falling in love with him too."

Grace and Lauren both gasped. "Holy fucking shit balls, this is huge!" Grace said as Lauren chuckled.

"This is beyond huge, Grace! Meg's in love! Meg. Is. In. Love!"

I rolled my eyes as I pulled my knees up to my chest and wrapped my left arm around them. "Gesh, Lauren. Why don't you make it seem like I'm not capable of loving?"

"No, Meg I think it's great. I'm just surprised."

"I'm not, I heard the two of them having sex before."

"Gross, Grace"," Lauren said while making a gagging sound.

"You're gagging? Bitch do you know how many times I've heard Meagan calling out while getting fu—"

My legs dropped as I jumped down. "Okay, can we just stop now? What am I going to do y'all?"

"About what?" Grace asked.

I lifted my hand and waved it around like a crazy person. "This! This whole Grayson thing where he told me he loved me when he was falling asleep. How do I even know if he meant it?"

Lauren sighed. "I've got this one, Grace. Let's see, he told you earlier he was falling in love with you. He gave you an amazing day where y'all didn't focus on sex, but instead on just being with each other, and then he told you he loved you. It doesn't matter if he said it while he was nodding off. Meg, sweetie, Grayson is in love with you and has probably been wanting to tell you for some time now."

I felt my cheeks instantly blush as I smiled. "Grace?"

"I totally agree with Lauren. The fact that he spent an entire day with you, dog-ass tired, from lack of sleep I might add, and to tell you he was falling in love with you. Oh, Meg, honey I see the way the two of you look at each other. Babe, I think you met your lobster."

"Yes!" Lauren said with a giggle. "Your lobster!"

"Oh my God," I whispered. "I'm in love with him. I'm so in love with him, y'all. What if he ends up hurting me? I don't think my heart could take it."

"That's what love is, Meg. It's a risk and a scary one at that. But if you just let go and fall, I promise you the landing is so worth it."

Tears built in my eyes as I fought for the words to say. Clearing my throat, I smiled as I said, "Lauren, when did you become so wise?"

"Jesus H. Christ, Lauren. You made me cry you little bitch," Grace said as she sniffled.

"It's the pregnancy hormones, Grace," Lauren said.

"Yeah, probably"," Grace said as she blew her nose.

I looked at myself in the mirror as I slowly shook my head and sat down on the toilet again. Putting my head in my hand, I moaned. "So what do I do now? What if he doesn't remember saying it?"

"He'll remember"," Grace and Lauren said at once.

"What if he doesn't? Do I say something? I mean what do you say in a situation like this? Oh hey, Gray, last night before you passed out on me you changed my entire world, do you remember that because I'll never forget it for as long as I live. Do you remember telling me you loved me?"

"Yes."

My head snapped up as my eyes widened in surprise. Grayson was leaning against the door frame with a sexy smile plastered across his face.

"Holy shit! Was that Gray?" Grace shouted. "Sorry, Noah! Go back to sleep, baby!"

"Yep," I whispered into the phone.

"Does he look hot?" Lauren asked. "I bet he looks hot."

"Oh yeah," I said as my eyes raked over his body.

"Girl, get you some of that now before the little bastard falls back asleep," Grace said as Lauren giggled.

"Gotta go girls, bye."

"Bye, Meg! Call us in the morning!" Lauren said as I pulled the phone from my ear and hit End.

"Hey," I whispered as I stood up.

Grayson's eyes swam with passion as he stared at me. "Hey. I woke up and you weren't straddling me anymore."

With a grin, I tilted my head. "You fell asleep."

He took a step closer to me while my eyes roamed his perfect body. Those black cotton pants that hung just low enough to have a girl's imagination going crazy.

"I'm awake now."

I swallowed hard while his muscles flexed with each movement. I longed to let out a moan but suppressed it. "Yep. You are."

Holy crap. Really, that's all you've got Meagan?

Stopping in front of me, Grayson placed his finger on my chin and lifted my eyes to his and softly spoke. "Are you ready to fall?"

My heart slammed against my chest as Lauren's words replayed in my head.

"Will you catch me, Gray?"

His hands cupped my face as his eyes stared intently into mine.

"Yes. Meg, I meant what I said. Spending today with you just made it all the more clear. I love you."

My knees felt weak as my heart hammered. Closing

my eyes, I followed Lauren's advice. I was ready for the jump.

I opened my eyes and took in a shaky breath as I whispered, "I love you too."

His smile caused me to smile as our lips pressed together. Grayson's hands moved into my hair as he deepened the kiss. After a few minutes of nothing but kissing, he picked me up as he carried me to his bed and gently set me down, never once breaking apart from one another.

Slowly pulling his lips from mine, Gray's eyes looked deeply into mine. "Let me show you how much I love you, baby."

Chapter TEN

Grayson

MY HEART HAD never felt like this before as I watched Meagan's chest rise and fall as I slowly stood and undressed myself. Waking up alone, I searched for her as I made my way to my bedroom. When I heard her voice coming from my bathroom, I slowly opened the door and stood there frozen as I listened to her talking.

I thought I had dreamed I told her I loved her; truth be told, I'm glad I said it out loud. It needed to be said.

"You're wearing my robe," I said as I sat down on the bed and untied it.

The moment her tongue slid across her teeth, I knew I was fucked. I'd never be able to live without her. "I was going to take a um . . . take a shower."

With a quick move of my hand, both sides of the robe fell open to reveal her beautiful body. Crawling onto the bed, I moved the robe out of the way as I lightly kissed her stomach. Meagan's body trembled as I moved slowly over her body, pressing one light kiss after another until I reached her neck.

"You're so beautiful, Meg. You take my breath away."

I wanted to make her feel how much I cared for her. How much I loved her. With everything that had happened to her in the past, I needed her to know that what we had was real. "I'm going to make love to you all night long."

Meagan lifted her eyebrow and flashed me a sexy as hell smile. "Or at least until you fall asleep again."

With a chuckle, I peppered her face with kisses as I pushed my hard dick against her body. "I've gotten my seventh wind."

"I see that," Meagan said as her hands moved gently over my back. "Gray, my body is shaking I want you so much."

With a smile, I rubbed my nose against hers as I whispered, "We have our whole lives to get lost in each other. I want to take my time with you tonight."

Meagan's hands moved to the back of my neck where she pulled me closer to her lips. Kissing her was what I imagined heaven must be like. I'd never in my life had a woman affect me the way Meagan did.

My hands slid between her body and the robe as I cupped her ass and pulled her hips closer to me, my cock teasing her entrance as Meagan moaned.

"Gray . . . condom."

I pushed in a little more; the feel of her pussy on my bare cock was almost too much to stand. I'd never in my life had sex without a condom, and I had never in my life wanted to so badly. I pushed in more as I squeezed her ass harder.

"Gray," Meagan whispered.

My lips brushed over hers as I said, "Meg, you've been my only partner in over two years."

Her hands stopped moving and her body stilled.

"W-what?"

I knew this was a conversation that needed all my attention, but her pussy was practically pulling me in. "Grayson, you've only been with me since we met?"

Stopping my motions, I pulled my hands out from under her and held myself above her as I gazed into her eyes. "Just because I was a stripper, doesn't mean I was a manwhore. I broke up with my last girlfriend a few months before I saw you again in Austin. I always used a condom with her and everyone before that. I've never not used one."

Meagan gnawed on her lip as her eyes searched mine. "What makes you not want to use one with me?"

With a smile, I kissed her lips softly. "That's easy. Because I love you and I want to give my whole self to you and I want you to do the same."

Meagan's eyes glistened with a mist as she grinned. "I've never had sex without a condom and you're the only guy I've been with in over three years . . . if not longer."

My heart slammed against my chest as I positioned myself and slowly pushed the head of my cock through her wetness. "And I'm going to be the last guy you're ever with, Meg."

Passion filled her eyes as she lifted her hips and wrapped her legs around my body, pulling me further into her as we both moaned.

Slow was something Meagan and I had never really done before. Sex with her had always been hot . . . really fucking hot . . . and passionate. The moment she was around me all I could think of was burying myself inside of her and hearing her call out my name.

This was different. Tonight was different. Nothing would ever be the same after this.

I pushed as far into her as I could as Meagan wrapped her legs around me tighter.

"Oh God, Gray." She spoke softly while her back

arched up. Grabbing her hands, I laced my fingers with hers and took my time pulling out and pushing in. As slow as we were taking this, our bodies quickly were covered in a sheen of sweat. I wasn't sure how long I would be able to keep this up. The urge to grab onto her hips and fuck her was overwhelming. The feel of her without a condom was mind blowing.

My lips found their way to Meagan's as she whispered, "Feels so amazing, so perfect."

I wanted this night to be perfect for her and if perfect meant going slow, then that was what I would do.

As I pushed in, I circled my hips, causing Meagan to moan. I repeated it and this time Meagan moved her hips up to allow me to go deeper. With another circle, Meagan called out my name as her entire body quivered with her orgasm.

With a smile, I buried my face into her neck while she softly repeated my name while grasping onto me tightly.

"Oh God, I've never . . . that was . . . Grayson."

I loved that she was so overwhelmed by what we were sharing she couldn't even talk. "Faster, Gray. I want it faster."

My eyes about rolled to the back of my head as I pushed up and lifted her legs over my shoulders. Grabbing onto her hips, I moved faster, trying like hell not to go too fast.

Meagan's hands grabbed onto the sheets as she hissed through her teeth, "Yes!"

"Fuck, Meg. I can't hold out much longer, baby."

Her eyes opened and captured mine. That was my undoing. I pulled out and slammed back into her, causing her to cry out. Then I lost all control and fucked her hard and fast. My body trembled as I felt my own build up starting.

"Grayson! I'm going to come again!" Meagan cried out as I pushed in hard and grunted, spilling my cum into her body. The feeling was unlike anything I had ever experienced.

Pulling out, I rolled over onto the bed and pulled in one deep breath after another.

"There is nothing I love more in this world than being inside of you, Meg."

Fingers slowly moved across my chest as I felt my eyes grow heavy. With a smile on my face, I drifted off to sleep one happy and satisfied man.

∞⁂∞

The game played quietly on the television as I whisked the eggs and watched my favorite team, the Dallas Cowboys, run the ball in for a touchdown.

"Yes!" I said as I fist pumped and got back to making omelets. "I'm totally going to win this week."

Meagan stood at the doorway of my bedroom, wearing nothing but one of my T-shirts as she yawned and slowly made her way into the kitchen. "Oh man. Mr. Bennett, you wore me out last night."

With a chuckle, I kissed her fast on the lips and got back to cooking us a late breakfast. "I can't believe it's almost noon," Meagan said as she reached up and took down a coffee cup.

"Well, once you finally stopped seducing me in the middle of the night, we were able to fall asleep around what, three or so?"

Meagan giggled as she blew on the coffee and scrunched her nose and took a sip. "I seduced you? Really? Because the way I remember it you seduced me, then passed out cold, only to wake me up with your dick slipping back into my body."

"The sergeant needed his Wonder Woman."

Meagan rolled her eyes and sat down on the barstool. "Scrambled eggs?"

My mouth dropped open as I stared at her. "Fuck no. I'm making omelets."

"Really? Huh."

"What's that supposed to mean?"

With a shrug of her shoulders, Meagan attempted to hide her smile. "I just never pictured you . . . cooking."

Narrowing my eyes at her, I shook my head. "I'm a good cook." Pointing at her with the spatula, I said, "Probably better than you."

"Is that right?" Meagan asked with a serious expression.

"Damn straight it is. I'd cook circles around you, Ms. Atwood."

Meagan stood up and took another sip of her coffee before setting it down on the island and walking over to me. Her hands landed on my chest as they slowly made their way up. Wrapping her arms around my neck, Meagan tilted her head and looked at me. "Want to make a wager?"

My dick jumped as I stared back at her. "What kind of a wager?"

"We each take one dish and make it. Someone neutral has to judge it."

I was liking the sound of that. I knew Meagan wasn't much of a domesticated kind of girl. She'd rather go to a nice restaurant over cooking any day. This was in the bag for me.

"And if I win?"

"I'll do whatever you want to do."

My second head kicked in and talked for me. "Anything sexual or anything not sexual?"

Biting down on her lip, Meagan flashed a sexy smile. "*Anything* you want."

Oh hell yeah.

"So, if I said I wanted to bend you over, tie your hands to something and fuck you in the ass, you'd let me?"

Meagan licked her lips. "I've never had anal sex before, so I'm guessing you're going to have to start me with something smaller than this to get me ready."

Running her hand over my rock hard dick, I moaned. "And . . . if you . . . win?"

"You have to give me my own private dance show. I want to see what all those other lucky women got to see when you used to dance."

I couldn't help but smile. There wasn't anything I wouldn't do for Meagan. If she asked me right now to do that for her, I would.

"It's a deal. Who picks the meal?"

Meagan lifted her eyes in thought as a warm feeling spread through my body while I looked at her beautiful body. "Melissa."

My head pulled back slightly. "Your boss?"

With a nod of her head and a chuckle, she said, "Yep!"

I blew out a deep breath as I thought about it. "All right. Then I get to pick who judges."

"Fair enough."

Meagan was rubbing her foot up and down her leg, causing my dick to throb. "Diana."

Meagan laughed like I was kidding. Once she saw I was serious, she stared at me with a look of disbelief. "Your old boss? The owner of the strip club?"

"Yep. I'll even ask her if I can use the club if, and that's a big if, you win."

Something passed over Meagan's face and I knew in that instant, she would be winning this bet, but I'd still be claiming that ass as mine.

Meagan reached her hand out to mine as we shook. "Deal," we both said at once.

"Do I have time to take a quick shower?"

Reaching around her, I slapped her perfect ass and laughed. "You have about ten minutes."

Shortly after Meagan got into the shower, my front doorbell rang. I turned the fire down on the eggs and made my way through the living room, yelling for the quarterback to throw the ball. Still looking at the television, I opened the door and felt someone push me out of the way. Turning, I watched as Claire made her way into my apartment.

What the fuck?

"Grayson, I can't even believe you were with that vile girl last night."

It took me a few seconds to figure out what in the hell she was talking about.

"I mean, I didn't say anything the first time I saw Meagan at lunch that day. I thought you were just friends. But then to see you with her and dancing with her like you were. I think it's only right for me to tell you I know her, Grayson. We went to Baylor at the same time and let's just say, you might not want to be messing around with her."

I couldn't believe my ears. This girl was insane if she thought I'd even entertain her.

"Claire, you can leave now," I said as I motioned for her to head back through the door.

Claire stood with her hands on her hips. "Grayson. I'm only trying to shed some light on this. I'm not angry you stood me up for our date; you had your reasons, although I pray they weren't Meagan Atwood. She's a whore."

Anger began to build as I tried to remain calm. Before I even had a chance to say something, Claire shot off again. "She was known on campus for giving guys blowjobs. I also heard she had unprotected sex almost every night. Who knows what kind of diseases she is carrying." A total fake look of horror came over Claire's face. "Please tell me you haven't had sex with her."

Leaning against the doorframe, I smiled. "Oh Claire, Meagan and I have been having sex for some time now. Hot amazing fuck fests."

Anger moved swiftly across her face. "Well, girls like that make guys like you not think clearly. You should be making love to someone, Grayson. Not having, what did you call it?"

"Fuck fests," I said with a wink. "And believe me, Claire, I've made love to her plenty of times. So, if you'll take your poor pathetic excuse for a person and get the hell out of my apartment, I'd really appreciate it. I'm actually trying to make breakfast for my girlfriend."

Claire swallowed hard. "G-girlfriend."

"Hey, Claire," Meagan said as she strolled over toward me in a long blue T-shirt of mine. "I see some people never seem to step out of the role of bully."

With a nervous laugh, Claire looked between Meagan and me. "I don't know what you're talking about."

Meagan took a step closer to Claire, causing her to take a step back. "See, Claire, all those years of torture by you and your little flunky friends taught me a thing or two. The first thing, anything that comes out of your mouth is vile. I actually feel sorry for you because you must have had a really shit-filled life to try to make someone else's life miserable. That's the only thing I can come up with for people like you."

Shooting Meagan a dirty look, Claire lifted her chin. "People like me?"

"Bullies, Claire. You see, you don't have to be in elementary school to encounter one. They come in all walks of life, any age, any size, and any color. The difference is now you don't threaten me because I know who I am and what I've always been. I pray that someday when you have a child they don't encounter someone like you."

Claire opened her mouth to talk but quickly shut it. Turning to me, she shook her head and pushed past both of us and out the door. Shutting it, I turned to see Meagan smiling.

"Thank you for not believing her lies."

I went to talk right as the smoke alarms went off in the kitchen. "The eggs!"

Meagan and I ran into the kitchen as smoke filled the

small space. Grabbing the eggs, I tossed the pan into the sink and frowned.

With a sexy smile, Meagan walked up to me and ran her finger along my jaw. "I'm still hungry," she purred.

Twenty seconds later, Meagan was sitting on the counter as I moved in and out of her body fast and hard.

Perfect breakfast.

Chapter
ELEVEN

Meagan

"EARTH TO MEAGAN."

Fingers snapped in my face as I directed my attention over to Melissa. "Are you even listening to me?"

With a grin, I nodded. "Yes."

Melissa cocked her head to the left and looked at me like I was full of shit. "Please. You were off in a dreamland and didn't hear anything I just said. You haven't been able to wipe that smile from your face for the last two weeks."

Biting on the corner of my lip, I attempted to keep my happiness at bay. "So I'm happy. Is that a bad thing?"

"Heck no it's not a bad thing, I'm happy for you, Meagan. I just need you to focus on the task at hand and not drift off into a daydream about your boyfriend. Your rather good looking boyfriend, I might add."

The light tap on the door caused Melissa and I both to turn and look at Jennifer. "Meagan, I wanted to remind you of your appointment with Mitchell."

With a quick nod of my head, I stood. "Thanks, Jennifer."

As I gathered up my notebook and pen, Melissa stood. "How are things with Mitchell going?"

"Good. If he's being honest with me, which I think he is. He comes in once a week and it appears things have calmed down at school. The rest of the football team seems to be treating him as a member of the team now."

"That's good news. What about the coach?"

Stopping what I was doing, I glanced up at Melissa. "The coach is a real asshole and I'd give anything to be able to tell him that. When I asked him to educate his team on the effects of bullying, he practically laughed in my face. Claimed no one on his football team was bullying anyone and if they were, he'd kick their ass. The guy wears blinders to everything that happens."

My boss pushed out a deep breath. It was a constant struggle in our profession. Parents, teachers, coaches, all claiming it isn't their kids causing the trouble. No one ever wants to admit something is wrong until it's too late. My job was to make sure it was never too late.

With a smile, I hugged my notebook to my chest. "Mitch has a girlfriend. I think that's helped."

Melissa frowned. "That can be a good thing or a bad thing. If things end badly with the girlfriend, that might not be such a great thing. Keep that in mind, Meagan."

My heart ached a bit because I knew she was right. I also remember thinking I wish I had had someone to save me from all the shit that was happening to me in college. The lump in my throat grew bigger as I walked back to my office. Why me of all people thought a girlfriend would be the answer to all for Mitchell confused me. I knew better and had to make sure Mitchell knew that as well.

Before I had time to even sit, three knocks on the door signaled Mitchell. "Hey, Meg!"

Turning to face him, I smiled when I saw his dimpled smile staring straight at me. He reminded me so much of Grayson it wasn't even funny.

"Hey there. You're a little early."

Mitchell shrugged. "You said we were heading out on a field trip and I'm all about field trips."

I couldn't wait for Mitchell to find out we were headed to the police station. His dream was to become a cop, like his father was. Unfortunately, his father died in the line of duty, leaving his mother to raise three boys on her own. That was the main reason they left California and moved back to Colorado, so Mrs. Haus could be close to her family to help with the boys.

"Yep, we are for sure headed out on a field trip today. Have you had lunch yet?"

Mitchell shook his head. "No ma'am."

Grabbing my purse, I motioned for Mitchell to follow me. "Good, because I'm starving."

~❦~

I decided to take Mitchell to one of my favorite places to eat lunch. Snow was slowly falling, making it a bit tricky to drive for me, seeing as I was still new to driving in this stuff. If it snowed in Texas, everything shut down and you stayed home.

"I hope you like pizza!" I said as we walked into Fired Up Pizzeria.

Mitchell laughed. "Who doesn't like pizza?"

"I can't argue with you on that one. Let's grab that table over there before someone else snags it."

After sitting down and ordering our drinks, Mitchell and I settled into a casual conversation about how school was going. His grades, how his little brothers were adjusting to life in Colorado as well as how his mom was doing.

Mitchell glanced up and smiled as I felt warm breath

hit my neck. "Hey beautiful," Gray whispered as he placed a kiss on the side of my face. I instantly felt my cheeks flush as I glanced over to Mitchell. The goofy smile on his face spoke volumes.

"Ah, Meg has herself a boyfriend!" Mitchell teased as Gray reached out and shook Mitchell's hand.

"Indeed she does. You must be Mitchell, Meg speaks very highly of you."

Now it was Mitchell who turned red. "Mitchell, this is my boyfriend, Grayson, but everyone calls him Gray."

"The pleasure is all mine, sir," Mitchell said. It didn't take long for both men to get lost in the talk of sports as I watched Mitchell. Seeing him so happy was a far cry from a few months ago when his mother sat across from me in my office and told me her son hated life.

The adjustment from being one of the best high school football players in Sacramento, California and a super popular kid, to someone who had to fight to get onto the football team and was hated almost instantly by a group of jealous guys, had been a hard one. The fact that Mitchell was so good had intimidated the other players. Instead of them welcoming him in . . . they shunned him. It didn't help matters any more when recruiters from colleges kept showing up to watch him play.

"So you've already had colleges interested since your sophomore year? Man dude, that is impressive."

Mitchell grinned. "Yeah, it was crazy. When we told my football coach we were moving, I was almost positive I saw a tear in his eye."

Grayson and I both laughed. "It was hard at first moving here. It didn't help that a scout from Stanford showed up to talk to the football coach before I was even here."

Mitchell looked down. "I think that's why I had all the trouble when I first moved here. A lot of guys on the football team gave me hell."

"Why?" I asked with a frown.

Mitchell shrugged. "A few of them accused me of coming here to get away from the competition in California. Like I was looking to catch recruiters' eyes here better or something. It's all so stupid."

"How are things now?" Grayson asked. Mitchell seemed to be so at ease with Gray. I was stunned at how openly he was talking about all of this to him. I had to practically pull it out of Mitchell and that was after hours of working to gain his trust.

"It's better. Once I actually got on the team and started playing. Casey helps though."

With a smile, Grayson asked, "And who might Casey be?"

"Casey is Mitchell's girlfriend. Things going okay with y'all?"

Mitchell laughed. "Dude, I'm still not used to you saying y'all. But to answer your question, things are going good. Casey's been a big help with me getting settled in and feeling accepted."

Grayson frowned. "I'm sure you'd fit in just fine though without Casey."

Mitchell shrugged. "Yeah, probably."

The rest of lunch was spent mostly with Grayson and Mitchell talking football.

After paying the waitress, I grinned and said, "You ready for my surprise?"

Mitchell chuckled. "Surprise? I thought we were going on a field trip."

"It's both!" I said as I slid out of the booth while Grayson held onto my hand. Lifting the back of my hand to his lips, Grayson kissed me softly and winked before turning to Mitchell and reaching for his hand to shake it.

"I'll meet you both over at the station."

Mitchell looked between Grayson and me confused. "O-okay see you at the . . . station?"

As we walked out to my car, Mitchell laughed. "So

what station are we going to? Like the police station?"

Hitting the button to unlock my car, I glanced over to Mitchell. "That's exactly where we're going."

Chapter
TWELVE

Grayson

I'D NEVER MET a kid like Mitchell before. He seemed sure of himself, yet so unsure of himself. I couldn't really read him. Meagan had already filled me in about Mitchell's father and all the bullying he had gone through when he first moved here.

"When did you know you wanted to be in law enforcement?" Mitchell asked me as we headed back to where Meagan had set up shop with her laptop and worked while I showed Mitchell around.

Taking in a deep breath, I blew it out and thought for a moment. "I'd have to say when I saw a woman being robbed. God it pissed me off so much. I ran after the asshole and knocked him to the ground and buried my knee into his back until the police showed up. The woman kept thanking me over and over. When the cop shook my hand and told me they needed more people like me, it just kind of clicked. I grew up with a single mom, so I was used to keeping her safe."

Mitchell nodded his head as he stared down at the floor while we walked. "What about you?"

In a nonchalant kind of way, he grinned. "I guess it's just always been something I wanted to do. My father was a cop and I remember him coming home at night and the way my mother looked relieved at first to see him . . . and then proud as hell. He used to sit me on his lap and tell me how I was going to follow in his footsteps, so that's what I'm going to do. Make both him and my mother proud."

I could see it in Mitchell's face. As much as he wanted to believe this was his calling, I had a feeling it was far from what he wanted to do.

"There hasn't been anything else you'd like to do?" I asked as we stopped outside the vacant office Meagan was working in.

"Oh I don't know. I guess I've tossed around a few ideas. I've always loved football. Before we left California I used to coach a fifth grade football team. I loved it. I mentioned once to my mother about playing college football and if I'm lucky, pro. Then after that I'd love to coach."

Mitchell let out a gruff laugh and shook his head as he combed his hand through his short blond hair. "That didn't go over so well. She was pissed and said that was no way to make a living."

I raised my eyebrows, surprised at his mother's response. "Coaching huh? I did that for a bit while volunteering at an outreach place for boys from abused and neglected homes."

Mitchell's curiosity peeked. "Really? Wow, that's really cool of you."

Placing my hand on his shoulder, I gave it a light squeeze. "I get wanting to make your parents proud, Mitchell, but in the long run it's your life and you have to do what makes you happy."

With a forced smile, Mitchell nodded his head. "Yeah, tell that to my mother."

My heart hurt for this kid. He had a talent for football, yet he was being blocked from every single side.

Mitchell reached for the door and pushed it open. Meagan was typing away on her computer when she glanced up and smiled. "Hey. How was the tour?"

Mitchell put on what I was assuming was the masked face he had gotten used to using around everyone. A weird feeling passed over me as I made a mental note to talk to Meagan about what I talked to Mitchell about.

"It was awesome. Thank you, Meg, for arranging this."

Meagan smiled bigger, clearly thinking this was something Mitchell wanted to do.

"Well my gosh, I better get us back to the office so you can get home." Meagan turned to me and flashed me a heavenly smile. "Thank you, Gray, for doing this for us."

"Anytime. Mitchell, you have my number if you ever want to talk."

Meagan's eyes lit up as she gave me an adoring look. With a quick kiss goodbye, I watched as Meagan and Mitchell left the station. A terrible feeling came over me as I wondered how much longer Mitchell would be able to keep up this happy front of his.

～✖～

"Hey there, handsome."

Glancing up, I saw Claire standing with her hands spread across the desk and just the right amount of cleavage hanging out to make a guy do a double take.

"What do you need, Claire?"

Ever since the encounter a few weeks back at my place, Claire had kept her distance. Except for today. She saw me walking in with Meagan and Mitchell and something must have come over her because she had come up with every excuse under the sun to come talk to me today.

"It appears we don't have your next of kin's address correct in the system. I'm going to need you to come to my office and update that."

I narrowed my eyes at her. She clearly was up to no good. "I'll email it to you."

With a pout of her lips, she batted her eyes and said, "What's the matter, Grayson? Afraid to be alone with me?"

A gruff laugh came from my lips as Derrick chuckled. "I'll send the information over to you, Claire, and copy HR on the email."

Claire's smile dropped as she stood up and glanced over to Derrick and then back to me. "You have no idea what you're missing out on."

Deciding to ignore her comment, I pulled out my phone and saw I had a voicemail from my mother. I turned away from Claire and hit play.

"Hey! I was wondering if you and Meagan would like to come for lunch or dinner this weekend. I'd love to see you both again. Let me know. Love you, Gray and please be careful."

Opening up my messages, I sent my mother off a text message.

> *Me: Hey, Mom! I'd love to come for lunch or dinner this weekend. Let me check with Meg and see how her schedule looks. I'll let you know tonight or tomorrow.*

My mother quickly responded back.

> *Mom: Sounds good, Grayson. Stay safe and I love you.*

"How's your mom doing?" Derrick asked as he typed up a report from yesterday's attempted robbery.

Letting out a deep breath, I got back to what I had been doing before Claire walked up. "She's doing good. Loves her place up in the mountains and loves her new job working at the elementary school as the art teacher."

Derrick gave me smile. "That's great."

Our sergeant poked his head out of his office and called out our names. "Winn, Bennett, we've got a 187 down on Westgate."

My heart stopped. That wasn't far from Meagan's office.

Jumping up, I grabbed my jacket and followed Derrick out of the building and to the car.

Fifteen minutes later, we pulled up to the crime scene and walked over to Dalton Murphy with CSI. "Looks like another rape/murder."

My stomach turned as I saw the victim on the ground, long brown hair, and slender build, mid twenties.

"Same as the other two?" Derrick asked Dalton.

"Yeah, looks like it. I don't want to say we have a serial rapist murderer out there, but it appears he left the same calling card," Dalton said as he pointed to the belt wrapped around the woman's neck.

"Fuck," I whispered as I pulled out my phone and called Meagan.

"Hey, what's up?"

Taking a few steps away, I let out a sigh of relief. "Hey, baby. I just wanted to make sure you got back to your office okay."

"Yep. Sorry, I should have sent you a text. Still getting used to this whole *my boyfriend is a cop and worries nonstop* thing."

With a shallow grin, I nodded my head and looked around. "Will you stay at my place tonight?"

"Sure. Is everything okay, Gray?"

"Yeah, everything is fine. I just want to sleep with you wrapped up in my arms, that's all."

Meagan purred through the phone. "I like the sound of that. I'll call you when I'm leaving."

Turning, I glanced back over to the body of the young girl. "Okay baby, I'll see you later. I love you, Meg."

"I love you too, Gray. Bye."

I made my way back over to the scene. Derrick and I both talked to the woman who found the body and made arrangements for her to come in and give a statement. The whole time I felt the hair on my neck rising. One look around showed a small crowd gathered around trying to see what was going on.

"Winn?" I asked as I hit him on the arm.

"What's up?"

"Why do I have the strangest feeling the killer is watching us from somewhere close by?"

Derrick looked around at the crowd and then around the buildings. "He might be. Probably some sick bastard who gets a kick out of watching us figure out who in the fuck he is. You're gonna find out there are some fucked up people in this world, Bennett."

My eyes scanned the crowd and stopped on a younger man. His blond hair was barely seen under his knit cap. When our eyes met, he smiled. Something about him didn't sit right with me as I made my way over to him.

"Detective Bennett; your name is?"

The young man reached his hand out to mine and shook it firmly. "Joshua Black. I live up in the condos right over there."

Joshua pointed to the building on the corner. "You see anything out of the ordinary."

He frowned and shook his head. "No, sir. I didn't."

With a nod, I looked around and then back into his eyes. "Any particular reason you smiled when I looked at you?"

Joshua seemed to be taken aback with my question. "Hell, I don't know. The polite thing to do I guess? I mean you looked directly at me. What was I supposed to do, give you the finger?"

Realizing I was most likely overreacting and that this whole detective thing was still so damn new, I let out a chuckle. "I guess you've got a point. If you think of anything that you might remember later on, be sure to let us know."

"Yes sir, of course."

I turned to start heading back to the crime scene when Joshua called out for me. "Detective Bennett!"

I stopped and looked back at him. "Do you know who she is? I mean, do you know what happened to her or why it happened?"

With a shake of my head, I turned and walked away.

Chapter
THIRTEEN

Meagan

ONE QUICK LOOK in the mirror and I was happy with what I saw. Grayson and I were headed up to his mother's house today for lunch. My hands moved over the light-blue dress as I drew in a deep breath and tried to calm my nerves. I'd met Ashley once before, but now it was official; Grayson and I were dating, practically living together. I spent most of my nights here at Grayson's place and only went home to grab more clothes.

"Meg, are you almost done?"

Frowning, I leaned in closer. "Damn it, is that mascara?"

"No, it's not. Let's get going or we're going to be late. My mother does not like late."

Panic set in as I quickly spun on my heels and grabbed my purse. "Shit! Why didn't you tell me we were running late?"

Grayson laughed. "I did, when you said you only had one more piece of hair to curl."

"How late are we?" I asked as I pushed past him and ran into the kitchen. I opened the refrigerator and reached for the seven-layer dip Grayson had asked me to make. The moment I felt his hands on my ass, I knew we were both in trouble.

"Damn, Meg. You look so fucking hot in this dress."

Turning, I set the casserole dish on the island. My body was on fire just from his touch. His finger came up and traced along my jaw line as his name passed softly through my lips.

"We're late," I giggled as his hands moved down my body.

"So what, my mother can wait."

I shook my head as I sucked in a breath while Grayson lowered his body and ran his hands up my legs then he pushed my dress up and around my waist.

His eyes lit up when he saw the black lace panties. His head moved in as he kissed me through the thin lace. "Oh God," I panted as my head dropped back.

His fingers slowly pulled my panties off as I gave in to my desire. I could practically feel the wetness growing between my legs.

Grayson stood and brought the panties up to his face and took in a deep breath. "Fucking hell, it smells like heaven."

My tongue ran along my lips as I fought to breathe.

"Tonight I'm fucking you, Meagan."

I swallowed hard. "Why tonight? Why not right now?"

Grayson slipped my panties into the back pocket of his jeans and grabbed my hand, pulling me to him. Our lips were inches apart from each other. "Because you took too long curling your hair."

The drive to Ashley's house was getting me hornier by the second. Grayson would run his hand along my leg, just barely slipping it under my dress, causing me to breathe heavier and silently will him to finger fuck me.

His hand would move up my inner thigh and stop just inches from where I needed relief, then slowly come back down.

Ugh! I can't take this.

My head dropped back against the headrest as I let out a frustrated sigh.

"Something wrong, baby?"

Lifting my head, I looked into those baby blues. My eyes drifted down to his smile and then to those dimples. Oh. Oh he knew exactly what he was doing to me. Okay . . . two can play at that.

"Nope. I'm perfectly fine. We did forget the dip though."

Grayson lifted an eyebrow and gave me that look that said he knew I was spilling out bullshit.

"That sucks," was all he said as he turned back to the road and punched it when the light turned green. I decided my neck was stiff, and I needed to roll it some to loosen it. I also decided I needed to be vocal about how good it felt. *Very* vocal.

"Oh God," I said in the most seductive voice I could, "that feels *so* good."

I could see Grayson tighten his grip on the steering wheel as he kept his eyes forward. Rolling my head the other way, I said, "Yeah, oh right there, that stretch feels so good."

Grayson cleared his throat as I forced my smile back. My hands came up as I dropped my head toward my chest and rubbed my neck. "Mmm . . . oh yes . . . the stretch is so . . . deep."

Grayson reached over and turned on the AC as I pressed my lips together to keep from laughing. It was thirty-six degrees outside and he had the air conditioning on.

My hands dropped down as I dragged them slowly over my chest and down my entire body. Reaching for his dick, Grayson adjusted himself as he cleared his throat again.

I innocently looked over at him. "You okay, baby?"

Without so much as a peek my way, he nodded his head and said, "I'm perfect. Hungry."

Oh hell. He walked right into that one.

"Oh me too," I purred. "Mmm . . . I hope there is something *hot* for me to warm my body up against."

"Jesus Christ," Grayson mumbled.

"What was that?"

"Nothing," Grayson said as he reached his hand over and placed it on my knee, causing my entire body to tremble.

I looked out the passenger side window quickly and tried to think of anything else besides Grayson's hands on my body and the fact that I just made myself even hornier than I was before.

When I saw Ashley's house coming into view, I silently said a prayer. The second Grayson stopped, I jumped out of the truck and took in a few deep breaths. The chilled air on my body instantly cooled my libido down. Now all I had to do was ignore the devilishly handsome man walking up to me with a shit-eating grin on his face. And ignore the fact that I was sans panties and that they were tucked into his jeans pocket.

"Interesting drive up here wouldn't you say?"

With a sexy smile, I tilted my head. "Seemed like any other drive."

Grayson's mouth dropped open. "Is that so?"

"Yep," I said as I popped my p and tried like hell to remember how to breathe.

Grayson's eyes were on fire as he wrapped his hand around my waist and pulled me into him. His hard dick was pressing into my stomach as his eyes landed on my lips. "Don't count on the drive home being like any other drive."

My lips parted and for one moment, I forgot how to talk. "Why's that?"

Grayson reached his hand up under my jacket and dress while he pushed two fingers inside of me as he pushed me against his truck. I should have been shocked and worried if anyone saw us, but I was too worked up to care. He slowly moved his fingers in and out as I pushed my hips into him, trying to gain friction. "Oh God," I whispered as I grabbed onto his coat.

And just like that, he stepped away and I felt empty. My breath hitched as he pushed his fingers into his mouth and moaned. Slowly pulling them from his mouth, he winked at me. "It's time to eat."

My body could barely move as I felt the wetness between my legs. "Wait, Grayson. May I please have my panties back?"

With a laugh, he tugged me along and right into the house. We stopped dead in our tracks when we came upon Ashley kissing someone in her living room.

"Mom?" Grayson said as Ashley quickly stepped away and tried to hide her embarrassment. Her cheeks were flushed, and I was positive she was worked up as much as I was.

"Oh, Grayson! Meagan darling. I didn't even hear you come in."

"Obviously," Grayson said with disgust laced in his voice.

Reaching for his hand, I squeezed it. "Ashley, it's so wonderful seeing you again!" I said as I walked toward her. She quickly pulled me into an embrace and said, "That was not how I wanted that to go."

With a reassuring hug, I pulled back and looked at an older handsome man standing awkwardly in the living room.

"Oh, um, James, this is Grayson, my son." James reached his hand out for Grayson's as they shook quickly.

"It's so nice to finally get to meet you, Grayson," James said as Grayson flashed his mother a confused look.

Ashley took James' hand and moved him closer to me. "And this is Meagan, Grayson's girlfriend."

Our hands shook as I gave him a big toothy grin. Hopefully I wasn't over doing it by trying to make up for Grayson's reaction.

"Ashley has spoken fondly of you, Meagan."

My face blushed as I said, "Please call me Meg."

James nodded, "Meg it is."

"So, it seems to me you know a lot about us but I've got to be honest here, I've never heard my mother mention you once, James."

Ashley glared at Grayson while I shot daggers at him. I got that he was upset, but to embarrass his mother was just wrong.

"Grayson, may I speak with you in private please?" I said as I tugged on his jacket.

James cleared his throat and turned to Ashley, "I'll go check the chicken on the grill."

Grayson chuckled. "You're grilling in the middle of winter?"

Another tug on Grayson's jacket and his mother glaring at him had Grayson taking a step toward the stairs.

Ashley looked lovingly back at James. "I'll join you." Snapping her head back toward her son, Ashley spoke softly. "Grayson, when you remember how I raised you, please join us in the kitchen."

We watched James slip a coat over Ashley's shoulders as they retreated through the kitchen.

Turning, I shook my head. "Oh my God. Could you be any more of a dick?"

Grayson grabbed my hand and pulled me up the stairs and down the hall. The door to the guest room flew open and then slammed shut. I was about to lay into Grayson and the way he behaved but his lips pressed hard against mine.

Something came over both of us. It was the raw passion we had when we first started sleeping together. The need to get inside one another and we couldn't do it fast enough.

"Gray, we're in your mother's house." I panted.

"I need you, Meg. I need my cock inside of your wet pussy now."

I loved when Grayson talked dirty to me. My body shook as Grayson unzipped his pants and pulled out his dick. He quickly stroked it as I licked my lips and got ready for what he was going to give me.

His hand lifted my dress as two fingers pumped fast and hard, building up the orgasm I had been fighting to hold back.

"Gray," I whispered as he pulled his fingers out and lifted me, positioning his dick at my entrance. When I sank down and he filled my body, we let out a rumbled growl.

"I'm going to fuck you, Meg, and don't make a sound."

Walking into the guest bathroom, he shut the door and pressed my body against it as he moved in and out with one purpose and one purpose only. To fuck me fast and hard, and I loved every single second of it. Then I came to my senses.

"Gray, stop!"

His dick grew bigger and I knew we were both on the edge of coming. "Gray . . . oh God, we can't."

"Meg, fucking hell, I need to feel your pussy come on my cock."

Jesus, I loved it when he talked to me like this. My orgasm hit me hard as I dug my fingers into Grayson's shoulders. I could feel his body tremble as his face buried into my neck and he came just has hard as I had.

I wasn't sure how long we stayed with Grayson still

buried inside of me while I was pressed against the bathroom door.

When he finally pulled his head back and pulled out of me, he looked into my eyes. "I'm sorry I was so rough."

With a smile, I placed my hand on the side of his face. "You weren't rough. I loved every second of it. Well, except for the fact that we're in your mother's house, and you just fucked the living hell out of me and I had to keep as quiet as possible."

Grayson laughed as he grabbed some toilet paper and cleaned between my legs. My legs shook as my stomach dropped at the loving gesture.

Once he cleaned himself off, he took my panties out of the back of his jeans and slipped them over my legs. "I can't even bear the idea of you being with no panties and not being able to touch you."

Smoothing my dress out, I took a look at myself in the mirror and smiled. I had a just-fucked glow over my skin and I was positive Ashley would know what we had done. Maybe she'll just think I jumped all over Grayson for acting the way he did.

"I wasn't prepared for him," Grayson said as he walked out and sat down on the bed. Following him, I sat down next to him. Taking his hand in mine, I kissed the back of it.

"Is that why we just had our little fuck fest in there? Was that your way of dealing with this?" I asked as I waited for his response.

"No, that was because you had me so damn worked up that I knew I wouldn't be able to keep my hands off of you another minute."

I lifted my eyebrows. "Really?"

"Okay, there might have been some small part of me that knew if I fucked you I'd be able to forget about everything that happened a few minutes ago."

I reached up and ran my finger along his stubble. "It

was a nice distraction, but that's all it was. Grayson, your mother is a beautiful woman who deserves to find her own happiness, just like we have."

Grayson's body sank as he dropped his head. "I know. Believe me I know and I want her to. I just didn't want to walk in on it."

"They were just kissing."

Grayson moaned and dropped back onto the bed. There was a light knock on the door and I prayed like hell I looked the same as I did when we first walked in.

The door opened and Ashley walked in. "Grayson?"

Quickly sitting up, Grayson stood and walked over to his mother. "I'm sorry, Mom. I just wasn't prepared at all for walking in and seeing you sucking face with some strange guy."

Ashley blushed as she looked over to me and smiled before turning back to Grayson.

"Ever since your father walked out on us, Grayson, I've been so afraid to open up my heart to anyone else. When I finally felt like I could let someone in, I didn't want to get my hopes up. I wasn't sure how to tell you about James once I knew how strongly I felt about him."

"How long have you been dating him, Mom?"

Ashley rubbed her lips together in a nervous manner. "About five months."

Oh. Shit.

"Five months? What the hell, Mom? I don't even know this guy and walk in and see you all over him. Now you're telling me this has been going on for five months!" Grayson said as he took a step back.

Ashley's faced looked pained. I knew it must have been hard for her to keep this from Grayson and I quickly wondered why she would have kept it from him for so long.

"I understand you're upset I kept this from you, Grayson. First off, I wasn't all over him when you walked in. We were kissing."

Grayson rolled his eyes as I took his hand and squeezed it. From his reaction it was safe to say Ashley hadn't dated much when Grayson was growing up; that could be why she hid James for so long.

"Don't roll your eyes at me, Grayson. You will go downstairs and be polite to James because I . . . I . . . oh lord this is harder than I thought."

My heart began to pound against my chest. I knew exactly what Ashley was about to say, I could see it in her eyes. I also knew Grayson was about to freak the hell out.

"What? Oh God don't tell me you're having sex with him!"

A look of horror washed over Ashley's face as I silently moaned. "Gray, maybe you should take a deep breath and count to five before you talk," I said as I pulled on his hand.

"What I do in my private life is none of your business, Grayson Bennett. I'm a grown woman and am free to kiss and have sex with any man I please to."

Grayson's body trembled as he jerked his head back. "I didn't need that visual."

Ashley's hands came up to her hips as she glared at Grayson. "Well, get used to it because you will be seeing a lot of James from now on. I love him, Grayson."

Grayson's legs gave out as he stumbled back and sat on the bed.

Oh. Holy. Shit.

Things were about to get interesting.

Chapter

FOURTEEN

Grayson

THE ROOM SPUN as I sat down on the bed. The air in there was getting thick as I cleared my throat and tried to breathe. I shook my head and tried to erase what my mother had just said. Not that I didn't want my mother to find happiness, because I did. I just wasn't prepared to walk in on that happiness and see it sucking her face and his hands all over her ass.

I closed my eyes and thought back to a few moments ago when I was lost in Meagan. I'd give anything to be there again.

My mother is having sex. Oh God. I'm gonna puke.

"Gray? Baby, look at me."

Meagan's voice pulled me from the depths of hell I was currently in. Her blue eyes searched my face as she took my hands in hers. With one look, she told me to snap the hell out of it. My mother had finally found someone to make her happy, and I was acting like the world was ending.

My hands cupped Meagan's face as I pulled her closer to me and kissed her quickly. "I love you," I whispered on her lips.

"I love you, too."

Dropping my hands, I stood and took my mother in my arms and held her. For as long as I could remember, it had always been my mother and I. I needed to make myself understand that she deserved to find love just like I had. The fear that another man would hurt her was far less than the desire for her to find happiness. "I'm happy for you, Mom. I needed a few moments to process it all."

Her arms held me tighter as I felt a few sobs escape as we stood there. "Grayson, I've never met anyone like James. He is so good to me and I'm not sure I deserve him."

I held my mother out at arms length and gaped at her. "Don't ever say that again, Mom. If anyone deserves to find love, it's you. And if James is the one, then I'm excited to get to know him and let me tell you right now, he is the lucky one to be getting you."

Relief washed over my mother's face as she reached for Meagan and pulled her into our embrace. "Everything is perfect!" she said as Meg and I both laughed.

My mother stepped away from the embrace and took in a deep breath while smiling so big I couldn't help but smile back. "Okay, let's head on down there before James thinks we all took off and left him."

I reached for Meagan's hand as we followed my mother out of the bedroom and downstairs.

Before we reached the kitchen, Meagan pulled me back. "Be nice, Gray. You know he means a lot to your mom."

Flashing her an *I don't know what you're talking about* look, I winked and said, "Don't worry, baby, I'll be good . . . ish."

Her mouth dropped open as she watched me walk into the kitchen. Mumbling something about she should have kept her panties off, I laughed and glanced at her over my shoulder. Meagan gave me a behave look as we walked into the kitchen.

My attention was drawn to James as I walked up to him and stuck my hand out. "Let's try this again. James, it's a pleasure to meet you. I'm Gray, and I'm going to try really hard not to threaten you in any way with bodily harm if you hurt my mother in any way what so ever."

James grinned and shook my hand firmly. "And that is the response I would expect from any son who loves his mother."

"And I do love her. Besides Meg, my mother is the only woman I've ever loved, so it's hard for me to give her up."

James nodded his head. "I'm not asking you to give her up, Gray, I'm just asking that you let me have a piece of her heart."

Ah hell . . . a romantic son-of-a-bitch.

Meagan and my mother both sighed behind me as I fought to keep from rolling my eyes.

Turning, I faced my mother and pointed to Meagan. "Right, so Meg forgot the dip."

Meagan's eyes widened in surprise as she looked between my mother and me. "What? I had it in my hands and you distracted me with your—well um yeah, I forgot it." My mother brushed it off with a wave of her hands, saving Meagan from digging herself in deeper.

"No worries, Meg. We have so much food. James made potato salad, and beans and I made homemade fries along with steamed veggies. We will have plenty of things to eat. Not to mention the apple, cherry and pecan pies James and I made."

With a chuckle, I shook my head. "My gosh, Mom. Why did y'all make so much food for just the four of us?"

Turning away from me, she pulled out the plates as she gave James a quick peek. "Oh well, we have a few more people coming over."

"Who?" I asked as I popped a piece of cut up cheese into my mouth.

James took that has his cue to step in. "My daughter and son. Sandy and Rick."

"Your kids?" I asked slowly. "Wow, do they at least know about my mom, or are they walking in blind as well?"

With an awkward smile, James shook his head. "I told them this morning. They're both thrilled and excited to meet everyone."

Meagan walked up and helped my mother set the table. "That's wonderful! Isn't it, Gray?"

I wanted to yell out no, but I was almost positive my mother would frown on that so I forced a smile. "Yeah, how old are they?"

James flashed a proud smile across his face. "Sandy is twenty-six, and Rick is twenty-two."

With a quick nod, I grabbed a handful of cheese and headed toward the door. "I'm gonna see how your chicken is doing."

James laughed and stepped out of the way as I headed outside. I hadn't bothered putting on a jacket.

The cold air felt good as it hit my face. I lifted the grill and cursed.

The chicken was of course fine since James had recently checked on them. I needed a few moments to collect my thoughts. Everything with my mother and James seemed to be happening all too fast. Truth be told, she needed to find love again and if James was the guy, then I'd try like hell to be supportive.

The back door opened and I turned to see Meagan. "Hey, James's kids are here, you want to come back in and out of the freezing cold?"

Taking in a deep breath, I tried to not let any of it bother me. "Yeah," I mumbled as I walked up to Meagan.

Reaching up on her toes, she kissed my lips. "I'm sorry. I know this is all so fast and you weren't expecting it. Just remember your mom is happy and that's all that matters."

I knew she was right and I pulled her into my arms. "I'd be lost without you, do you know that?"

With a wiggle of her eyebrows, Meagan replied, "You can show me later when we get back to your place."

My eyes closed as I exhaled a breath while thinking about being with Meagan again.

"Come on, let's go met Sandy and Ricky."

With a moan, I shook my head. "They sound like they should be from the movie Grease."

Meagan giggled as she lightly hit my chest. "Stop it."

Less than a minute later, Meagan and I were being introduced to James's kids. Ricky was tall, about six two and built pretty big. He was attending college in Denver and had come home for the week to meet my mother. By the look on his face, I'd say he was just as surprised as I was to find out about all of this.

Sandy was for sure not from Grease. She wore tight jeans and a shirt so tight and low cut, I was sure her tits were going to fall out just from me shaking her hand. I tried desperately to stay focused on her nose. That felt like the only safe zone to look at.

"So, Grayson, what do you do for a living?" Sandy asked as she flashed me a fuck-me smile.

"Gray, you can just call me Gray. I work for the Durango Police Department."

Sandy widened her eyes. "Is that so? What do you do there?"

"He's a detective," my mother responded as I glanced over to her. "Sorry sweetheart, I'm just so proud of you I have to brag."

111

"It's okay, Mom."

I couldn't help but notice the way Sandy was staring at me. I've had lots of women eye fuck me before, but this was different and I couldn't put my finger on it. Meagan was helping my mother pull out food as they brought it into the formal dining room. I decided to ignore Sandy and talked to Ricky.

"So, Rick, what are you going to school for?"

"History major. Trying to decide if I want to go into law like dad here, or maybe take it in another direction."

My eyes lifted as I looked over to James. So he was a lawyer? That was good; at least he could take care of himself.

"Like what other kind of direction?"

Ricky glanced over to his father and then back at me with a weak smile. "I haven't decided yet."

Huh. Interesting. Sounds like Ricky is being pushed into law school and he might want to do something different. That reminded me of Mitchell. I still needed to talk to Meagan about him.

"James, will you go grab the steaks, I think we're about ready to eat," my mother said as she smiled and motioned for everyone to sit down. "Meg, sit down. I've got the rest of this."

Meagan smiled and headed over to where I was about to sit.

I pulled out a chair and began to sit down when Sandy took the seat next to me. Meagan tried not to show her look of shock as she moved and took the seat on the other side of me. Turning to say something to Meagan, Sandy talked.

"So, how did you get to move up for a promotion so fast? You must not have done a lot of patrol work before moving up."

"I did a few months on patrol but tested high on my state licensing test, and well, they needed more detectives."

"Wow. Impressive how far you've come."

My eyes narrowed as I looked at her with a confused look on my face. With a wink, she leaned forward and talked to Meagan.

"Meagan, how did you and Grayson . . . sorry . . . Gray, meet?"

With a smile, Meagan took my hand in hers. "My best friend is married to Gray's cousin, Noah. They live in Texas."

Sandy leaned back in her chair and took a sip of her water. "What a small world isn't it?"

Meagan laughed as we looked at each other. "Yeah it is," she said as she leaned over and kissed me on the lips.

"Time to eat!" Mom called out as she walked into the room.

Everyone glanced over as my mom and James brought in a huge plate full of steaks. The rest of the dinner was everyone getting to know each other. Sandy seemed to lose her interest in me fairly quickly, which was a sigh of relief.

After James, myself, and Ricky cleared the table, we headed into the living room while the girls cleaned up the kitchen. I had to admit, I liked James. He was smart, looked at my mother like she was his everything, and appeared to have normal kids.

Everything on the outside looked good. I made a mental note of his last name of Kennedy and when Ricky mentioned his dad was turning forty-eight in six days. I made plans to run a background check on his ass first chance I got.

While everyone sat in the living room and talked, I got up to get some fresh air. The whole idea of one big happy family wasn't sitting right with me at the moment and I needed a few moments to let it all sink in.

Leaning over to Meagan, I spoke softly against her ear.

"I need a few minutes. I'm stepping out back."

Meagan's expression turned to worry. "Do you want me to go with you?"

I wanted to pull her into my arms and tell her how much I loved her. The sooner we got out of there and home, the better. The only thing I wanted to do was wrap Meagan in my arms and sleep. I didn't want to think about my mom dating this guy or the fact that they were trying to mash us all together at once.

"Nah, you didn't bring a coat and I only need a couple minutes."

Her eyes softened as she whispered, "Okay."

I stood and headed into the kitchen and out the back door. Taking in a deep breath of cold air, it burned my lungs as I held it in. The pain felt good as I tried to make sense of the feelings I was having. I was happy for my mother, yet I didn't like the idea of James.

"Fuck," I whispered as I dropped my head back and closed my eyes.

"Feeling a little tense? I bet a dance from you would ease both of our tension."

My head jerked up as I spun around to see Sandy standing on the back porch wearing a smirk on her face.

Fucking hell. "What did you say?"

Sandy tilted her head and smirked. "I'm guessing you don't remember the private show you did for me and my friends during her bachelorette party."

Sandy made a tsk-tsk sound as she moved closer to me. "Such a shame, that big ole cock sure felt good rubbing up against me."

Trying to make light of the subject that my mother's boyfriend's daughter knew I had been a stripper, I let out a chuckle. "Well, this cock has rubbed up against a lot of women."

Her smile faded some. "How would your pretty little girlfriend like to know her man was a male stripper? After all, she seems pretty innocent."

Okay, that's funny.

With a roar of laughter, I shook my head. "Oh Sandy, Meagan is far from innocent and she's actually seen me in action, so she is well aware of what I did while trying to get through college."

"What about your mom, Gray? Does she know about this little side career you had going on?"

I felt the anger begin to build as I stared into her eyes. "What are you getting at, Sandy?"

She took a step closer and went to place her hand on my chest, but I backed away as she let out a laugh. "I'm not getting at anything. I just find it kind of funny that we met before under different circumstances and now our parents are dating. That's all."

Lifting her hand to touch me again, I grabbed it and pushed her away. "Well let's get something straight. What I did in the past is in the past. I'm very happy now with Meagan and I'm trying really hard to get used to the idea that our parents are dating. So, unless you've got something else on your mind, I say this conversation is over."

Sandy narrowed her eyes at me as she took me in. The way she was eye fucking me certainly was going to make the rest of the evening awkward. With a deep breath in, she slowly blew it out. "I won't deny I'm a bit disappointed. It would have been fun going down memory lane with you."

Pushing past her, I started toward the back door and came face to face with Meagan, who looked between Sandy and me. Fuck. The last thing I wanted for Meagan to worry about was running into women I've danced for in the past. "What's going on?"

Taking her hand in mine, I glanced over my shoulder at Sandy standing there with a smirk on her face. "Nothing, let's go say goodbye to Mom and get out of here."

Meagan remained silent the entire drive home. I wasn't

sure how much of my conversation with Sandy she heard, if any. I knew I needed to tell her what happened so she didn't get the wrong idea, but I was pissed off and tired.

By the time we got back to my apartment, Meagan had had enough of the silence.

"Do you want to tell me what you and Sandy were talking about? The tension was so thick in the air, I could have cut it with a knife."

I rubbed my hand across the back of my neck and sighed. As much as I didn't want to talk about it, I knew I needed to. "Turns out a few years ago Sandy and some friends of hers had a private party at the club I used to work for."

"Okay, so why are you so angry? Because she recognized you?"

I was somewhat stunned Meagan took that bit of information as well as she did. "I'm angry because I don't want to be running into women I've danced for, and I'm pissed she came on to me."

Meagan's eyes widened in surprise. "What do you mean she came on to you?"

I blew out a breath and looked away. "She tried touching me a few times and mentioned something about going down memory lane."

"What?" Meagan shouted as I glanced back over to her. "Oh my God, I wish I had heard that." Meagan balled her fists up and shook her head. "Oh . . . oh . . . I really want to punch her in her—"

I anxiously waited to hear where she wanted to punch Sandy. "In her what?"

"Her throat!"

Well, okay then.

Lifting my eyebrows, I asked, "Her throat?"

"That little cunt licker. I cannot believe, with her own father in the house, she had the nerve to make a move on you! Wait until our next family get together."

God, I love this woman.

"Babe, did you call her a . . . *cunt licker*?"

Meagan snarled up her lip as she narrowed her brows. "Ugh. Yes!"

"Is Sandy a swinger?"

Meagan's mouth gaped open. "How the hell would I know?"

Shrugging my shoulders, I let out a chuckle. "I don't know, you called her a cunt licker."

Meagan pursed her lips together as she shook her head and let out a frustrated breath. "That's just something Grace said once, and it seemed like a good time to use it."

"Because you think she's a swinger?"

Her hands flew to her hips. "Jesus H. Christ, Gray! I don't have a damn clue what she is and I don't give a flying fuck. All I know is she tried to get you to sleep with her and I want to punch her in her throat!"

Laughing, I pulled Meagan into my arms and pressed my lips to hers. It didn't take long before we were all over each other and in bed naked.

It was the perfect way to end a perfectly shit-filled day. Meagan wrapped up in my arms as we drifted off to sleep.

Chapter

FIFTEEN

Meagan

I LOWERED THE book I had been reading and stole a peek at Grayson. He was buried in files that were laid out in front of him. He worked so hard and I knew he was trying to prove to everyone he deserved to be the youngest, fastest promoted detective on the Durango force.

"You hungry?" I asked as I stood up and stretched.

"Nah, you go on ahead and eat something, babe."

With a frown, I slowly turned and headed to the kitchen. Opening the refrigerator, I glanced around.

Nothing.

Ugh. Single men never keep food in their houses. Shutting the door, I made my way to the pantry. *I wonder why I just don't talk to Grayson about moving in together. What am I afraid of?*

I stood there mindlessly looking at ten different boxes of cereal as I contemplated talking to Grayson about living with him. It was the middle of March and we had been going strong as official boyfriend and girlfriend for two months.

Two months. Maybe that's too soon?

Chewing on my thumbnail, I leaned against the island as I thought this through. Maybe having our two separate spaces was a good thing for right now. Even though I spent ninety-nine percent of my time here, I still had my apartment to go to.

My phone buzzed in my back pocket as I pulled it out and smiled.

Mitchell.

Mitchell: Hey Meg. Are we still on for Monday afternoon?

Me: Yep! I'll see you at the office around 3:45.

Mitchell: Okay good. See you then. Bye.

I stared at the message and thought it was kind of strange for Mitchell to text me just for a reminder. I often gave my cell phone number to my patients. Melissa frowned on it, but I felt like it allowed them to trust me a bit more. Almost all of them communicated through text for their appointments or when they were faced with a tough time.

"What are you doing staring at your phone?"

My head snapped up as I smiled at the handsome man in front of me. My eyes roamed his perfectly toned body as I felt a pull in my lower stomach.

Struggling to find my voice, I grinned and said, "It was Mitchell."

Grayson lifted his eyebrows. "I've been meaning to talk to you about Mitchell."

My interest was piqued. "Oh yeah? What about?"

The refrigerator opened and Grayson pulled out a

beer. With a quick twist of the cap, the bottle hit his lips and caused me to moan internally. What I wouldn't give to have those lips kiss my body. My breasts. My stomach. My throbbing wet—

"Meg? Are you listening to me?"

I shook my head to rid me of my dirty thoughts. "What? I'm sorry what did you say?"

"I asked you if you knew Mitchell didn't really want to be a cop?"

Staring at Grayson like he was insane, I let a quick chuckle out. "What? Of course he does. His mother said Mitchell wants to be a cop just like his father was."

Grayson leaned back against the kitchen sink and looked intently at me. "Has Mitchell ever told you that?"

I went to answer when I slammed my mouth shut as I thought about it. In all the meetings I'd had with him, he never once really told me he had a desire to be a cop.

"He hasn't has he?"

For some reason this bothered me, knowing I hadn't caught on to the fact that Mitchell hadn't ever said his true desires. Grayson caught on to it just by spending one afternoon with Mitchell.

"How . . . what makes you think you know what he wants?" I asked as my body flushed with anger.

Grayson pushed off the counter. "Don't get your panties in a twist, Meg. He told me."

My mouth dropped. "He told you what exactly?"

Pulling in a deep breath, Grayson blew it out. "That it was his mother's dream for him to follow in his dad's footsteps. Mitchell wants to play pro football and would like to be a coach after college."

I was positive Grayson heard the slamming of my heart against my chest. "He's never once mentioned that to me."

"Have you asked him or did you just assume?"

My eyebrows pinched together as I glared at Grayson.

"Are you saying I don't do my job well?"

A look of shock moved across his face. "No! I'm not saying that at all. Maybe the kid just felt more comfortable telling me."

"That's just you covering up for saying I'm doing a shitty job with Mitchell."

Grayson closed his eyes and shook his head before opening them again and looking directly into my eyes. "Meg, that's not what I was saying. I'm just telling you what he told me. You do what you want with it, but honestly I'm exhausted and I don't feel like turning this into an argument with you."

Lifting my hands up, I slowly shook my head. "Oh, by all means let's just stop talking about it because that's what you like to do when things get a little complicated for you. You either clam up or you fuck the hell out of me. I guess you're too tired for option number two."

I spun on my heels and headed to the living room where I grabbed my book and purse. Slipping on my tennis shoes, I reached for my jacket.

"Where are you going?"

Not even bothering to look at Grayson, I said, "Home."

"Meg. Come on, what in the fuck is bothering you?"

Not even wanting to respond, I pulled open the door and quickly walked through it as I gave it a hard pull. It slammed behind me as I heard Grayson yell out and glass hitting the front door.

Keeping my tears at bay, I headed down to the parking garage and out to my car. Once I got in, I started it and headed toward my place. The moment I pulled into my parking spot, I started crying. Pulling out my phone, I ran my finger down the list of names and stopped on one. Hitting it, I dropped my head back onto the headrest.

"Hey, Meg! How's the weather there? Dare I say it's a chilly sixty-two here?"

Just hearing Lauren's perky voice made me smile.

"Hey, Lauren. You lucky bitch. It's thirty fucking hell here."

Lauren giggled. "What's up? I figured you'd be skiing since it's the weekend?"

I wiped my tears away and laughed. "When have you ever known me to ski?"

"Oh my glitter! What did you move to Colorado for then?"

I pressed my lips together to keep from sobbing.

"Meg? What's wrong?"

"Gray and I had our fist fight and I egged it on. I don't know why I did it. I was upset and I took it out on him."

"Sweetie, it's okay. Life isn't always hot sex with ex-strippers. You're going to have some ups and some downs."

I rolled my eyes. "Do we have to keep bringing up the fact that Gray was a stripper?"

"Yes. Yes we do. Unless we're around your parents, then no."

"Lauren!"

"Okay! Okay! I'm sorry. So you picked a fight, I've done that before with Colt. It's just something I think women do when they get hormonal or something."

Pushing out a breath, I rocked my head back and forth against the headrest. "I'm not sure what's going on with me to be honest with you. I'm up one minute and the next I'm pissed off. Gray noticed something about one of my patients and it was like some kind of switch flipped. I was so angry at myself for not catching it, but he caught it just spending the afternoon with the kid."

"Meg, you're not super woman, and no matter how hard you try to help each and every one of those kids, you have to realize some you might not be able to help at all."

The realization of what Lauren had said hit me like a brick wall. "I know," I whispered as I pushed my car door open and headed to my apartment. "That doesn't make it any easier though."

"I know, but the one thing you can't do is take it out on Gray. I'm sure he only told you what he told you because it was something the kid felt comfortable sharing with him."

Lauren's words soaked into my brain as I stepped into my apartment and shut the door. Leaning back against it, I realized what an idiot I had been.

"I'm such a bitch."

With a chuckle, Lauren said, "No you're not. You weren't prepared for it is all. Just think if there was a case Gray was working on and he had gone over and over the evidence and couldn't find any clues and you walked up and pointed to a picture and said, *hey there's a license plate number.* He'd beat himself up for looking over it. That's what you're doing right now and Gray just happened to be in the line of your fist throwing."

Pushing off the door, I knew what I had to do. "Lauren, I love you so much. From now on I'm calling you when I need someone rational to talk to."

"Oh my glitter! Are you for real? 'Cause if you are, I'm totally rubbing that in Alex's face!"

With a laugh, I shook my head. "Go for it. But I've got a hot detective who I need to go apologize to."

"Oh! I have a feeling hot sex will be involved."

Feeling my cheeks flush, I said, "One can only hope. Bye, sweets! I love you! Give Colt a big hug and kiss for me. Plan on coming to see me soon!"

"I will and yes! Ski trip!"

I rolled my eyes and said, "Bye, Lauren. Love you."

"Bye, Meg. Love you more."

Hitting End, I reached for the door and pulled it open only to see Gray standing there getting ready to knock.

He came after me.

I couldn't help but notice how sad his eyes looked and that broke my heart in two. I did the only thing I knew to do, threw myself at him and kissed him like I hadn't seen him in weeks.

Grayson wrapped me up in his arms as we spoke against one another's lips. "I'm so sorry, Gray."

"Baby, don't ever walk out on me again."

And just like that, I felt like shit. Gray's father had walked out on him and here I did the same thing.

"I promise, I'm sorry. Gray, I need you!"

Those three words were all Grayson had to hear. I was in his arms as he moved into the living room. Placing me on the couch, Grayson ripped his shirt over his head and unbuttoned his jeans. I followed as I quickly stripped myself of my sweater, yoga pants, and panties.

"Fucking hell," Grayson whispered as he lifted my hips up.

Our lips crashed together as we kissed like we hadn't seen each other in weeks. Grayson pushed his pants down and pushed himself into me fast and hard, causing me to let out a gasp.

Burying his face into my neck, Grayson moved like he couldn't get enough of me. My nails dug into his back as our breathing quickened.

"Do not come," Grayson grunted as he pushed into me harder. I cried out as I felt the familiar feeling begin to build in my body as I squeezed down onto his dick.

"Fucking hell, Meagan. You're . . . killing . . . me."

His arm wrapped around my lower back as he pulled me even closer to him. His breath hot on my neck as I trembled with the anticipated orgasm.

"Gray," I gasped as cold air rushed over my sweat-covered body. I loved how sex could be so raw with Grayson, yet so incredibly moving at the same time. I'd never experienced the feelings I felt with Gray with any other man.

"Oh God . . . I'm going to come, baby."

His words were my undoing as I felt myself pulling out his orgasm while mine hit me hard.

Names were spoken against kiss-swollen lips as

Grayson slowed his pace down. His lips moved along my jawline and across my neck. I could feel the twitching inside of me as I smiled and memorized this moment.

Grayson kicked off his pants and lifted me as he made his way to my bedroom. I wrapped my arms around him and asked, "Where are we going?"

"We're taking a shower and then I'm holding you next to me all night and not letting go."

My heart about burst with the amount of love I felt for Grayson. Pulling my head back, I gazed into his eyes and said, "If we ever fight, we make up like this. No walking away ever again."

The way he looked at me had a surge of heat rushing through my entire body. Grayson slowly slid me down his body as he backed me up against the wall. With his lips inches from mine, he reached into the shower and turned it on as steam quickly filled the bathroom.

"Meagan," he barely spoke as he closed his eyes and softly kissed me. When he broke the kiss, our eyes met and I could feel the love between us.

Grayson placed his hand on the side of my face and brushed his thumb across my skin. His eyes traveled down to my lips and back to my eyes where he held me captive with those piercing blue eyes. "Marry me."

My lips parted open as my heart beat faster. "W-what did you say?" My mind was spinning. The way Grayson was looking at me was as if I was the very thing he needed to survive.

His smile grew over his face as he cupped both hands on my face now and looked intently into my eyes. "I want to spend every moment of every day being yours."

My hands came up and gripped his arms as I pressed my lips into a smile while trying to hold back my tears. "Grayson," I whispered as I felt a single tear roll down my cheek. "Nothing would make me happier than to be yours forever."

Before I knew what was happening, Grayson had pulled me into the shower and had me up against the cold tile while he slowly made love to me.

Chapter
SIXTEEN

Grayson

"YOU ASKED HER to marry you?" Derrick said as he shut his driver's side door.

With a grin as wide as the Texas sky, I nodded my head. "I sure as hell did."

"Why? You have hot fucking sex with her, anytime you want from the sounds of it. You both have your own apartments for when you need a break from each other, you have women falling at your feet all the damn time. Dude, what is wrong with you?"

I rolled my eyes and looked away as we walked into the jail. "Nothing is wrong with me. I love her and I want to know she's mine."

"Give her a promise ring or some shit like that. Don't do it dude, take it from me. If you do this, you'll be buying fucking BMW's for her when all you want to do is take a hunting trip to Canada."

With a chuckle, I looked straight ahead. "So what you're telling me is you'd rather go on a hunting trip to Canada than make your wife happy?"

Derrick placed his hand on my shoulder and gave it a squeeze. "You know, Bennett, I've never known a guy to come on to the force, patrol for a few months, take the test for detective and get promoted as fucking fast as you did. Call it a shortage of officers if you will, but I'm inclined to think you're just one hell of a smart guy."

"I'm going with I'm one hell of a smart guy."

Derrick laughed as I reached for the door and opened it. I saw him the second the door opened. Joshua Black. The guy from the murder scene was walking toward the front door. His head was down as he walked quickly.

"Joshua?" I called out as he glanced up and looked directly into my eyes.

"I'm sorry, do we know each other?" Joshua asked as he looked between Derrick and myself.

My eyes narrowed just a bit as something in my gut told me he knew exactly who I was.

"Detective Bennett. This is my partner, Detective Winn."

Joshua's face constricted as he thought for a moment. "Oh yeah, the murder outside of my condo. Have you gotten any leads on that? Find out any new information on who it might be?"

Derrick answered. "No, we're no closer now than we were before."

"Damn, that really sucks," Joshua said as he looked between us.

"Yeah, it sucks," I said. "So what brings you here?"

Joshua stood a bit taller. "I'm a lawyer, work for my dad," he said as he rolled his eyes. "One of my clients was arrested yesterday."

It was then I noticed he was dressed in a suit, but he wasn't carrying a briefcase, which I thought was strange.

"Well, we'll let you go. Have a good day," Derrick said as he motioned for me to follow him.

"Um, yeah, good luck on the case, detectives."

With a nod and tight smile, I said goodbye to him. "Have a good day, Mr. Black."

The second we stepped into the elevator, Derrick and I looked at each other.

"Something was off with that guy," he said.

I rubbed the back of my neck as I sighed. "Yeah. I thought so the first time I talked to him. Was it just me, or did it seem like he was fishing for information?"

Derrick laughed. "Oh he was fishing all right. I'm thinking we might need to find out a little more about this Joshua Black."

An uneasy feeling came over me as I nodded my head and said, "Yeah, I think you're right."

Walking into Meagan's office, I was immediately greeted by the receptionist.

"Gray!" Jennifer called out as she jumped up and flashed me a huge smile. "Would you like a cup of coffee or tea? Something to warm you up?"

I shook my head and returned her smile. "Nah, I'm good. Is Meagan busy?"

"I'm sorry, she's with an appointment currently. They shouldn't be much longer if you'd like to take a seat and wait for her."

Clapping my hands together, I sat down in the chair and grabbed a magazine. "I'll do just that."

Jennifer giggled and then awkwardly looked around the office before she sat back down. I knew she had been looking for an excuse to walk off before she quickly gave up.

Ten minutes of mindless chatter with the receptionist

was broken when a young girl about seventeen walked into the waiting room. Her eyes lit up and her cheeks instantly blushed when I smiled at her.

"Casey, your mom said she would be waiting in the coffee shop across the street."

"Thank you so much," the young girl said as she quickly high tailed it out of the office.

Jennifer glanced back to me and said, "You're more than welcome to head on back there, Gray."

With a salute of my hand, I stood and headed back to Meagan's office. I slowly opened the door only to see her standing at the window, staring out. Quietly walking up to her, I wrapped my arms around her and pulled her to me.

"Hey," I softly said as she continued to look out the window.

"I don't understand why kids are so cruel to each other."

I pressed my lips to the back of her head and closed my eyes. "Is everything okay?"

Meagan shook her head. "No."

"Anything I can do to help?"

Turning to look at me, Meagan worried her lip. "That girl was a girlfriend of one the kids I council. She's worried about him. He's doing things to try to fit in and changing because he is so afraid if he doesn't, they'll bully him again." Meagan looked away and shook her head. "She said she is going to break up with him if things don't change."

I placed my hands on her arms as she looked into my eyes. "Grayson, I'm so scared if she walks away from that boy, he'll give up on everything and what if I can't . . . if I can't . . . save him?"

My hands cupped her face as I forced her to look at me. "Meg, all you can do is help guide these kids. You can't save every single one of them."

A tear rolled down her face as she whispered, "I have

to." I knew her experience with bullying was what was behind the driving force for her to want to help each and everyone of those kids.

I blew out a deep breath and reached for her purse. "Come on, let's go grab a beer and a greasy pizza. My treat for my beautiful fiancée."

Her lip twitched at the mention of fiancée and I could see the smile trying to appear. "We have one stop to make first though. Can you leave for the day?"

Quickly wiping her tears away, Meagan nodded her head and smiled big. "Yeah. I can work on my case notes tonight in front of the fire."

"That's my girl," I said as I grabbed her coat while she gathered up a few files and put them in her briefcase. She reached for her purse and headed out the door and to the reception area.

"Jennifer, will you let Melissa know I'm going to be heading out early? If she needs me for anything, I'll have my phone with me."

The receptionist gave a smile as she said goodbye to us while I grabbed Meagan's hand and led her down the street.

The temperature had warmed up enough that she didn't need her coat.

"Where are we going?" Meagan asked as I rounded the corner and made my way to the little shop I'd been passing for the last few months.

Stopping outside the jewelry store, I turned to Meagan and grinned. "I need to put a ring on it, baby."

Meagan's eyes widened in shock as she slowly smiled. "A ring?"

Tugging her into the store, I laughed and said, "Yep. A ring."

I'd catch heat for this when Derrick found out, but I didn't give two shits. I wanted to see Meagan smile and more than anything, I wanted to see a ring on her finger.

Chapter
SEVENTEEN

Meagan

MY HEAD WAS spinning as I stared down at all the engagement rings.

My heart felt as if it was fluttering about in my chest. *Is this really happening to me?*

"So? Is there one you like?"

My lip was going to be bruised and swollen by the time I picked out a ring. "Um," was all I could respond with as Grayson stood there with a goofy grin on his face.

The moment our eyes caught, I couldn't help but smile. "I can't pick," I said with a giggle.

With a smile that melted my panties, Grayson said, "Close your eyes."

Snapping my eyes shut, I held my breath.

Grayson's hot breath near my ear caused me to jump. "Breathe, baby."

Letting out the breath I was holding, it felt good to

take a moment after all the stress from work the last few weeks.

My entire body came to life as Grayson took my hand in his.

"Open your eyes, Meg."

Slowly opening my eyes, I took in a shaky breath as I looked at Grayson down on one knee. A beautiful princess-cut diamond was in his hand as he cleared his throat. "Meagan, will you do me the honor of becoming my wife?"

Everything about this moment was perfect. It felt spontaneous and real. It was Grayson reacting to his feelings, and that was more romantic to me than if he had planned some elaborate proposal.

Nodding my head, a sob escaped from my lips as I whispered, "Yes."

Grayson slipped the ring onto my finger and stood. His arms twisted around me as he lifted me up while pressing his lips to mine. The entire store erupted into cheers as we got lost in our kiss.

Grayson set me down and gently wiped my tears from my face. "I love you, Meg. More than you'll ever know."

"I love you too. So very much."

"Dare I say that was the most romantic thing I've ever seen!" the saleslady said as she clapped her hands in front of us.

Grayson frowned and said, "I could have made that better."

With a shake of my head, I looked deeply into his eyes. "No . . . it was beautiful. Perfect. So very perfect."

Still lost in each other's eyes, the sales lady took my hand and checked the fit of the ring. "My goodness. It fits like a glove, like it was meant to be!"

"It was," I whispered as I glanced down to the ring. It was breathtaking and I couldn't wait to tell the girls and my parents.

Oh. God.

My parents.

"That look of horror can only mean one thing."

I swallowed hard. "My parents."

Grayson shuddered as I giggled. "I should have asked your dad's permission first."

The sales lady quickly stepped between us. "In the meantime, shall we go ahead and wrap up this purchase?"

Grayson and I looked at her as if she had lost her damn mind. It was obvious she was more concerned with the sale over the fact that my father was most likely going to flip a gasket when he found out I was marrying a man they didn't even know I was dating. Everything had been going so well with Grayson, and I knew the moment I told my parents, my father would be on the first flight out to check out Grayson and scare him away.

Grayson took out his wallet and handed her his American Express card. "Talk to me, Meg."

"My parents don't even know we are dating. My father is going to freak out, Gray."

Grayson took my hands in his as he gave me the sweetest smile. "Whatever happens, we're in this together now. If you want, I'll fly to Texas and ask your father for your hand in marriage."

All the tension left my body as I looked into Grayson's eyes. The idea that he would risk his life for me had me longing for him. My lower stomach pulled with the instant desire I was feeling.

"He'd kill you if you showed up and asked to marry me."

The left corner of his mouth rose as my insides quivered. "I'm willing to take the risk."

The saleslady handed Grayson his credit card back along with her card. She was talking a mile a minute, and all I heard was something about bringing the ring in every six months to check it out and clean it.

I turned to her and nodded as I flashed her a polite

smile before grabbing Grayson's hand and pulling him out of the jewelry store right as it began snowing. Where in the world did the snow come from?

"Jesus, Meg. Where is the fire and where the hell did the snow come from?"

Spinning around, I pierced his eyes with mine. "Between my legs, Gray."

Grayson started choking as he pulled me to him. "What? The snow came from between your legs?"

Frowning, I looked at him. "No. I want you."

"Oh yeah?" he asked with a come get me look on his face.

My eyes frantically searched his face. I wanted to say so many things to him. I wanted to tell him I was scared and excited, but more than anything, I was so turned on it felt like my insides were going to explode. There had been plenty of times I wanted to jump this man in public and right now was one of them. "I want you."

"Now?"

Pressing my lips together, I softly spoke. "Now."

It was Grayson's turn to pull me now. "My truck is around the corner."

Walking carefully without slipping on the freshly snow-coated sidewalk, Grayson reached down and picked me up as I let out a giddy yelp. He opened the passenger door and practically threw me inside as I laughed.

Fifteen minutes later, the door to Grayson's apartment flew open as we stumbled in, lips pressed together and hands all over each other.

"Fucking hell, Meg."

My hands shook as I quickly stripped my clothes off while watching Grayson do the same. His hard dick sprung out of his pants as I let out a moan.

Dropping to my knees, I took him in my mouth as he pumped his hips and grabbed onto my hair. "Jesus . . . ahh . . . damn it, Meg! You need to stop."

Grayson lifted me by my shoulders and pulled me up as his hand made its way between my legs. My breathing was erratic as I anticipated the feel of his fingers inside of me.

"Tell me how you want it, Meg."

His fingers pushed deep inside me as I gasped. "Fuck me, Gray. I need you to fuck me."

When his lips crashed into mine my hands tunneled through his thick brown hair and grabbed a handful. Grayson let out a rumbled growl from the back of his throat as he lifted me while walking me toward the wall. One quick movement of his hand and he pushed everything off the new wood table he had bought for his foyer. My ass landed on it with a thud as Grayson's eyes roamed greedily over my body. Grasping my breasts with both his hands he bent over and sucked on one of my nipples as I dropped my head back and cried out in pleasure as my own hand found its way to my throbbing clit.

"Fucking hell, that is so hot watching you play with yourself, Meg."

With a whimper, I lifted my fingers and pushed them into his mouth. Grayson's eyes burned with desire as he grabbed my hips and pulled me to the edge of the table where he quickly buried himself inside of me.

"Yes!" I cried out as Grayson fucked me in earnest while my orgasm built. I loved when we lost control like this. It was raw, pure, animalistic pleasure that turned me on more than I could ever express. My legs wrapped around him as I pulled him in deeper. Grayson lifted me off the table and spun us around until I was pressed up against the wall with my right hand pinned above my head as Grayson continued to fill me full as I felt him grow bigger.

"Baby, I can't hold it back any longer," Grayson called out as his dick throbbed inside of me.

"Grayson!" I cried out as the intensity of my orgasm

hit me full force.

"Oh God, Meagan . . . fucking hell."

The sounds of our pleasure echoed off the walls as we both came hard. I could feel Grayson's dick twitching inside of me as I squeezed down and milked every ounce of cum out of him.

Minutes passed as we both fought to regain our breathing. My heart was beating crazy in my chest as Grayson carried me over to the couch, still buried inside of me. When he sat down, I dropped my forehead to his and waited for my breathing and heartbeat to return to normal.

"My God, Meg. Each time with you is so fucking amazing."

I lifted my head and smiled. "It was amazing, wasn't it? It felt so good, I didn't want you to stop."

Grayson's hand came up as he pushed a piece of my brown hair behind my ear. "I didn't want to stop. I never want to stop when I'm making love to you."

With a chuckle, I bit down on my lip. "That was not making love, that was fucking."

Grayson's eyes turned dark and then softened. "Yeah it was, but at the same time, it felt so damn intimate. Like I was a part of you and you were a part of me. We were one, and I loved every second of it."

Bending down, I softly kissed him as I moved my hips. I could feel Grayson's dick twitch as it was coming back for round two.

"You greedy little girl."

Pushing off his chest, I sat up and ground my hips onto him as my hands cupped my breasts while my head fell back. "I want more."

His hands grabbed onto my hips as he moved along with me. "Holy shit what are you doing to me? You're like a drug that I can't get enough of."

With a smile, I lifted my body as I rode him. I couldn't

believe how fast my orgasm was building.

Grayson moaned as he began to grow harder and hit the spot I needed for my release.

My hands landed on his shoulders as I fucked him as fast as I could while I called out his name. Grayson's head dropped back onto the couch as he dug his fingers into my hips.

Warmth spread through my lower body as I collapsed onto him, my breasts pressed against his chest as we both fought for air.

"I'm spent. I don't think my dick is ever going to recover from this."

Giggling, I kissed his chest and lifted my head. "Oh somehow I find that statement to be false."

Grayson winked and cupped my ass. "Yeah me too. Now get your beautiful ass off of me so we can go take a shower."

Crawling off Grayson, fear set in again. "Gray, what about my parents? They're going to be so upset with me."

"You're a grown woman, Meg. You're not obligated to let them know about every single detail of your life."

"I would think dating someone might be something I'd share with them."

I glanced down at my engagement ring. How in the world would I tell my father about Grayson and I seeing each other for so long and now we were engaged? He was going to lecture me . . . I just knew it.

No. That was not going to happen. I needed to stop letting my father's expectations guide me.

After taking a hot shower, I thought I would feel better, but I felt worse. My head began to pound and I felt sick to my stomach.

Grayson wrapped a towel around my body and carried me to the bed where he gently laid me down. Crawling in next to me, he pulled my body close to his.

"Love you, baby."

My heart felt as if it was going to combust. I was instantly calmed and in that moment I knew all I would ever need was this right here, Grayson's arms wrapped around me . . . protecting me and loving me.

I cared about what my father thought, but I was going to follow my heart. I was in love with Grayson and that knowledge instantly calmed me.

"Love you too."

Chapter
EIGHTEEN

Grayson

"DETECTIVE BENNETT?"

Turning, I saw Joshua Black standing with his arm around a dark haired girl.

"Mr. Black, how are you this evening?"

His eyes moved from me over to Meagan, where he looked a bit too long for my liking.

"I'm doing good. Taking my girl out to a movie." Gesturing over to Meagan, Joshua smiled. "I see you're doing the same."

Reaching his hand out for Meagan's, Joshua said, "Joshua Black."

Meagan went to say her name when I cut her off. "This is my fiancée, Meagan."

Meagan turned to look at me as Joshua chuckled. "This is Christy, my girlfriend."

I quickly looked the girl over and gave her a friendly

smile. "Nice to meet you. If you'll excuse us, we're late; nice seeing you again, Mr. Black."

"Joshua, call me Joshua."

I nodded my head and led Meagan to another movie. "Gray, what's going on? Why didn't you let me talk?"

Guiding her into the movie, I led us up toward the top row.

"I don't trust that guy. Neither does Derrick. Something about him is off, plus we found out he's been snooping around asking questions about a murder case."

"Oh, what does he do for a living?"

"He works for his father's law firm."

"Lawyer?"

"Yeah. Derrick checked him out. Something isn't right though. He never brings any of his cases to trial. They're all settled."

Meagan made a face like she was intrigued as I said, "Let's grab a bite to eat instead of a movie."

"Are you sure? I thought you wanted to see a movie."

"Nah, not anymore."

A few minutes later we were sitting in a café drinking coffee and waiting for our dinner. "So, have you talked to your parents yet?"

The coffee cup froze at Meagan's lips. "Um . . . well I did tell them about you. Of course they already know you, but I broke the news that we had been dating."

Ouch. Broke the news. I had to admit that felt like a knife in my chest. I wasn't sure why Meagan was so afraid to tell her parents we were dating. I'd met Brad and Amanda plenty of times, and every time they were super nice.

Maybe it was my past she was afraid would come out. I could see how they wouldn't want their little girl dating an ex stripper.

"You make that sound like it's a bad thing."

Meagan jerked her head back. "No. Not at all. It's just,

my parents aren't used to me dating."

"Their reaction?"

"My mom acted as if she already knew. She said she noticed the way we always looked at each other. She figured something was going on. My father on the other hand, he went on about dating a cop and the stress that would add to my already stressful career. All that kind of stuff."

"Damn, does your father ever let up on you?"

Meagan shrugged her shoulders. "It's not as bad as it used to be. Now that Taylor is going to be graduating college, my father will ease up on both of us. At least I hope he will."

"I heard he was always a little harder on you though."

With a lift of her eyebrow, Meagan flashed me a smile. "So how much did Grace tell you about me before we started officially dating?"

Leaning back in the chair, I flashed her my crooked smile that I knew she loved. "She told me you were bullied in college and that your father rode your ass pretty hard. Compared you to Taylor all the time and wanted you to be the perfect example for her."

Meagan's head tossed back with her laugh as I reached for my drink and took a sip. She exhaled a breath and nodded. "Ahh yes, all of that is very true. Although, he did let up for a little while when he realized I was moving to Colorado. I think he might have thought he pushed me away."

"Did he?"

Meagan sat up a little taller as if she was still trying to prove something to her father. "I really did fall in love with it here when we came for our girls' trip, and maybe I was running away from something I didn't want to face."

My elbows rested on the table as I looked into her eyes. "Isn't that what you council kids to do . . . not run away from things. Face them head on?"

Her lips parted open as if she was going to argue with me. She didn't though. My words must have been swirling around in that beautiful mind of hers because she was soon lost in her own thoughts.

Reaching for her hands, I rubbed my thumbs gently across her delicate skin. "Hey, look at me, Meg."

Her eyes slowly looked up into mine. "You're not that girl anymore, Meg. You're a smart, beautiful, confident, amazing, woman and I'm so damn proud to be a part of your life."

Tears pooled in her eyes. "My dad is coming to visit me and I guess I'm so afraid he is going to judge every single thing I've done and then he'll judge you and I don't want him to scare you off . . . and oh my God. Why is this bothering me so much?"

The waitress walked over and set our plates down as I pulled my hands back. "Is everything okay, sweetheart?"

Meagan quickly wiped her eyes and nodded. "My gosh, I don't cry. Ever. Yes, yes, everything is perfect. Just emotional today."

Giving Meagan a wink, the waitress glanced at me and asked, "Can I get anything else for you?"

With a polite smile, I shook my head. "No thank you."

"Let's eat and head back to your place. We can snuggle up and watch a movie."

"When is your dad coming, Meg?"

Without so much as looking up at me, she softly said, "In a week. He's staying for four days."

So much for getting rid of her apartment.

"After that you'll get rid of your place and move in with me, right?"

Meagan's eyes softened as she looked at me. "Yes. Gray, there's nothing more I want than to be with you. I just need to figure out how to do this and I need a bit more time."

I nodded and took a bite of food. "But you're going to

tell him while he's here that we're engaged, right?"

Pressing her lips together, Meagan looked down at her food. "Maybe."

I quickly grew frustrated. Whatever issues Meagan had with her father needed to be worked out during this visit. I was tired of feeling like I was a bad secret she needed to keep locked away.

"Meg, you can't hide this forever. At some point I am going to want to actually marry you and have your family there."

"I know! I know! Just let me worry about it when he gets here. For now we have a few days to prepare."

I couldn't help but feel like it was more than just Brad being a tough father. It was my past that was stopping Meagan from saying anything.

❧

"Damn it, Bennett. Did you not learn a damn thing from me at all?"

Looking up, I stared at my partner. "What's up, Winn?"

"A ring? You bought her ring? You're in all the way now."

Laughing, I shook my head. "Stop acting like you don't believe in marriage. I see the way you look at your wife."

"It's too late for me. I have to be happy, but you. My god, son, you're young, good looking, and women are falling at your feet. Mainly the chick up in the main office. What's her name? Claire?"

I rolled my eyes. "Don't even go there with me. Claire is not anyone I want to get myself hooked up with. I love Meagan."

Derrick smiled a goofy-ass smile as he slowly shook his head. "Damn straight. I just needed to make sure my partner was on the up and up. Lana wants to invite you and Meagan over for dinner if you're free Friday night."

I stared at him in disbelief. "I'll never understand you."

"Good. That's the way it should be."

"Bennet, Winn, we've got another 187 near Wilcox Road."

Derrick looked disgusted as he grabbed his jacket and said, "Shit, let's go."

As we walked to the car, I punched the address into my phone. "That's two blocks over from the last one."

"It's looking more and more like we have a serial rapist murderer out there."

"I need to talk to Meg about staying at work late. They all need to make sure they leave as a group."

Derrick nodded his head. "Yeah, make sure she keeps her eyes and ears open and pays attention to who is around her."

Pulling up to the scene, I couldn't help but look around for Joshua Black.

"You looking for him?"

"Yeah. Don't see him anywhere though," I said as I rubbed the back of my neck.

"Come on, let's go talk to Murphy, see what his first thoughts are."

The hair on my neck stood as I glanced around. That feeling of being watched swept over me again as I searched the crowd.

"I'm right behind you," I said as I followed behind my partner.

Chapter
NINETEEN

Meagan

"I'LL BE AT the airport early, Dad. Stop worrying."

"I'm not worried, Meg. I just don't want you rushing through traffic to get there if you're running late."

Rolling my eyes, I bit my tongue to keep from saying what I really wanted to say. "It's not Austin, Dad. It'll be fine. I'll see you in a few hours."

"All right, sweetheart. Can't wait to see you and meet Grayson."

"You've met him a number of times."

My father laughed. "Yeah well, that was before he was dating my daughter."

Great. Just great.

"I've got to go, Dad, my appointment is here."

"Bye, Meg. Love you."

Glancing up at the clock, I knew my next appointment wasn't until noon, but he didn't have to know that. "Love you too, Dad."

As I hung up the phone, I blew out a deep breath. "Jesus, help me get through this weekend and I swear I will do good things until I can't do good any more."

Melissa knocked on my door and pushed it all the way open.

"So, I picked the dishes."

My headed pulled back as I gazed at her. "What are you talking about?"

"The challenge you have with your hotter-than-hot fiancé."

My eyes rolled. "When are you going to stop calling Gray that? Plus that was forever ago, I forgot all about it."

"First off, I'll stop calling him that when he becomes ugly, and second, your hotter-than-hot fiancé was the one who called to remind me about it. Seems like he wants to win this pretty bad."

Giggling, I shook my head. "You're so bad and yes, I'm sure he does."

Melissa lifted her eyebrow and said, "I will get it out of you what the winner gets."

I leaned back in my chair and chewed on the end of my pen. "So, what's the dish?"

An evil smile spread over her face. "Beef tenderloin with cognac butter, shaved broccoli apple salad with tarragon and bacon, and chocolate almond cheesecake bars."

My mouth fell open as I dropped the pen. "What the hell? That's an entire meal and I don't even know what half that shit means."

Melissa laughed. "Oh man, I just wanted to see your reaction. Okay seriously, it has to be a meal made with beef tenderloin."

"What's a beef tenderloin? A type of steak?"

Staring at me with a stunned expression, Melissa shook her head. "Jesus, I hope whatever you agreed to if Grayson wins it isn't anything too crazy."

My face blushed as Melissa's eyes grew wider. Leaning toward me, she dropped her mouth open. "Oh. My. God. Meagan Atwood you have to tell me what it is."

"Two words . . . hell no."

With a pout, Melissa dropped back against the chair. "Okay this is not fair. You can't ask me to be a part of this and not tell me what the stakes are."

"Nope. It's too personal."

"It's anal sex isn't it?"

I sat there with a stunned expression on my face. "W-what? Why is that the first thing you think of?"

Melissa shot me a *please* look. "I may be older than you, but I've been out with you and I've seen you with guys."

"What's that supposed to mean?" I said as I gave her a dirty look. "Are you calling me a whore?"

With a laugh and a brush of her hand, Melissa dapped at her eyes. "No! I'm just saying you're . . . friendly . . . with the boys and I would have to guess you've had your fair share of sexual encounters, but I don't take you for the kind of girl that would let any guy dive into the deep dark world of anal sex."

Who was this person sitting across from me?

"Who are you? The deep dark world of anal sex? You make it sound forbidden."

"Isn't it?"

I shrugged my shoulders. "I don't think it's something you'd sit around the table and tell your mother about, but no, I don't think it's forbidden. I also don't think it would be something I would attempt to do with just any guy."

Leaning forward, Melissa gave me a wink. "And we both know, Grayson is not just any guy."

My face flashed hot again. "No. He most certainly is not."

My phone buzzed as Jennifer came over the line. "Meagan, Mitchell called and asked if he could come in earlier. Your schedule was clear, so I said yes."

Hitting the button, I said, "Thanks, Jennifer. When will he be here?"

"Thirty minutes."

Melissa stood and looked down at me. "How are things going with him?"

With a smile, I stood as well. "I think good. His girl-friend came to see me not too long ago. Said Mitchell was starting to get involved with some of the football guys who were pulling pranks and such. Looks like she was able to pull him away from it. He seems to be doing good."

With a smile and nod, Melissa made her way to her door. "Pay close attention, Meagan. Sometimes these kids have a way of hiding things when they're hurting the worst."

My heart dropped to my stomach as I gave her a weak smile while she retreated out of my office.

I loved my job, but sometimes I felt so helpless. The only thing I could do is pray like hell that they listened to what I talked to them about. There was something about Mitchell though that I felt such a connection with.

Burying my face in my hands, I let out a moan. "I need something strong to drink."

Grabbing my jacket and purse, I headed out of the office. Walking past Jennifer, I smiled and said, "I need a quick Starbucks run before Mitchell gets here. I'll be right back."

Jennifer lifted her hand and called out, "Get me my normal!"

The Starbucks was less than a minute walk from my office. I wasn't sure if that was a blessing or a curse. I pulled out my phone and sent Grayson a text asking how his day was. I knew he was just as nervous as I was about my father's visit.

My face blushed as I thought about last night and this morning. We had fucked like rabbits both times. The thought of not sleeping in the same bed with Grayson for four nights killed me as much as it did him.

"Must be something good you're thinking about."

Looking up, I saw the guy from the movies that Grayson had a funny feeling about.

"Excuse me?" I asked as I took a step back. Something about the way he was looking at me had me on edge.

"It's Meagan, right?"

My phone went off in my hand while I attempted to smile politely. "Yes. I'm sorry I don't remember your name."

"Joshua. Joshua Black."

With a quick nod, I said, "That's right."

"I was just commenting on your flushed cheeks. You must have been thinking about something good."

My head jerked back. He did not just go there.

"Must just be the weather outside."

With a smirk, Joshua nodded his head. "You meeting Detective Bennett?"

Glancing toward the door, I shook my head and turned back to the front. "Um, yes. I work around the corner so it's an easy place to meet."

"Really? I live right across the street in the new condos."

This guy was really starting to bug me and I had no idea why. If he took one more step closer to me I was going to tell him to back the fuck off.

"I've heard they're really nice. My boss was thinking of buying one."

Joshua grinned. "Yeah well, they are nice and they are very expensive, but worth it. The amenities are amazing. Hey you ever want to take a look, I'm more than happy to show you mine."

Uh-huh. I bet you are, you pervert.

Glancing at my phone, I couldn't read Grayson's reply. I simply typed in 77 and hit Send. It was Grayson's code he came up with for when I needed him to call me as soon as possible if anything was ever wrong.

My phone rang almost immediately as I held up my finger and said, "So sorry, I've been waiting for this call."

"Hello?"

"What's wrong?"

"Hey, are you almost here?"

"Are you at the office?"

"No silly, Starbucks."

I peeked over to see Joshua was texting someone on his phone. Turning away from him, I lowered my voice.

"I'm fine, just a little uneasy."

"Is someone bugging you?"

I cleared my throat and moved a bit closer to the front when the line moved up. Joshua was now talking to someone on the phone. "Oh, you know, the same reason you wanted to leave that movie."

"Joshua Black is there?"

"Bingo."

"I'm on my way."

"No! Honestly, that's not necessary."

Grayson's heavy sigh told me he was not happy. "Meg, you fucking text me your distress code and then tell me some asshole guy I have a bad feeling about is bothering you and you *don't* want me to come there? Why text me then? Are you no longer feeling uneasy?"

His condescending tone pissed me off. "Sorry to have bothered you then. My mistake."

I ended the call and tossed the phone into my purse. Joshua was still talking to someone on the phone as I stared straight ahead. When it was my turn to order, I placed my order and stood off to the side. Joshua made no attempt to come over and talk to me at all which allowed me to breathe a sigh of relief. Although my phone going off in my purse was seriously causing me to stress. I knew Grayson would be pissed I hung up on him and left him hanging.

I quickly grabbed the two coffees when they were called out and headed toward the door. Joshua appeared before me as he opened the door and smiled. "Have a good day, Meagan."

My entire body stiffened as I forced a smile and nodded. "You too."

Walking out of Starbucks I never looked back, although I was almost positive Joshua was watching my every move. As I rounded the corner I took a chance and glanced back. I let out the breath I was holding when I didn't see Joshua anywhere.

The moment I stepped into the office, Jennifer jumped up. "Grayson called here looking for you. He said to call him the second you got back."

Snarling my lip up, I handed Jennifer her coffee. "If he calls again, tell him I'm in meetings up until I have to pick up my father."

Jennifer's eyes widened. "Whoa, what happened? You get in a fight?"

I headed back to my office as I called over my shoulder, "Something like that."

Slamming my door shut, I dropped my purse and set my coffee down. "Ugh! He gives me some stupid code and tells me to use it whenever I need him. Then he goes all caveman crazy on me when all I needed was to hear his voice." My hands landed on my hips. "Well fuck that."

My phone buzzed again in my purse. Chewing on my lip, I pulled it out and read Grayson's text messages.

Gray: Meg, are you okay?

Gray: Meg, please answer your phone or at least text me!

Gray: Meagan. Fucking text me back!

Gray: Stop acting like a child.

My mouth dropped open. "A child? Oh, no he didn't."

The phone buzzed in my hand as I swiped it without looking at who was calling.

"How dare you treat me like a child! I've made it perfectly fine on my own without you trying to boss me around. I don't care to talk to you at this moment, so if you'll excuse me I—"

"Meagan? It's your father."

Fuck. My. Life.

Swallowing hard, I quickly sat down. "Oh hey, Dad. Did you land in Dallas?"

"Yep."

Squeezing my eyes shut, I cursed under my breath as I tried to calm my pounding heart down.

"Great. I'm sorry your layover is so long."

"What did he do?"

Son-of-a-bitch. "He didn't do anything."

With a fake laugh, my father mumbled something away from the phone before saying, "He obviously bossed my daughter around and that doesn't sit well with me. I'm glad to hear you had the sense to set him straight."

Oh. My. God.

"I had the sense to set him straight? What in the hell is wrong with men? How dare you think I'd actually let a man boss me around! I'm not a child. I do know how a man should treat a woman. My own father!"

"Wait a minute here, Meagan. You answered the phone clearly pissed off at Grayson and now you're taking it out on me."

"He didn't do anything wrong. He overreacted to a situation I had under control and I certainly don't need you telling me how to live my life anymore, Dad. I followed that plan my whole life and have no desire to continue with that."

Silence filled the phone as I realized what I had just said. "You think I tried to tell you how to live your life?"

I almost wanted to laugh at his statement. My phone beeped as I pulled it away and saw it was Grayson. "Dad, I have an appointment in a few minutes I need to get ready for. I'm sorry, I'm just angry and I didn't mean to take it out on you. I really am looking forward to spending the weekend with you."

"Okay, sweetheart. I'll see you in a few hours."

My heart hurt as I pictured my father upset. "I love you, Daddy."

"Love you too, pumpkin."

The line went dead as I pushed out the breath I had been holding in. "Damn it," I whispered as I tossed my phone onto the desk.

Dropping my face into my hands, I took in one deep breath after another. Mitchell would be here in a few minutes and I needed to put my own problems on the back burner to focus on him.

Ten minutes passed and Mitchell arrived early. My phone was sitting in front of me as we got caught up on things going on at school. When the text popped up on my phone, I felt all the air leave my lungs.

Gray: Tried to call again. I won't be at dinner tonight. Sorry.

Chapter
TWENTY

Grayson

I HATE STAKEOUTS. It was probably the only thing about my job I hated.

"You're mumbling over there, Bennett."

I drew in a breath and released it before saying, "This is a waste of our time."

Derrick nodded in agreement as he lifted the binoculars and looked at the building across the street. "Someone thinks it's not."

"Yeah well, I can't imagine we're going to find anything on this guy."

"Want to talk about it?"

Looking away, I rubbed my hand along the back of my neck as I paced across the room. "Nothing to talk about."

Derrick laughed as he dropped the binoculars and looked at me. "You called Meagan and ever since then you've been pissed at the world. If that doesn't scream fight, I don't know what does."

My throat tightened as I thought about Meagan hanging up on me earlier and then ignoring my calls and texts.

Derrick went back to watching the house as I shook my head. "I gave Meagan a code that she could text whenever she was feeling uncomfortable or scared."

"Okay," he said as he continued to watch the house.

Letting out a breath, I tried not to let myself get upset again. "She used it today."

He turned and looked at me as he lifted a brow.

"She ran into that Joshua Black and I guess he made her feel uncomfortable. I told her I was on my way and she told me no, that everything was fine so I asked her why she used the code then if everything was fine."

"Oh hell," he said as he made a face.

"What? Was that wrong of me?"

Derrick motioned for me to take the binoculars for a bit. "Here, you watch while I explain women to you."

Grabbing the damn things from his hands, I let out a snort. "I know plenty about women, asshole."

"Obviously, dude, you don't. So you gave your girl a code to use when she needed you, whether needing you was maybe just needing to hear your voice or actually physically needing you. In this case, she wanted to hear your voice and was possibly using your call to get out of talking to the creep. You pulled the *I am caveman and will protect you* bit and she got pissed. Now, I don't know Meagan all that well, but from what I can tell, she's tough and not one to overreact to things. Maybe she thought you were treating her like she was weak."

I turned to look at my partner as my mouth dropped open. "Weak? Meagan is the last person I would consider to be weak."

Derrick shrugged. "Gray, women want to be strong and independent, but at the same time, they want to know that you'll be there for them if they need you. So maybe

Meagan just needed to know you would have been there for her if she needed you to be."

"Why are they so complicated? I'm so fucking confused. So I did something wrong?"

With his head thrown back, Derrick laughed his ass off. I couldn't help but laugh along with him even though I had no clue what in the hell we were laughing at.

He finally got himself under control when he said, "Dude, we're always in the wrong. The sooner you learn that the happier your life will be."

My eyebrows drew together as I thought about my last text to her. "I think I fucked things up big time."

Derrick dropped his head. "So. Much. To. Teach. You." Shaking his head, he looked up at me. "What did you do?"

"Well, I um, I sent her a text when I found out about the stakeout and just told her I wouldn't be making it tonight."

"Was tonight important to her?"

With a shrug, I whispered, "Maybe, sort of."

"Maybe sort of?"

"Her father was flying in tonight and we were supposed to have dinner."

Derrick jumped up. "You blew her off with a text on the night her father was coming into town? You realize you need to make a good impression with him right?"

"Yes I know that, Winn! We got called out on this stupid ass stakeout. I tried calling her, but she refused to take my calls. What was I supposed to do?"

Derrick stood up and gave me a look of disappointment. "Dude, I didn't take you for such an asshole."

Even though I knew he was right, I balled my fists and walked to the other side of the empty room while I tried to calm myself down. I wasn't angry with Derrick, I was angry with myself.

"Hey cap, this is Winn. Bennett isn't feeing so great and heading home for the night. Nah, there are a few uniforms here. We can switch out . . . right . . . I'll let him know."

Hitting his phone, Derrick motioned with his head for me to take off. "It's early and I bet you can still make dinner."

With a smile, I walked over to him and held my hand out. "Thanks, Winn."

"It's called experience, brother. Plus, you're my partner and I'll always look out for ya."

The lump in my throat was very real as I nodded and said, "That goes for me too."

Lifting his hand, Derrick waved for me to get going. Turning, I quickly headed out of the building as I looked at the time. The reservation for dinner was for ten minutes ago. Waving down a taxi, I jumped into the cab and prayed like hell Meagan wouldn't tell me to fuck off.

∾⧈∾

"Welcome to the Ore House, do you have a reservation?"

I scanned the restaurant quickly looking for Meagan and her father. When I turned back to the hostess, I couldn't help but notice the smile on her face. "Gray? Oh my God, is that you?"

With a slight frown, I looked her over to see if I could place her. Her blonde hair was pulled up into a bun and the tight black dress left nothing to the imagination.

"I'm sorry, I'm not sure how we know each other?"

Her mouth parted open as her face flushed. With a quick look around she said, "You did a private bachelorette party for my best friend a couple years ago. You and I . . . well . . . we got a little cozy after the party in my car."

It was in that instant I saw Meagan. She was staring directly at me with one seriously pissed off look on her face.

Fucking hell. How many women am I seriously going

to run into that I've danced for at some point? "Um, sorry sweetheart, I don't remember."

My eyes darted back to Meagan as the hostess leaned closer to me. "Don't worry, we didn't have S. E. X. or anything. But you did give me one amazing org—"

"Okay, well, I see my fiancée is already here so I'll make my way over to her."

The hostess pouted as she mumbled, "Lucky girl."

Luckily, I dressed in dress pants and a button down shirt almost every day. Today I dressed a bit nicer knowing I'd be coming to dinner with Meagan and Brad.

Meagan watched my every move as I made my way over to the table. Leaning down, I kissed her cheek softly. "I'm sorry, I didn't think I would be able to make it."

Brad stood and reached his hand out for mine. "Mr. Atwood, it's a pleasure seeing you again."

Giving me a once over, Brad forced a smile. "It's good seeing you again, Grayson. Please, call me Brad and you're just in time. We haven't ordered yet."

With a quick nod of my head, I said, "Brad it is and please call me Gray. Great, I'm glad I'm not too late."

I pulled out the chair and sat down as the waitress asked for my drink order. I remembered Meagan telling me once that her father dealt with a drug and alcohol addiction in the past so I played it safe. "I'll just start with a water, thank you."

Smiling, I looked between Brad and Meagan. If looks could kill, I'd have fallen over when Meagan lifted her glass filled with red wine to her lips and glared at me.

Fuck. Now I want a drink.

"So, I thought you weren't going to be joining us?"

With a forced grin, I went to talk but let my eyes move down to Meagan's hand. It felt like I had been sucker-punched when I saw her engagement ring gone. Meagan must have noticed me looking because she quickly pulled her hand back and placed it in her lap.

I tried to find my voice as the waitress set my water down. "I've changed my mind. I'll have a scotch on the rocks please," I said as I took a long drink of water.

Brad cleared his throat as I looked at him and grinned. "We got a stakeout last minute, a guy we got a tip on that might know or have something to do with an ongoing murder investigation. Turned out my partner and I both didn't need to be there, so I headed this way as quickly as I could."

The waitress set the drink in front of me as I picked it up and forced myself not to down the whole damn thing.

Brad leaned forward and gave me a long hard look as if he was giving me an assessment. "Wow, so tell me, Gray. How is it you were able to pretty much skip doing patrol like every other officer has to do and move right into a detective position? Who does your father know on the force?"

"Dad!" Meagan said with a stern look on her face.

I reached up and loosened my tie some as I let out an amused laugh. "Nothing like cutting to the chase, sir."

"I'm just curious how you moved into a position like that so quickly. It's also very clear to me that my daughter is pissed off at you as well, so we might as well get all the dirty shit out of the way while we're at it."

Meagan moaned and dropped back in her seat while folding her arms across her chest. "Dad, I can't even right now."

I quickly glanced over to Meagan and winked as I focused back on her father. "You're right on almost everything you've said, Brad. Meg is angry with me and I don't blame her. I overreacted with a situation earlier today, but that is something she and I will work out later . . . privately."

Seeing Meagan from the corner of my eye, I could tell she was staring at me. "As far as my career with the Durango Police Department goes, I graduated with a masters in criminal justice and tested for the police department. I didn't have to go through their program because of my high scores and I indeed started on the force patrolling just like everyone does. There was a major shortage of detectives, so I immediately applied for a position, took the test and passed with a perfect score. I've been with my partner, Derrick Winn for almost eight months now. I don't profess to be the best at my job, but every day I'm learning more and more and my goal is to be the best damn detective Durango has ever had."

Brad took a drink of his water as he nodded his head. Every now and then he'd steal a look over at Meagan, whom I was guessing was still sitting with her arms folded.

I continued to focus on Brad. The last thing I wanted him to think was that he could intimidate me like he did his own daughter. "As far as knowing anyone, that is where you're wrong. My father left my mother when I was very young. I've earned my way in everything I do. My mother wouldn't have it any other way and neither would I, sir. I work for everything I get and nothing in my life has ever come easy to me. Including your daughter's love."

Brad lifted an eyebrow and then cracked a smile. "Good to know. I'm sure your mother is very proud of you. That had to have been hard for her trying to raise a son on her own."

"If it was, she never complained."

Meagan cleared her throat and said, "Dad, I was thinking we might take a drive up to meet Gray's mother. She's an amazing woman and I can't wait for Mom to meet her."

My head snapped over as I looked at Meagan. Brad looked between the two of us as he barely said, "I'd love to meet Gray's mom."

The waitress came back over to take everyone's orders as Meagan started talking about her job and how much she liked it.

"I'm glad you're enjoying it so much, Meagan. When

do you think you'll be heading back to Texas? Your sister is graduating you know; it would be nice to have my girls close to home. I'm sure your sister would love to have you back in Texas. Set a good example for her on starting her own career."

Oh hell. Here we go.

Meagan moved about nervously in her seat. "I like it here, Dad. I don't have any plans on leaving anytime soon and why can't I be an example to her here?"

Brad sighed. "Of course you can set an example for her, but, Meagan, there is nothing here for you. Your entire family is back home in Texas."

Glancing down at my salad, it was my turn to move about in my seat nervously.

"Stop. Dad you have to *stop* doing this."

"Doing what, Meagan? Wanting you to be home and near your family?"

Meagan tossed her napkin onto the table. "No. I'm not doing this anymore with you. My whole life you've told me what I can and can't do. When all my friends went to A&M, you told me I had to go to Baylor. Set an example for Taylor by being your own person you said. When my grades would slip, you would ride my ass. By God I had to set an example for Taylor by getting stellar grades and being the perfect daughter who listened to everything you told me to do."

"Meg," I whispered when her voice grew louder.

Her head snapped over to me. "I'm sorry, Gray, but I can't do this anymore." Turning back to her father, I watched as a single tear rolled down her cheek. "For years I did nothing but chase after the person I wanted to be. I was stuck though, stuck in a world you painted for me. Stuck in a world I hated so much I did nothing but cried myself to sleep most nights."

Brad's face dropped as he stared at his daughter.

"Newsflash for you, Dad. I didn't have a perfect life, I

hated college, I hate Texas and I never want to move back there. I'm not that perfect daughter you strived so damn hard for me to be. I'm the daughter who made mistakes, has regrets and was so beaten down by your expectations that I let myself be miserable in college because I couldn't stand up to you or the people who made my life a living hell. Well not anymore. Everything I need and want is right here. Matter of fact—"

Meagan reached into her purse and pulled her engagement ring out and slipped it on her finger. "I love Gray and when he asked me to marry him, I finally felt like I was happy and safe. For the first time in a long time, I felt like I was exactly where I belonged."

Meagan stood and looked down at her father. "I'm not perfect, Dad, so please stop trying to make me be. And by the way, I like my hair brown and have no intentions of ever going back to red!"

Meagan grabbed her coat and her purse. "If you'll excuse me, I've lost my appetite and will be sitting at the bar drinking a very strong drink and I don't give two shits if you approve or not."

Both Brad and I watched as Meagan retreated over to the bar.

After a few minutes of silence, Brad shook his head. "My God. She is her mother's daughter."

I couldn't help but smile as I watched the love of my life stomp over toward the bar and sit her sexy ass down on the bar stool.

"Gray, I have to ask you something."

Turning, I looked directly into his eyes. "Anything."

"Will you please allow me to spend some time alone with my daughter this evening? I not only need to process what she just hit me with, but I also need to process she is engaged and right now all I want to do is hit you."

With a grin, I pulled out my wallet and placed money on the table. "Of course. I'll go let Meagan know I'm heading home and I certainly don't want to have to arrest you for assaulting an officer."

With a smile and a nod of his head, Brad said, "Thank you, son. That means a lot to me."

Chapter

TWENTY-ONE

Meagan

WHEN THE BARTENDER set the drink down in front of me, I raised my hand to grab it. My hand was shaking so bad I had to make a fist. Could my life get any crazier?

I felt him before I saw him. "Hey," Grayson whispered as he leaned down and kissed my cheek. "I'm so damn proud of you, baby."

My eyes burned as I fought to hold in the tears I wanted so desperately to let out. "I just told my father everything I've been wanting to say for years and I'm scared shitless he's going to hate you."

"As long as you're not mad at me anymore."

Turning, I gave Grayson a bemused smile. "I'm a little mad at you still."

"How can I make it up to you?"

With a lift of my eyebrow, I let the naughty thoughts I was having invade my mind. "I need to relax before I talk to my father. How are you going to make that happen?"

Grayson's eyes turned dark as he swallowed hard. "Your father just asked me to leave so he could spend some time with you."

"You better think fast then, Mr. Bennett; time is running out."

An evil smile spread over Grayson's face. "You naughty girl."

"You bring it out in me."

"Excuse yourself to use the restroom; I'll take care of it from there."

My cheeks burned as my body hummed with anticipation.

With a quick kiss on my lips, Grayson walked away as I sat there, horny as all get out and pissed beyond belief.

Motioning toward the bartender, I asked, "Will you please add this to the bill for that table?" I asked as I pointed at my father.

"Yes, of course."

I picked up my jacket and purse and then grabbed the vodka and cranberry juice and made my way back to my father.

"Meagan, please sit back down and let's talk."

With a dramatic sigh, I set my drink, jacket, and purse down. "I need a few moments to calm down, Dad."

My father nodded his head. "You're not angry I asked Gray to leave, are you?"

A part of me was angry he asked my fiancé to leave. But that was a battle I wasn't ready to fight. "I'm not happy about that, but I understand. If you'll give me a few minutes, I'll be right back."

My father stood and said, "Of course, sweetheart. Your meal should be coming out soon, though."

It was then I realized Grayson had paid for the meal and left without eating. The idea of him rushing over here to be with me only to be asked to leave had me longing to see him even more and say how sorry I was for earlier to-day. My emotions were all over the place lately.

Ugh. I need a girls' weekend.

Turning on my heels, I quickly made my way to the restrooms. Right as I was about to walk into the ladies' restroom, Grayson grabbed me and pulled me down the hall and through the kitchen.

"Gray!" I whispered as he guided me out through the kitchen and down a hall. "Where are we going?"

"I told the manager I had to question you regarding a case. He graciously offered me the use of his office."

My stomach dipped at the idea of doing something naughty with Grayson as my father sat in the restaurant. Covering my mouth, I tried to hide my smile as Grayson stopped at the door marked General Manager. Opening the door, he pulled me in, shut and locked the door.

His hands were up my dress and his lips pressed to mine before I could even utter a word. Warm fingers dipped into my panties and slid effortlessly between my lips.

A low moan vibrated between our mouths as I pushed my hips against his hand. Being with Grayson meant forgetting the world. We were both guilty of using sex as a way to forget the now, and I was totally okay with that.

"Gray, fuck me. I need you to fuck me now."

His eyes roamed over my body like a hungry lion waiting to eat his prey. "Goddamn it, Meg," Grayson said as he unzipped his pants and pulled out his hard dick.

"Yes," I hissed as I walked up against the wall opposite the door and pushed my panties out of the way and.

Grayson lifted my leg and teased my clit with the head of his dick. "Gah! Grayson! Now!"

With one quick move, he was balls deep as we both gasped.

"Tell me you're not angry anymore."

My eyes widened as he stood there, buried inside of

me in some stranger's office in a restaurant where my father was sitting at a table waiting for me. "W-what?"

Barely rotating his hips, he grinned. "Tell me you're not angry with me anymore."

Narrowing my eye at him, I smiled. "Unless you pull an orgasm out of me in the next three minutes, I'm not going to say that."

The smile on his face caused my body to tremble. "Challenge accepted."

Holding my leg up, Grayson moved in and out of my body like he couldn't get enough of me. It was raw, hard, fast, and the hottest fucking thing I'd ever experienced as his lips moved across my neck.

"Oh God," I whispered as I buried my face into his neck and rode out my orgasm while I felt Grayson's own release pouring into my body. Nothing felt as amazing as Grayson's cum inside of me.

Pulling out, Grayson gently let go of my leg as he moved my panties back into place and zipped up his pants.

My head dropped back as I fought to catch my breath. "That was almost *too* fast."

With a laugh, Grayson pulled me to him and cupped my face with his hands. "I love you so fucking much."

His lips brushed gently over mine as he stole one last kiss before turning and walking over to the door. I peeled my body from the wall and walked over toward the man I would do anything for. The man who helped me find a piece of myself I had buried away for so long I almost forgot who she was.

"Will you be coming by my place later?"

Grayson frowned as he jerked his head back. "What about your father?"

With a shrug of my shoulders, I winked and said, "Give me two hours with him and then bring a pint of Ben and Jerry's and a movie."

Grayson opened the door and motioned for me to take the lead. "If that's what my girl wants, that's what she'll get."

❦

An hour later, my father and I were still sitting at the table at Ores. The conversation started off shaky as I finally told my father everything that happened at Baylor. I had let my parents know some things, but I never fully told them everything and how bad the bullying got.

Now we were on the subject I was most afraid to talk to him about.

"So . . . Grayson."

His name caused me to smile and my father noticed it right away.

With a frown he slightly shook his head in disbelief. "Engaged? I'd say this is pretty serious."

My stomach fluttered as I looked down at my ring. "He makes me happy, Dad. I can't explain how I feel about him without smiling like a silly teenager."

"Meg, why didn't you tell us about him sooner? Why wait until you're engaged or one of us was coming to visit you?"

Glancing down at my dessert plate, I shrugged as I moved the last piece of cheesecake around mindlessly. "I guess I was afraid you might try to push him away from me."

My father reached across the table and squeezed my hand. "I'm so sorry I made you feel that way, Meagan. I really wish you had come to talk to me. My heart hurts knowing I was the one who pushed you away from us."

I shook my head, "No, Dad. Please don't feel that way. I never pictured myself moving back to Mason after college. I know everyone else wants that life and that's great. I'm so happy for all of my friends and happy that most of our family is right there. For me though, I needed something different. I didn't want to marry a cowboy and live on a ranch and play the rancher's wife. I wanted the life I have right now."

"And Gray? Being married to a cop who puts his life on the line every day, you're okay with that?"

"Yes. Dad, I'm not going to live my life in fear of the unknown. I love him so much, and I know he loves me. I feel complete when I'm with him. I laugh, have fun, dream of kids with him."

"Kids?" my father asked, nearly choking on his own spit.

With a shy smile, I nodded. "We um . . . we're moving in together, by the way."

My father released my hand and sat back in his chair as he exhaled a long breath. "I figured as much. You're a grown woman and you don't owe me any explanations but, Meg, you've hit me with a lot tonight." Tears formed in my father's eyes as he pinned me with his stare. "That doesn't make it easier for me though. Letting go of you is hard, baby girl."

I tilted my head and studied my father. "Why were you so hard on me?"

His eyes turned sad as he looked away for a moment before turning his attention back on me. "I don't know, Meg. I wish I had a solid answer for you, but a part of me thinks it was my own failures that drove me to make sure you never failed. The moment I held you in my arms I promised myself I would push you to do great things, but never once thinking about how that would affect you. I'm so sorry, baby. I never meant to compare you to Taylor or make you think I thought any less of you. You're my everything, Meagan. The very air I breathe is because of you. I never told you this, but you saved my life."

My heart jumped to my throat as I felt a single tear drop from my eye. "What do you mean?"

"Your mother left me when she was pregnant with you. I missed a good portion of her pregnancy because of some serious stuff. But I had two things that kept me going and kept me fighting to get clean. Amanda, and my unborn child. The first time I ever felt you move in your mother's stomach my life changed. The one little kick opened my eyes like never before. I'll never forget the feeling that washed over my body. Everything I did from that point on was for the two of you. Then when we were blessed with your sister, it made the circle complete. The three of you are my world. I don't ever want you to have to say the things you said to me earlier tonight. I want you happy, Meagan. And if living here in Colorado makes you happy, and Gray makes you happy, then I'm happy."

"Daddy," I whispered as we reached across the table for each other's hands. "I love you so much."

"I love you too, pumpkin. Now, how about we head home and watch a movie."

My heart felt as if it were about to burst. The idea of being with the two men I loved left me breathless. "I'll text Gray and tell him to bring a movie."

Standing, my father flashed me a smile. It was the same smile I used to see when I would get off the bus and run toward him when he would surprise us by coming home early. The same smile that always made me feel like everything was going to be okay. "Tell him to bring popcorn if you don't have any."

With a chuckle, I nodded. "Sounds good."

Taking my arm, we left the restaurant. "Meagan?"

"Yeah, Dad?"

"I need to be prepared for something."

With a deep breath in, I held it for a second before releasing it and asking, "What's that?"

"Will your fiancé be staying the night at your apartment while I'm there?"

My face flushed as I chewed on the corner of my lip.

"Um . . . he was going to, but if it makes you feel uncomfortable he doesn't have to."

Holding up his hand, he shook his head. "No, you're a grown woman who is engaged to be married and I'm not stupid to fool myself into thinking my little girl has never had sex before." His body shivered, and he frantically shook his head as if trying to erase a thought. "Fully clothed and I don't want to hear a sound coming from your room."

For a moment, I thought back to a few hours ago when Grayson and I were having sex not but a few yards from my own father. Hearing my father talk like that though caused me to let out a roar of laughter until I had tears streaming down my face. The valet driver pulled up with my car as my father shot me a dirty look and got into the passenger side of my car as he said, "I'm glad you find that so funny. Wait until you have kids one day, Meagan."

The mentioning of having kids caused my stomach to dip.

"Oh man. Whoa . . . I must have needed that laugh," I said as I buckled up and started heading home.

"Ha ha. Some day the shoe will be on the other foot and you just wait."

Peeking over at my father, I smiled. This was what I wanted our relationship to be like. Open and honest. This was turning out to be the best night of my life.

Chapter

TWENTY-TWO

Grayson

STANDING IN THE kitchen, I flipped the bacon and then checked the biscuits. Smiling, I stood and said, "Perfect," as I tended to the eggs.

"So you cook too huh?"

Glancing over my shoulder, I flashed a smile over to Brad. "Good morning, Brad. Coffee is on and hot."

Lifting his hand, he mumbled something as he made his way over to the coffee pot and poured himself a cup.

Getting back to breakfast, I started to heat the pan for the sausage.

"Whatcha making?"

"Breakfast tacos and biscuits and sausage gravy for my girl."

Brad cleared his throat. "*Your* girl? I do believe she is still mine."

A wide smile moved across my face as I turned and

leaned against the counter next to the stove. Brad was staring me down, trying to intimidate me. "So this is where it's going to happen?"

Brad lifted the cup to his lips and took a small drink before raising an eyebrow and saying, "I guess so."

"I love your daughter, sir."

"You think by getting up early and making us breakfast I'm going to just fall in love with you and hand her right on over?"

I stayed completely relaxed while I took on the death stare Meagan's father was giving me. I'd never let on that my mouth was now completely dry and my pulse was about to pound my heart out of my chest.

"I think Meagan is worth a little more effort than a breakfast."

"Confident little bastard aren't you?"

My smile faded some as my eyes turned serious. "I just know your daughter is worth the fight."

Brad tried to hide his smile as he gave me a quick nod. "She means the world to her mother and I, and cop or no cop, you hurt her and I will kill you."

"Fair enough."

"I expect you to treat her with respect."

"She deserves nothing less than to be treated like a princess, sir."

He snarled his lip slightly. "You realize you are all she has here."

"I do. I also know how much her family and friends mean to her and I would never hold her back from anyone or anything."

With a huff, Brad crossed his arms over his chest. "I'm not happy with this."

I attempted to hold back my smile. "I see that."

"Breakfast isn't going to fix this situation."

Now I was intrigued. "How do you propose we handle this so that you are happy?"

Brad let out a gruff laugh. "Oh, Gray, I'll never be happy about this. Ever."

Swallowing hard, I pushed off the counter and turned my focus back onto the food.

"You hunt?".

Jesus, that subject just got changed fast and I'm not so sure I like where it is going.

"Yes, sir. I've been hunting since I was about five."

"That so?"

I took a chance and glanced over my shoulder, only to find Brad pinning me down with his stare. "Um . . . yeah. My best friend's father took us all the time."

"Really," Brad said as he pulled the chair out at the island and sat down. "There a shooting range around here anywhere?"

Panic filled my body at the idea of giving this man a gun with me in the same room.

"Morning to my two favorite men!" Meagan said as she practically skipped up and gave me a quick kiss on the lips before heading over to her dad.

"Why did he get the first kiss?"

Meagan froze as she looked between the two of us. Lifting my eyebrows, I turned back to the eggs that were now done. "Um . . . gosh I don't know, Dad. I saw him first?"

"Huh," Brad said as I attempted to hold back my grin.

"I was just asking Gray here if there is a shooting range we could hit up today."

"Oh fun!" Meagan said as I snapped my head over to her. "Yeah, there's a few, plus Gray has access to the range they use as well. He's taken me there a couple times."

Stop. Talking. Meagan.

Brad leaned back in his chair and looked at me. "Is that so? I say after this wonderful breakfast your fiancé made for us, we head to the range. Get some shots in."

"Ahh—"

Meagan poured a cup of coffee and then reached into the refrigerator for the orange juice. "That sounds like fun. Doesn't it, Gray?"

"Ahh—"

The smirk that spread across Brad's face said it all. He'd won round one, but I'd be damned if he was going to win round two.

～�֍～

Meagan jumped when I hit all my shots in the dead center of the bullseye. I engaged the safety and turned to look at Brad. I was almost positive I saw steam coming from his ears. "You want to go another round?"

His mouth pinched into a scowl as he muttered something under his breath. "I'm thinking we can call it a day."

I would have given anything to do a fist pump and flaunt the fact that I had just out-shot the hell out of him for the last hour and a half. Seeing that pout on his face was reward enough.

"At least I know you have a good aim," Brad said as he handed me the gun and I returned them both to their cases. Locking them, I grabbed one and Brad took the other while Meagan reached for my hand.

"What do you want to do now, Dad?"

Please say go to the airport and fly home.

"How about we grab some lunch, my treat."

Meagan smiled and I groaned internally. It's not that I didn't enjoy Brad's company, I just hated the fact that he was judging every single thing I did and he made it pretty damn clear he was not happy about our engagement.

"Sounds great! Gray, where should we take, Dad to eat?"

For some reason I remembered Meagan saying her father hated Chinese food. With a wide grin, I said, "How about May Palace. Best Chinese food in Durango."

176

"Oh yum, but Dad doesn't like Chinese food."

Brad shot me a smirk. Fine you won that one.

"All right, let me think."

"How about Steamworks Brewery? They have great hamburgers."

My body stiffened. I'd never told Meagan this, but Diana not only owned a male strip club right outside of Durango, but Steamworks Brewery as well.

Brad tilted his head and looked at me intently. I was positive he saw my reaction. "That sounds amazing, pumpkin. I'm in the mood for a good burger."

Meagan did a little happy dance and laced her arm with her dad's and grabbed onto my hand. "This is turning out to be the best day ever!"

❧

Inhaling a deep cleansing breath, I held the door open to Steamworks as Meagan and then her father walked in. Closing my eyes, I quickly said a prayer no one said anything to me.

Eyes open, and I walked in with a straight posture.

"Oh. My. God! If it isn't Grayson!"

Fuck. My. Life.

Diana came walking over and engulfed me in a hug. I could see Meagan's confused expression quickly replaced with one of fear.

"Hey Diana, you remember Meg, my fiancée?"

"Of course, but I didn't know you had moved up from girlfriend to fiancée! I'm judging the tenderloin dish! When am I getting those by the way?"

Meagan and I both fumbled over our responses as Diana zeroed in on Brad. "Why hello there, handsome. Who might you be?"

Brad chuckled and shook Diana's hand. "Brad Atwood, Meagan's father."

Diana lifted her eyebrow as she snuck a quick look at me before turning her attention back to Brad. "Well, welcome to Steamworks. Dad, you look like you need a drink. We have the best brewed beers in Colorado."

Lifting his hands up, Brad took a step back. "No thank you. I don't drink."

Diana quickly backed off and grabbed three menus. "Totally get it. Let's go have a seat, shall we."

I followed behind everyone as I scanned the restaurant. Waiting tables in the other section was Georgia.

Shit.

Turning my head, I avoided looking at her. Pulling Meagan's chair out, I smiled and squeezed her shoulder before sitting down. She leaned over and whispered, "Sorry, I didn't know."

With a fake smile, I nodded and buried my face in the menu.

"Georgia will be over to take your drink orders here in a second. Enjoy your lunch." I didn't bother looking at her as Meagan and Brad thanked her.

"I take it you know the manager, Gray?"

Not wanting to lie, I gave a nod of acknowledgement and said, "Owner. Diana is the owner. She owns a few places around the area."

Brad lifted his eyebrows in surprise. "Well, that's great for her. She must be a smart business woman."

Meagan giggled as she lifted her hand over her mouth and whispered, "Sorry. Thought about something that made me chuckle."

"Afternoon, folks. What can I get you to drink?"

"Iced tea please," Brad said.

"Same for me, thank you."

Not wanting to be rude, I pulled the menu down and said, "I'll have the same."

Georgia's mouth dropped open as she ran around the table and wrapped her arms around me. "Gray! Holy crap.

I haven't seen you in forever! How's the new life treating you?"

My stomach felt sick as I forced a smile. "It's good. All is good."

"Oh, I'm so glad. I was so worried when I found out you were going to be a cop."

One peak over to Brad showed him looking through the menu. Thank God.

"Yeah, crazy."

It was then I saw him.

Joshua Black. Meagan must have seen him at the same time because she grabbed my hand.

"Crazy running into you here, Detective Bennett."

Dropping his menu, Brad looked at Joshua. Meagan grabbed my hand and held it tightly as my adrenaline shot up fast.

"Mr. Black, how are you this evening?" I asked. Brad must have noticed the tone in my voice had changed.

Joshua smiled as his eyes bounced over to Meagan. "I'm doing good. Meagan, how are you?"

Clearing her throat, Meagan said, "Doing well. Out to lunch with my father."

"Is that so?" Turning to Brad, Joshua held out his hand and shook it. "I'm an acquaintance of the detective's."

What the fuck?

"It's a pleasure, Brad Atwood."

Son-of-a-bitch. Now Joshua knew Meagan's last name.

With a quick smile, Joshua turned back to me. "Is this as close to your old stomping grounds as you could get?"

Meagan froze as Brad looked between Joshua and me. "Excuse me?" I asked as I balled my fists.

Joshua looked back at Brad and said, "It's crazy to think that the owner of this fine establishment also owns a male strip club on the outskirts of town."

"What are you doing?" Meagan asked as she glared at Joshua.

Brad looked confused as hell. "Um, well, I guess as long as everything is legal it's all good."

Joshua slowly turned and stared at me. "Well I don't know, lets ask the detective. After all, he used to work there."

Standing, I rounded the table and grabbed Joshua as Meagan jumped up. "Gray, don't."

Pulling Joshua closer to me, I gritted my teeth together. "I don't know what your play is, but I suggest you leave now."

With an evil laugh, Joshua pulled his arm from my grasp. "Better watch out detective, you wouldn't want to have anyone thinking police brutality is going on."

"Fuck you, asshole!" Meagan shouted as Diana came walking back over.

"Problem?"

Taking another step toward Joshua, I looked directly into his eyes. "Yeah, Di, the trash needs to be taken out."

Less than thirty seconds later, Joshua was being walked out as I followed behind them. Meagan stayed back at the table with her father while I stepped outside and stood in front of this piece of fucking shit.

Joshua flashed me a cocky ass grin as he shook his head. "Stripper turned cop. Pretty interesting story."

"You snooping around in my life?"

His eyes turned dark as his grin dropped. "You're snooping in mine so I thought I would return the favor. Want to tell me why you're so interested in me?"

"It's part of an investigation."

"For what?"

"Murder."

Joshua's face turned white. "You're barking up the wrong tree, detective. I suggest you look elsewhere or I'll have my father slap you with a harassment charge."

With a laugh, I asked, "Harassment charge?" I took one step closer to him. We were practically standing head to head. "Listen here you little fucker, you mess with me and I promise you you're gonna pay for it. And as far as Meagan goes, don't you even utter a word to her or you'll be hit with a restraining order."

Joshua's eyes narrowed as he gave me a dismissive nod. "We're done here then?"

"You bet your fucking ass we are."

Taking a step back, Joshua glanced over my shoulder before turning and walking out the door.

My heart was pounding so hard in my chest it felt as if I couldn't breathe. I motioned to Meagan for one second. She looked frazzled and I couldn't help but notice how angry Brad looked.

Great. Just fucking great.

Pulling out my phone, I hit Derrick's number.

"What's up?"

"I just had an interesting run in with Joshua Black. I want a tag on him twenty-four seven."

"All right. Want to tell me what in the hell happened?"

Sighing heavily, I pushed my fingers through my hair and cursed. "Can I fill you in later? I have serious damage control to do with my future father–in–law."

"Oh hell. Yeah, no worries. Call me later. Meanwhile, I'll get on it."

"Thanks, Winn. I owe you."

Hitting End, I looked around for the little fucker. If he walked up to me I'd bash his fucking head in.

Before I had a chance to head back into the restaurant, Meagan and her father came walking out. Meagan was clearly pissed off and Brad didn't look any happier.

"My father is being an asshole."

"Meagan!" Brad and I both said at once.

Brad glared as Meagan stepped between us. "Dad, you promised me you would wait until we got back to the apartment."

"You were a stripper? A male fucking stripper?"

181

My hands clenched and unclenched as my anger grew. "Dad!"

"Yes, I was. I worked my way through college being a male stripper. That says nothing about who I am, though."

Brad let out a contempt laugh. "The hell it doesn't." Turning to Meagan he pointed to me. "You really want to marry a guy who's slept with lord knows how many women? Seriously, Meagan, where is your head at?"

Now it was Meagan's turn to get angry. "How dare you judge him, Dad! You don't know anything about Gray, except for spending a few hours with him talking and shooting guns. So he worked at a strip club; why do you think that automatically makes him a manwhore? Tell me, Dad, how many women have you slept with? Have you ever looked twice at a woman after you married Mom?"

Brad immediately looked away as Meagan took a step back and covered her mouth. Turning back to Meagan, Brad shook his head. "It's not what you're thinking, Meagan."

"Oh my God. Is that why she left you before I was born? Because you cheated on her?"

Shit. This was turning south and fast.

"Can we all just go ahead and get back into the car and head back to your apartment? It feels like the temperature is dropping out here and this is not the place to have this conversation," I said while trying to prompt Meagan back to the car.

Meagan glared at her father as she made her way over to her car. I was taken aback when she handed me the keys and got in on the passenger side. No one said a word as I drove us back to Meagan's apartment. I could see she was trying hard to keep her tears at bay.

Damn it all to hell. I should have suggested another restaurant.

Not even letting me get the car fully parked, Meagan jumped out of the car and slammed the door shut.

I slowly got out of the car and followed her while Brad followed behind me.

"Meagan," I started to say when she held her hand up to stop me. When she opened the door to her apartment, she rushed in and went straight to her room where she slammed the door so hard a picture came off the wall.

Spinning around, I looked at Brad. I was done being nice. "Listen, whatever you may or may not think I was like at one point in my life, you know nothing about me. I did what I had to do so that my mother didn't have to worry about how in the hell she was going to afford for me to go to college."

"And stripping was the best you could come up with?"

"No, I worked plenty of other places. It was when I finally opened my eyes to see the struggles my mother was going through that I decided I needed to do something else. A friend of mine was working at the club and told me about it. I checked it and decided it was worth it."

Brad drew his mouth into a straight line, stopping himself from saying anything.

"It's not like what you're thinking. I didn't sleep around with women. I went in, I did my job and I left. I never did anything illegal and I certainly didn't fuck a different girl every night. I did a few private parties and yeah, I messed around with a girl or two that caught my eye. When you can stand here and tell me you led a perfect life, I'll let you judge mine."

Brad looked away for a brief second as the reality of my words sunk in before turning back to look at me.

"I was able to pay for all of my college, no loans needed. I paid off the debt my mother had, bought her a car and a house. I've got a pretty large nest egg in the bank as well. All with the money I earned stripping."

"Does your mother know what you did?"

"Of course she does. She wasn't happy about it, but it was my life, my decision."

Brad turned and walked over to the sofa where he sat down and buried his face in his hands and let out a frustrated grunt.

"Son-of-a-bitch, I messed up again."

I wanted more than anything to agree with him, but I kept my mouth shut as I made my way to Meagan's room. Knocking lightly, I said, "Meg, baby it's me."

I could hear her crying on the other side of the door and the way it made me feel shocked me. That sound was something I never wanted to hear, and I'd do anything to make that happy. "Come in," she softly spoke.

Slowly turning the knob, I walked in and about dropped to the floor when I saw her bloodshot eyes and mascara running down her face. Shutting the door, I quickly walked over to her and fell to my knees.

"No, don't cry, Meg."

Cupping her face in my hands, I kissed all over her face as she sobbed harder.

"I'm. So. Sorry," she whispered between sobs.

My eyes searched her face as I smiled at her. "I love you." Pressing my lips to hers, I pulled her down to the floor with me. Her arms wrapped around my neck as she pulled me closer to her. I would have given anything to not have her father on the other side of her bedroom door.

"I love you," I whispered against her lips.

"Gray."

Pulling back, I looked into her eyes. "You need to talk to your father."

Meagan shook her head. "I don't have anything to say to him."

My finger came up to her chin as I made her look into my eyes. "Meg, your father has paid for his past mistakes and your parents moved on. You can't blame him for being upset because he found out about my past job. If I was your father, I'd flip a fucking lid as well."

She shook her head as her eyes fell to my lips. I knew

what she wanted. What she needed. I felt the same way. Getting lost in each other was what we did, but not now. Now we both had to face this head on.

"I'd give anything to be with you, Meg, but baby, we need to go out there and talk to him."

The moment her teeth sunk down into that plump bottom lip, I moaned and adjusted my growing dick.

"Gray," she whispered.

I quickly stood and backed away from her. "No way, Meg. Your father is right there," I whispered as she stood up and made her way to me.

My hand came up to stop her. "No!"

"Please, Gray. I just need to feel you."

I looked away. Don't look in her eyes! Stay strong!

My body shivered the moment her hands touched my chest.

"Just for a second. I need to feel you for one second."

God why can't I resist this girl?

My hand landed on her hip to stop her.

"We need to go out there now, Meg."

The knock on the door had Meagan stepping away from me as she pouted.

"Meagan? Pumpkin, please come out and let me talk to you."

Giving her a wink, I walked up to her and kissed her on the forehead. "Let's go talk to your dad, together."

Meagan laced her fingers in mine as we headed to the door. We could face anything, as long as we were together.

Chapter

TWENTY-THREE

Meagan

MY BODY ACHED as I rolled over and stretched. The sun was pouring into my bedroom lighting up the whole room and telling me I had slept in much longer than I wanted to.

Feeling to my right, the space was empty. I sat up and rolled my neck a few times before swinging my feet out and stumbling out of bed.

We had stayed up late last night talking to my father and then watching a movie. Dad had given up on the movie only twenty minutes into it, but Grayson and I watched it till the end.

Today was the last full day to spend with my dad. I was so glad we talked last night and got everything out in the open. I wasn't sure if my father was going to be able to move past the whole Grayson being an ex stripper thing, but he did and they actually laughed and joked around a good part of the evening.

"Gray?" I called out as I walked into my bathroom.

Quickly changing into some sweat pants and a T-shirt, I threw my hair up into a ponytail and brushed my teeth. Five minutes later I was walking into the kitchen where my father was already sitting at the kitchen island with the newspaper in one hand and a cup of coffee in the other.

"Dad, you're the only person I know who still reads an actual newspaper."

With a chuckle, my father laughed. "Not true. Gunner and Jeff still read a newspaper."

With a roll of my eyes, I sighed and reached for my favorite coffee mug. "I wish Mom could have come with you."

"I know, but her sinus infection was just too bad. Plus I think she knew I wanted to spend some time with you."

Lifting my cup to my lips, I blew on my hot coffee. "I miss her."

"She's mentioned coming up here next month so the two of y'all can spend a girls weekend together."

My heart felt light as the idea of spending the weekend with just my mother filled me with excitement. "I love that idea!"

My father chuckled. "I thought you would."

After taking a sip of coffee, I glanced around. "Where's Grayson?"

"He got a call, said it was an emergency and he had to go into the office."

A shiver ran through my body. I prayed they hadn't found another girl killed. "I hope it wasn't anything serious."

"I think he mentioned it was a suicide. At least that's what I thought I heard him say to the person over the phone."

I covered my mouth to hide my yawn. "Oh no. Well I hope not. I wouldn't think they would call him for a suicide unless it was a murder suicide. I could be wrong though."

"Sounds like Gray is pretty good at his job."

I sat across from my father and smiled. The slight chill in the air had me wishing I had put on my fuzzy socks. I was ready for spring. March in Texas is shorts weather, so still bundling up was weird to me.

My father's cell phone rang as he jumped up and quickly made his way to where it sat on the coffee table.

"Hello?"

His eyes immediately came up to mine with a look of concern. Setting my coffee mug down, I stood up.

Something was wrong.

"Taylor?" I asked as my father smiled weakly and shook his head.

"Okay. I understand. Okay."

He hit End as he placed his phone in his back pocket.

The entire time he walked back into the kitchen he avoided eye contact with me.

"Dad, is everything okay? You're scaring me."

Looking up, his eyes answered for me. "Meagan, that was Gray."

My breath caught has he lifted his arms. "No, he's fine sweetheart, but he needs us to come down to the police station right away."

My brow wrinkled as my throat constricted. "W-why?"

"I don't know. He just asked me to drive you down to the station as soon as I could."

Without even thinking, I grabbed my purse and keys and walked to the door with my father closely behind me.

"He didn't say what was wrong?"

"No, baby. I'm sorry."

Something was off. Why would Gray call my father who now wouldn't even look me in the eye as he talked to me? We made our way out to my car as I pulled the jacket I had grabbed on the way out over my shoulders.

"I'll drive, just tell me where to go."

I grabbed onto his arm and pulled him to a stop. "Dad, what aren't you telling me?"

His smile was soft and gentle, just like his eyes were. "Baby, I don't have anything to tell you. Let's get down there and see what Grayson wants."

Trying to smile, I forced a grin out and nodded my head.

Then entire time in the car, I clasped my hands together. My gut was telling me there was something terribly wrong, and I knew my father was trying to protect me from something. That or he really didn't know.

After parking, my father took my hand and we walked into the police station together. Glancing around, I saw a large group of kids, high school age, all standing off to the side.

"Meagan."

Grayson's voice caused my head to snap in his direction. He quickly wrapped his arm around my waist and led me away from everyone. "Brad, want to follow me please?"

"Sure," my father said with a cracked voice.

"Grayson, you're really scaring me, please tell me what's wrong."

He didn't look at me; he only kept his eyes trained straight ahead. We walked up to what looked like an investigation room. Grayson opened the door and led us inside.

He shut the door and looked between the both of us before his eyes landed on mine.

Was that . . . tears in his eyes?

Pressing my lips together and moving them back and forth, my heart began to pound in my chest. Something bad happened. Oh God. Melissa!

"Gray!" I shouted.

He jumped as he took another step closer to me and

placed his hands on my upper arms.

"Um . . . Meagan . . . I don't even know how to tell you this, baby. I wish to God I didn't have to."

My breathing hitched as I tried to figure out what he was about to tell me.

Closing his eyes, he slowly shook his head before looking back into my eyes. Heaviness grew in my chest as my chin trembled.

"Just tell me, Gray. Please."

"Mitchell shot himself this morning in his bedroom."

My hands covered my mouth as I sucked in a breath. "Oh my God. Is he okay? Is he going to be all right? Was it an accident?"

Grayson shook his head as he blinked back tears. He went to speak, but his voice cracked. My heart felt like it had ceased to beat as I stood there and waited for his answer. Everything seemed to stop and move in slow motion as I heard each breath I took.

"Meg, he died instantly."

My brain tried to comprehend what Grayson had said. "W-what?" I choked out as my hands came up to his arms where I held on for dear life. This was impossible. *It's a mistake. It's not Mitchell!* "No. Grayson, no! You have to be wrong. I just saw him yesterday and he was fine! He told me he was happy. Everything was good!" My entire body shook as I replayed our meeting yesterday in my head. Squeezing my eyes shut, I shook my head. Forcing them open, I pleaded, "Please . . . Gray . . . no. He would have told me if things where that bad." Hitting Grayson against the chest as hard as I could, I cried out, "He's not gone! You're wrong. You're wrong!"

"God, baby, I wish I was wrong. I'm so sorry. I'm so very sorry."

The soreness in my lungs burned as I tried to understand what was happening. "I . . . I don't understand why." My fingers pushed though my hair as I cradled my head and tried to make sense of all of this. My arms dropped and I looked at Grayson. "Mitchell." Pushing Grayson away from me, I covered my mouth as my shoulders quaked. "No!" I screamed as I stumbled back against the door.

"Meagan," Grayson called out as he reached for me.

Tears streamed down my face as I saw Mitchell's smile flash across my mind. *How did I miss this? How could I have let him down like this?*

My body trembled as Grayson placed his hands on my face. I was barley able to speak as I whispered, "Please tell me you're wrong. Please, Gray. Please."

Grayson pulled me into his arms as he held me tightly. "I'm so sorry, Meg."

My legs gave out as I screamed out Mitchell's name and collapsed to the ground as Grayson went down with me. Pulling me onto his lap, Grayson held onto me tightly.

The room slowly faded away as I heard Grayson and my father calling out my name.

I failed him.

I. Failed. Him.

❧

"Gray, why don't you go get something to eat?"

My father's voice sounded so far away as I fought to open my eyes.

"I'm not hungry, Brad, but thank you."

Turning my head, I saw my father and Grayson both sitting in chairs. Grayson's head was buried in his hands as my father stared out the window.

It was then I realized what had happened.

Mitchell.

Tears spilled from my eyes as I looked up at the ceiling and then around Grayson's bedroom confused. "What happened?" I asked as Grayson jumped up and was by my side in an instant.

"You passed out. We brought you back to my place."

My father stood on the other side of me and smiled sweetly as he took my hand in his. "Hey, pumpkin."

"Dad," I whispered with a smile.

Turning back to Grayson, I knew I had to ask the one thing I was praying had been a dream. "Mitchell?"

Grayson's chin trembled as he looked at my father. My heart dropped, knowing it wasn't a bad dream.

"Why?" I asked with a quaking voice. "Why?"

Sitting up some, I looked between my father and Grayson. "Is his mother okay? What about his brothers?"

Clearing his throat to speak, my father squeezed my hand. "She's doing the best anyone can expect and Melissa has been with Mitchell's brothers."

I attempted to swallow but my throat was so dry. Gripping my father's hand, I looked into his eyes. "Daddy," was all I could manage to get out.

My father kissed my forehead and mumbled against my skin, "I love you, pumpkin." Pulling back, he gave me a weak smile. "Let me go see what I can find out about how Mrs. Haus is doing."

I watched as my father quickly walked out of the bedroom.

Grayson reached his hand over and pushed a piece of hair behind my ear as I closed my eyes. Mitchell's face appeared and my eyes snapped back open. "Meg, Melissa is really worried about you. I told her I would call her when you woke up and let her know you're okay."

When I turned to look into Grayson's blue eyes, I saw nothing but sadness. "I don't know what to say, baby. I'm so sorry."

"How did I fail him? What did I do wrong? How could I have missed this?"

Grayson blinked back tears as he shook his head. "Meagan, you didn't do anything wrong, and you certainly didn't fail him."

A sob escaped as I whispered, "How can you say that? He killed himself because I couldn't help him."

"No," Grayson whispered as he pressed his lips to the back of my hand.

Grayson moved to the bed and sat while he pulled me to him. My arms wrapped around him tightly. "Why, Gray? Why didn't he talk to me about this?"

My body shook uncontrollably as I cried harder. "God, why did this happen?" I cried out as Grayson's arms held me tighter.

My mind was filled with images of Mitchell. His smile. His laugh. The way he told me things were starting to look up for him.

My body felt numb and I couldn't even imagine how Mitchell's family was feeling. "I should have known. It was my job to make sure something like this didn't happen. He must have felt so alone and in a place so dark he couldn't find a way out. How did I miss that? Gray, how?"

Gripping onto Grayson's shirt, I lost it as I buried my face into his chest.

Chapter

TWENTY-FOUR

Grayson

MY ARM WAS wrapped tightly around Meagan's waist as we stood and listened to Mitchell's eulogy. Meagan stared off with a distant look on her face as her father and mother stood on the other side of her.

Feeling Meagan's body tremble, I pulled her closer to me. When the service was over, it was Meagan and Mrs. Haus who didn't move.

"Meg? Do you need a few minutes alone?" I asked.

Snapping her head over to me, Meagan's eyes filled with panic. "No. Please don't leave me."

Glancing over to Brad, his eyes met mine. With a quick nod, he and Amanda headed back to my truck.

Meagan had had this fear of me leaving her the last few days and it was beginning to worry both her parents, as well as me.

"Meagan?"

Mrs. Haus stood to the side of us as Meagan immediately wrapped Mitchell's mother in her arms and told her how sorry she was.

Both women cried for a few minutes before Meagan took a few steps back. Mrs. Haus wiped her eyes and attempted to smile.

"I want you to know how much he cared for you. How much you helped him."

Meagan's lips trembled as she tried like hell to keep her composure. Wrapping her arms around her body, she nodded and said, "I cared about him so much and I'm so very sorry."

With a quick nod of her head, Mrs. Haus placed her hands on Meagan's arms. "I know. Um . . . Mitchell had written a few letters. One for me, Casey, his two brothers, and one for you."

"W-what?" Meagan asked with a disbelieving voice.

Mrs. Haus wiped a tear away before reaching into her purse and pulling out an envelope. Running her fingers over her son's handwriting, she handed the letter to Meagan. "I'm going to miss him so much. I can't help feeling like this is my all my fault."

Meagan's posture lifted as she dropped her arms and took a step toward Mitchell's mother. "No, you cannot think like that. Mitchell was in a darkness that he felt he couldn't get out of. We all wish we had seen the signs. There won't be a day that goes by where I won't ask myself if there was something more I could have done or said, but you cannot blame yourself."

"I moved him from California. If I had just stayed there, he would have been with his friends and he wouldn't have had to . . . to . . ." Her hands covered her mouth as she broke down crying.

Meagan engulfed Mrs. Haus in a hug and repeated how sorry she was. A young gentleman about twenty finally walked up and took Mrs. Haus in his arms and led her to a car.

We stood there for a few more minutes watching them drive away before Meagan turned and looked into my eyes. The sadness that filled them gutted me. I searched internally for answers on how to ease her pain but I kept coming up with nothing.

Glancing down at the letter, Meagan swallowed hard as she stared at it. "It's not always a good thing when those who have commited suicide leave notes."

"Why?" I asked.

Meagan swallowed hard. "It sometimes leaves you with more questions . . . or . . . more guilt."

Her eyes lifted up to mine. "Gray, can we go back to your place?"

"Of course we can."

She slowly handed me the letter. "Will you read it once we get there?"

My hand reached for the letter as I drew in a deep breath and placed my hand on her back while I guided her to the truck.

I prayed that Mitchell left some answers to the questions that were surely swimming in Meagan's head.

～✖～

The moment we walked into my apartment, Amanda went into full mom mode. "Why don't you sit down in the living room with your father, Meg. Grayson can show me around his kitchen."

Meagan walked a slow walk into the apartment and did as her mother said. Brad was right behind her as they both sat on the couch.

After setting the grocery bags down on the counter, I started showing Amanda where everything was.

I opened the doors to my kitchen island and showed her all the cookware I had. "My mother made sure I had plenty of things to cook with as you can see."

Amanda chuckled as she grabbed two pots and put them on the stove. "This is perfect. I normally make home-made sauce, but we'll let it slide this one time," she said with a wink.

With a grin, I pulled out the whole-wheat spaghetti and jar of sauce from a bag while Amanda filled up the pot with water. I was comfortable around Amanda. She accepted me without hesitation, and I could see how close her and Meagan were.

Pulling myself back to reality. I took in a deep breath and slowly blew it out.

"Should I read her the letter now?" I asked as I peeked into the living room. Meagan was sitting next to her father with her head leaned against his shoulder as they watched television.

Amanda followed my stare as she placed her hand on my shoulder and gave it a squeeze. "Maybe it's best to take care of it now."

I reached into my back pocket and pulled the letter out as I walked into the living. I attempted to find my voice as I cleared the frog from my throat.

"Um, Meagan."

Her beautiful blue eyes looked up into mine as she smiled. "Do you want to read Mitchell's letter now?"

Meagan swung her legs over and stood up. Looking down to her father and then over to her mother, she wrung her hands together as she spoke. "Would y'all mind if we stepped outside onto the balcony while Gray reads the letter to me? I kind of feel like I need to hear it alone with him first."

Brad stood and kissed Meagan on the forehead. "Of course, pumpkin. You do what you need to do. I'll help your mom with the spaghetti."

"Thank you, Dad."

Meagan took my hand in hers as she turned and

headed toward the double doors that led out to the balcony. It was unseasonably warm out today and the fresh air felt amazing as I dragged in a deep breath.

Without saying a word, Meagan sat down on the small outdoor couch and pulled her knees up to her chest.

Clearing my throat, I leaned against the railing to face her as I opened the letter.

Dear Meagan,

Please don't be upset. I did a good job at hiding my pain, but I also tried, Meagan, I really did try and I need you to know that. It was too hard. I felt like I didn't fit in anywhere and when I did try to fit in . . . I wasn't being myself.

No one really knows what it's like to be lost within yourself until it's too late. The darkness is such a lonely place.

Meagan, you pulled me from that darkness for the longest time. You were the light that was pulling me out. But the darkness can have a terrible hold on you and slowly starts pulling you back in just when you thought you were finally escaping it. I'm so tired of trying to fight it.

Keep fighting for kids like me, Meagan. Teach others that their words really do hurt.

I'm so sorry, but this is the only way I can get out of the darkness that fills me. I wish I had been stronger for you and my family.

Forever your friend,
Mitchell

Glancing up, I expected to see Meagan crying. She sat with her chin resting on her knee as she wore a thoughtful expression.

"Meg?" She lifted her head and stared at me. "You okay?"

Her brows pinched together as she barely opened her mouth to speak. "I'm not sure."

I dropped to my knees and got in front of her. "Talk to me."

"When this first happened, the only question I had was why. I asked myself that same question over and over. What could I have done different for him? The other day when I saw him, he seemed so happy, but when I think back to it, I keep trying to think if I missed something. Did he say something to me that I missed? Did his eyes look sad or lost?"

"What have you come up with?"

Chewing on her lip, Meagan shook her head. "Nothing. He seemed like he was happy. I asked him about if he had talked to his mother about not wanting to become a cop. His emotions never faltered. He smiled and said he was planning to soon."

I blew out a sigh as I shook my head. "What do you think he said in his mother's note?"

Meagan shrugged. "I'm not sure. Sometimes, I think it's best for the families not to have a note. Guilt is a powerful thing and one wrong thing said can play havoc on your emotions."

I nodded in agreement. "I can understand that."

Her legs dropped down as she looked into my eyes. "I'm going to miss him so much, but I'm not going to let his death be in vain. I never want to see this happen again, Gray. Ever. I also want the kids at his school to hear at least one part of that letter."

I placed my hand on the side of her face. "You know I will always be here and support you in whatever you do."

Her hand moved over mine as her eyes softened. It was the first time in days I saw something other than sadness in them.

"Thank you for that. You'll never know how much you being by my side through all of this has meant to me. I love you, Gray. So much."

My hand moved to the back of her neck as I pulled her lips closer to mine. Our kiss was slow and soft. The love I felt between us never ceased to amaze me. As our kiss broke, our foreheads rested against each other.

"I love you too, baby."

I stood and pulled her up with me as we stood there for a few minutes holding each other.

The door opened and Amanda peeked out. "Dinner's ready y'all."

Meagan gazed up at me one more time as she smiled before turning and heading toward her mother.

I started to walk in when something stopped me. Looking over my shoulder, I looked down at the courtyard my apartment faced.

Anger immediately built as I looked at Joshua Black sitting on a bench looking up at me.

~ ❧ ~

I slammed the door to the office as I pushed my hands through my hair.

"Bennett, you need to calm down."

I had been pacing when I stopped and looked at Derrick. "Calm down? This motherfucker is messing with my life. He showed up where I was having lunch with my soon to be father-in-law, and then I see him sitting on a bench looking up at my apartment? How do I know he's not following Meagan around, waiting for her to be alone?"

Chief Decker stood up and walked around his desk where he proceeded to lean against it. "I can't get coverage on Meagan unless he tries to do something."

I waved my hand off in a bit of frustration. "If this guy is part of the murders and he is willing to fuck around with a cop, who in the hell knows what he'll do."

Derrick nodded his head. "Have you told Meagan?"

"No. With Mitchell's suicide and everything she had been through with that the last few days, I didn't want to worry her. I did inform her boss though of my concerns about Black. She said she would let the front desk girls know."

Chief Decker pushed off his desk as he sighed. "First thing you need to do is tell her. She needs to be prepared if this guy tries to make contact with her. Then, the two of you need to figure out if this Joshua Black has played a role in these murders. The sooner the better."

Derrick and I looked at each other. "All of our leads have lead to nowhere."

"Keep digging. That's why you're detectives, goddamn it. This is your job."

Derrick stood and nodded his head as I made my way toward the door. I knew the first thing I had to do, and I needed to do it as soon as possible.

Chapter

TWENTY-FIVE

Meagan

THE KNOCK ON my office door pulled me from the file I was reading over. "Come in."

Melissa opened my door and walked in. "Hey, Meg. How are you doing?"

With a smile, I motioned for her to sit down. "I'm doing good. If I could just get over this damn stomach bug, I'd be even better."

Taking a seat, Melissa gave me a funny look before shaking it off. "So, the beef tenderloin?"

I fell back in my seat and started laughing. "I won."

Her mouth dropped open as she said, "You've got to be kidding me!"

"Nope, I smoked him. Diana said it was the best beef tenderloin she'd ever tasted."

Melissa leaned forward and wiggled her eyebrows. "So when is the big dance?"

My stomach jumped as I felt my face flush. No one could ever possibly have a boss as cool as mine. I had decided long ago I was never leaving my job. Ever.

"It's tonight actually. The club is closed for three nights. Something about the back dressing rooms being remodeled."

Melissa leaned forward and formed her fingers into a steeple as she looked like she was deep in thought.

"Before you ask, no. This is a private show."

Her hands dropped as she huffed. "Damn." With a shrug, she said, "Well you can't blame a girl for trying."

We both busted out laughing as the wave of nausea hit me and I immediately stopped laughing.

Oh shit!

Slamming my hand over my mouth, I jumped up and ran out to the bathroom.

Five minutes later, I walked back into my office and sat down.

"Ugh. This is the longest stomach flu I've ever had."

"Uh-huh. Hey, what are you doing for lunch?"

I snarled my lip at Melissa as I stared at her like she was crazy. "I just threw my guts up and you want to go eat?"

Melissa stood up and nodded her head. "Yeah, grab your purse and meet me up front. It's a beautiful April day so we'll walk."

Fear crept in as I thought about Joshua Black. The fact that he had been outside Grayson's apartment had me completely freaked out. I'd seen him once in Starbucks but he didn't try to even talk to me.

"Stop worrying. I can see the fear in your eyes. Let's just go have lunch and for once you're not going to worry about some random guy . . . right?"

I took in a deep breath and slowly pushed it back out. "Right. It's a beautiful day so let's enjoy it."

Melissa headed out to grab her things, so I sent

Grayson a quick text.

> *Me: Heading to lunch with Melissa. We are going to walk I think to Derby's.*

Grayson had been working long days the last few weeks. There had been another rape/murder and this time it was closer to my apartment. It didn't take me long to move everything out of my old apartment and into Grayson's. A week after my parents left, I started moving things into storage or Grayson's place.

> *Gray: Okay, baby. Are you ready for tonight?*

I couldn't erase the silly grin on my face. Hell yes I was ready. A private show from my sexier-than-hell fiancé. Fuck. Yes.

> *Me: Hell yes! I hope you have been practicing your dance moves!*

> *Gray: Oh don't worry sweetheart. I'll be teaching you something new tonight.*

My body instantly got hot as the throbbing between my legs hit me.

> *Me: I can't wait. Better go, I'm getting horny.*

> *Gray: God I love you.*

With a giggle I replied back.

> *Me: Love you the most! Bye!*

> *Gray: Bye. Be careful.*

Reaching for my purse, I tossed my phone into it and made my way toward the lobby to meet Melissa.

Jennifer waved goodbye to us as she chatted with

someone on the phone. The walk to Derby's was a quick ten-minute walk. Melissa was spot on about the weather. It was about sixty-four outside and beyond beautiful.

"I need to run into the drugstore really quick. Want to go ahead and get us a table?"

"Sure!" I said as I took off across the street. Derby's was a cute little sandwich shop that the office frequented often. Before I walked inside, someone called out my name.

Turning, an older woman with bleach-blonde hair and a body to die for, approached me. "Meagan Atwood?"

Not having a clue as to who she was, I gave her a polite smile. "Yes. I'm sorry, do we know each other?"

With a smirk, she shook her head. "Oh, we've never met, but I know you."

My heart started beating rapidly. "H-how?"

"You gave that amazing talk at the high school two weeks ago. My daughter is a senior there and was so touched by your words."

I let out the breath I had been holding in and smiled. "Well, I'm so glad she was moved by what I had to say. It's a subject very close to my heart and I'm very passionate it about it."

"I think that's amazing. There are a few moms who set up a little group after . . . well . . . after um."

"Mitchell's suicide?"

Her face dropped some as she tried to smile. "Yes. Anyway, we have a meeting coming up in a few days and I would be honored if you joined us. Your experience and knowledge on this subject would really help us to make more of an effort in the schools to stop bullying."

Feeling a sense of pride that I was doing something Mitchell had asked me to do, I nodded enthusiastically. "I'd love to!"

"Do you have a cell number or email I can send you the meeting details?"

"Oh of course, yes." I searched through my purse for my business card and handed it to her. "I'm sorry, I didn't catch your name."

"Susan Powell."

As I reached my hand out to shake hers, the hair on the back of my neck stood up. I quickly looked around for Joshua, but saw nothing. "Um, it was a pleasure meeting you, Susan. Tell your daughter—"

"Kate."

"Tell your daughter Kate I hope to get to meet her again."

Susan took my card and put it in her purse. "Will do. Have to run now though, I'm late for a nail appointment."

Susan took off across the street as I watched her walk off. Melissa walked up to me with a perplexed look on her face. "Who was that?"

My stomach was still feeling upset, but the walk and fresh air had helped. I rolled my neck around trying to shake off the nausea. "Just a mom from the high school I spoke at a few weeks ago. Her daughter told her about my visit."

My neck had gotten so stiff as I rubbed the back of it with my hand. "You ready to go in?"

Melissa looked over her shoulder at Susan as she made her way down the street. "She must have had kids late in life, she looked a little old to have a high school kid."

I watched as Susan bounced away. "I didn't think she was that old. Maybe this is her last kid in school or something."

"Maybe," Melissa said with a concerned look. "What was her name?"

I opened the door to Derby's and said, "Susan Powell. Her daughter's name was Kate. She invited me to a meeting a bunch of moms are putting together in an effort to stop bullying in school."

That made Melissa light up. "Really? That's awesome.

Maybe I can come along as well."

The hostess grinned as we approached her. "Welcome to Derby's. Just the two of you?"

"Yep!" I said as I turned to Melissa. "I think that would be great if you came. With your knowledge and connections in the community, you would be a great asset to them."

Melissa pulled out her chair and tossed the small bag onto the table as she thanked the hostess. "Onto other subjects now."

I rolled my eyes as I took the menu and looked it over. The only reason I was pretending to read it was so that I didn't have to look at Melissa. "You know damn well what you're getting to eat so stop avoiding eye contact with me."

My mouth dropped open as I lowered the menu. I gave Melissa a *I don't know what you're talking about* look.

Widening my eyes, I leaned over and stared at her. "There. Happy?"

Scrunching her nose, Melissa said, "I bought you something!"

I lifted an eyebrow. "Really? What?"

She pushed the bag over to me and said, "Open it."

I cautiously reached for the bag and pulled it over to me and opened it.

"What the fuck?" I said as Melissa started clapping and laughed.

Frantically looking around, I pulled out the box and stared at it. "Why did you buy me a pregnancy test?"

The waiter walked up and gave us a big toothy grin.

"Ladies, good afternoon. Oh! Oh wow." Pointing to the test, the waiter smiled. "So please tell me you're going to do that here."

Melissa and I both looked up at our waiter. "Here? As in right here?" I asked.

With a chuckle, he rolled his eyes and looked at Melissa

like he thought I had said the stupidest thing ever. "No, I expect you to at least go into the restroom."

A small laugh escaped my lips as I dropped the box onto the table. "No. I don't need a pregnancy test because I'm not pregnant."

Melissa and our waiter asked at the same time, "Are you sure?"

My eyes widened as I looked between the two of them. "Yes! I'm on the pill!" I said in a hushed voice.

Our waiter let out a huff and waved his hand in dismal. "Girl, that is not full proof. Unless your man shrouded his trout before he made you shout."

"What?" I asked as Melissa started laughing and my mouth dropped open as I stared at the waiter. A man I had never seen before, who was now not only talking about me taking a pregnancy test, but condoms and sex.

"Oh my gawd! I have to keep you!" she said as they high fived each other. "Even when I'm eager, I protect my beaver."

Closing my eyes, I shook my head. *No. Just no.*

"If you're gonna get between her thighs, condomize."

Melissa pointed to our waiter and said, "No glove, no love."

His head went back in a roar of laughter as I sat there stunned.

"Are the two of you about finished?"

Melissa pressed her lips together as she whispered, "Sorry."

The waiter turned and looked at me with a questioning look on his face.

"So?"

"So what?" I asked.

With a frustrated moan like I was wasting his precious time, he asked, "Did he cover the stump before he humped?"

Melissa lost it and laughed as I fought to keep my

smile in.

I had no idea why I felt the need to say what I said next to a complete stranger. "If it's any of your business, we stopped wrapping his pickle before each tickle a few months ago."

Our waiter grinned from ear to ear. "I like you girls. Now let's get your drinks, food order, and then we are taking one pregnancy test."

Melissa began jumping in her seat as I jerked my head back and said, "No. No we are not."

"Why not?" Melissa asked with a pout.

"Yeah, why not?" The waiter turned to Melissa and asked, "What are you drinking love?"

"I'll take a Pepsi. Oh and I already know what I want. Ham and swiss on rye with a side of fruit."

As the waiter wrote it down, my eyes drifted over to the pregnancy test.

There is no way I'm pregnant.

None.

"Okay, water for you and what would you like to eat?"

Pulling my eyes from the box, I said, "Wait. I didn't order water."

"Oh, honey, now that you're pregnant, you need to drink more water."

Melissa lost it laughing again as I shot our waiter a dirty look. "Stop it! I'm not pregnant." With a frustrated sigh, I rolled my neck again to ease the aching pain. "I'll take an iced tea with a cup of French onion soup and a turkey and swiss on wheat."

"All righty, I'll get this in and get those drinks."

Finally he was moving on from this pregnancy nonsense.

Melissa stared at me as I continued to pretend like she didn't exist.

When the waiter came back, he set our drinks down and grabbed the test.

"The name is David, ladies, and if you end up having a boy, I expect it to be named after me." Reaching for my hand, he pulled me up as Melissa jumped up like a five-year-old set loose in a candy store.

"Wait! This is mutiny!" I cried out.

"Sweetie, you're not in control here," David said as he pulled me along behind him while Melissa practically skipped behind us. Stopping outside the women's restroom, David handed me the test and said, "Pee straight!"

I was positive my expression was one of confusion. "Who are you?"

Looking at Melissa she was covering her mouth and fighting to keep her laughter in. "I hate you both and I don't even know you, David!"

I grabbed the box and pushed the door open as I walked to the end stall. Melissa must have decided to wait with David.

With a long drawn out groan, I opened the box and took out the test. Pulling my dress pants and panties down, I let loose and peed straight on the stick as instructed.

I grabbed toilet paper and pulled a bunch off as I placed it on the floor and the test on top of that. Pulling my panties and pants up, I flushed and sat back down on the toilet.

Smiling, I thought about Grace. She was due in August with her first child and I couldn't wait to go home and visit this June. Libby's little boy, Trey, was already four months old and it killed me I hadn't been home yet to see him.

I pulled my phone out and sent Grace a text.

Me: I want to see your pregnant belly!

Less than a minute later my request was filled by a picture of Grace's precious baby bump. As I stared at the picture, I was overcome with emotion and started crying.

The idea of having a part of Grayson growing inside

me someday had me leaning over sobbing. That's when I saw it.

"Holy. Fucking. Shit," I whispered as my crying came to a full on stop.

Picking up the test, I slowly shook my head.

"I'm pregnant."

Chapter
TWENTY-SIX

Grayson

"DUDE, WHERE IS the fire?" Derrick asked as I quickly gathered up my shit.

"Big plans tonight."

Leaning back in his chair, he wiggled his eyebrows. "Oh man, I remember those nights. Back when the sex was hot and sweaty."

"I didn't need that visual dude, really?"

With a chortle, he shrugged. "Tell me it's not true."

"Sorry, I cannot tell a lie."

His head fell back as he let out a moan. "Damn. The good ole days."

"I'm gonna be late. Call me if anything develops with anything."

Derrick rolled his eyes. "Yeah, I'm sure you'll be waiting by the phone."

⁓ ❧ ⁓

The knocking on my door was loud and fast and not letting up. "Just a second! Son-of-a-bitch!"

Wrapping the towel around my waist, I unlocked the door and pulled it open.

"This better be good!"

Claire stood before me with her mouth parted open while her eyes raked across my body.

Fuck.

"Claire? What are you doing here?"

When she finally managed to pull her eyes off my chest, she closed her mouth and looked into my eyes. "I didn't know where else to go, Grayson. You were the first person I thought of."

Cocking my head to the side, I raised my eyebrows. "This ought to be interesting."

Claire frowned and tried to take a step forward but I didn't budge. I knew Meagan would be walking up any second and there was no way in hell I was letting Claire into my apartment.

"I *really* need someone to talk to. I've just received the worst news I have ever gotten in my entire life. My parents . . . they . . . oh God!"

My stomach dropped a little. Shit, I hoped her parents weren't in a car wreck or anything.

"They're getting a divorce!" Claire cried out as she buried her face in her hands and sobbed. There was one thing I figured out quickly; Claire would never make it in Hollywood.

Blowing out a quick breath, I glanced down the hallway and then back to Claire. "Listen, Claire, I'm really sorry about your parents, but I think you might be better off talking to someone else, like a girlfriend or someone who can relate."

Claire's hands dropped to her side. "But I don't really

have any friends here, Grayson."

"Now I know that's not true, Claire. I've seen you out with them."

Her eyes lit up as she flashed me a seductive look while she took a step forward. "I was kind of hoping you might help me out in another way . . . if you know what I mean."

My eyes widened while my entire body stiffened. Was she for real?

"Um . . . listen, Claire, I'm very much in love with Meagan, so just you being here is inappropriate. I think the best thing for you to do is find a friend you can talk to about this."

"Meagan doesn't have to know, Grayson."

I could not believe my ears. With a dry laugh, I shook my head. "And you called Meagan a whore?"

Claire took a step back and as her mouth and eyes widened. "How dare you."

"You need to get one thing straight here, Claire. I am not interested in you. Stay the fuck out of my business and don't ever come to my house again."

Taking a step back, I shut the door in her face.

I couldn't help but smile. "Damn, I've always wanted to do that."

Heading back to my room to change, there was a knock on the front door again.

"Damn it all to hell. This girl needs to go!"

Yanking the door open, I went to talk and was stunned into silence. Standing before me was the most beautiful woman I had ever laid eyes on. Her smile was stunning, her body amazing, and her eyes were dancing with passion.

"I'd say you handled that very well, Mr. Bennett."

Placing my hand on the door frame, I let Meagan's hungry eyes look me over. "You heard that huh?"

She walked up and placed her hands on my chest,

causing a warm rush to race through my body.

"I so cannot wait until I get my little private show." Biting down on her lip, her fingers moved down my chest to the edge of the towel. "Do I get a preview?"

Knowing how weak I was for this girl, and how hard my dick already was, I grabbed her hands and pulled her into our apartment, kicking the door shut. My lips pressed against hers as I slammed her against the door. Her hands immediately dug into my hair where she pulled hard, eliciting a long deep moan from my mouth.

"Gray, I want you so much. Please."

With a naughty smile, I quickly pulled back, instantly missing the heat from her body. "Not yet, baby. I've got something special planned for you."

With a sexy pout, Meagan pushed off the wall. "I have something special planned for you too."

With a questioning look, I asked, "Do I get a hint?"

The look that moved over her face had my stomach flipping. Her cheeks flushed and her eyes lit up. I'd never seen her look more beautiful.

"Trust me, no matter how many hints I gave you, you'd never be able to guess it."

"Hmm, I'm intrigued."

Meagan lifted an eyebrow before walking up and kissing me on the lips tenderly. "I don't know if I've ever told you this before, but I've never felt this way with anyone else ever."

My arms wrapped around her waist as I pulled her to me. "The same goes for me, Meg. My heart belongs to only you. If I ever lost you, I'm not sure what I would do."

"Would you come find me?" she asked with a shy smile.

Kissing the tip of her nose, I leaned my forehead against hers. "I'd scale every wall looking for you and wouldn't give up until I found you."

Her eyes closed as she drew in a deep breath and

slowly blew it out. "I want to be in your arms forever."

"Meg, you saved my heart when you gave me your love."

Meagan pulled her head back and looked into my eyes as a tear spilled over and slowly ran down her cheek. Using my thumb, I lightly brushed it away before reaching down and picking her up. "I need to make love to you."

With a giggle, Meagan said, "I thought I wasn't getting a preview."

"Things changed."

❧

Meagan and I walked into the dark club as I reached over and flipped on the lights. I couldn't help but smile when I saw the chair and table set up in the middle of the stage.

Meagan walked further into the club and ran her hands along the rows of chairs while she took everything in.

"So . . . this is where you did your thing, huh?"

Taking a look around, I nodded. "Yep."

With a glance over her shoulder back to me, Meagan asked, "Do you miss it?"

Without skipping a beat, I answered. "Fuck no."

Meagan chuckled as she walked up to the stage and climbed the stairs. "Good answer, stripper boy."

I lifted my eyebrow as I walked toward her. "You've been dying to say that haven't you?"

Shrugging her shoulders, Meagan took a seat in the chair and gave me a come hither look that had my dick instantly getting hard.

"What do you have planned for me?"

Straddling the chair, I ran my finger down along her jaw. "To make your panties wet."

Meagan swallowed hard. "That should be rather easy for you since I'm so turned on."

I sat down some as I moved my lips along her neck and

kissed her gently. "Earlier wasn't enough for you, baby?"

Dropping her head back, Meagan moaned. "Not even close to being enough."

"You want it dirty, baby?"

Meagan's eyes widened as she sunk her teeth down into that plump lip.

I jumped up. "Let me make sure no one is here before we start. Stay here."

With a quick nod, Meagan smiled.

After making a quick round around the club to make sure we were alone, I locked the front door and made my way over to the sound booth.

Searching through the songs, I found one that I had danced to plenty of times. Loading it up in the queue, I quickly made my way back to the stage. I had two songs loaded, the first one was just to get us started.

Meagan looked over to me when the first song started. "The Fix" by Nelly started playing as I started to dance some. I would never forget her smile for as long as I lived.

I pulled out every dance move I could to impress her as I danced my way up to the stage. I pulled my T-shirt over my head as Meagan began to whoop and holler. Moving closer, Meagan reached into her shirt and pulled out money as she winked.

I couldn't help but laugh as I shook my head. Stopping in front of her, I leaned over and said, "You came prepared."

"I'm always prepared, Mr. Bennett."

"You ready?" I asked as I ran my tongue along her lower lip. Meagan gripped my arms as she let out a low rumble from the back of her throat. "Don't touch me, Meagan."

"W-what?"

The music changed and "Cookie" by R. Kelly started as Meagan's eyes lit up and I shook my head. "Don't. Touch. Me." I knew by telling her not to touch me, it would drive her desire up even more.

Backing up, I started giving her exactly what she wanted as I danced to the beat of the music. I moved back over her in the chair and rubbed my body against hers as I quickly got lost in the song. Had this been just some girl sitting in this chair, I wouldn't have been touching her like I was touching Meagan, I was pushing my hard dick against her every fucking chance I got.

Dropping to my knees, I pushed her legs wide open and smiled. Pulling her forward, I lifted her body and buried my face between her legs as I breathed my hot breath on her bare pussy.

The fact that she hadn't put panties back on had me fighting to keep control. Dropping down again, Meagan let out a yelp as I slowly laid her on the floor and moved my body over hers as I continued to dance to the song. Meagan's face never once broke her smile as I continued to grind and slide all over her, staying in perfect rhythm to the song.

Hovering over her body, my hand moved up her dress as her eyes burned with passion. "Gray," she whispered as I pulled the dress over her head.

Moving my lips to her ear, I whispered back, "No one is here, baby."

Picking her up, she wrapped her legs around my body as I continued to dance until the song finally came to a stop and there was nothing but the sound of our heavy breathing. My dick was rock hard, almost to the point of being painful.

"Baby, if I touch you, will you be wet?"

Her legs wrapped tighter around my body as she nodded.

"God, the things I'm going to do to you."

She dug her fingernails into my arms as she softly spoke my name. Walking over to one of the tables, I gently laid her down and unbuttoned my jeans. Pushing them down, I took my dick in my hand and stroked myself slowly while Meagan watched.

"Touch yourself. Show me how wet you are, baby."

Meagan sat up and pinned me with her eyes while she parted her lips and gasped.

Snapping my own eyes down, I watched as she worked her fingers in and out of her body. It had to have been the hottest moment of my life.

"Gray! I need you. Oh God, I need to feel you."

"Meg, I want to fuck you."

A fire burned in her eyes as she moved further to the edge of the table and ran her fingers over my dick. "Give it to me, please."

It was like another person entered my body. I grabbed her hand and pushed her fingers into my mouth as I tasted her sweet honey. Moaning, I pulled her to me and lined my cock up with her pussy. One quick move and I pushed into her. Meagan screamed out as I felt her pussy squeeze down on me. She was coming already and that threw me into a frenzy. Digging my fingers into her hips, I felt like I couldn't get enough of her as I moved in and out. She was coming again, or maybe it was the same orgasm, all I knew was I needed more of her.

"Yes! Oh God. Harder!" Meagan cried out. I loved when we fucked like we couldn't get enough of each other. It reminded me of the first time we were together, hearing Meagan calling out my name in a raw passion, begging me to give her more.

"I want you from behind," I said as I pulled out and motioned for her to lean over the table.

Doing as I asked, Meagan quickly turned around and laid over the table. "Goddamn, you have the nicest ass."

My hands moved over her ass as I spread her legs apart and pushed into her.

"Fuck," she hissed as I buried myself deep inside of her. I could feel her body working up to another orgasm.

"Gray! Oh God! Oh God!"

Her body trembled as I moved my hand up and pushed my finger quickly inside her ass as she screamed out and came hard. I was about to explode, feeling her fucking ass pulling my finger further into her.

The sound of our bodies hitting sounded fucking hot, but not as hot as her whimpers and moans.

"I want your ass, Meagan."

Meagan looked back at me with wide eyes as I put pressure on her ass. I swear to God if I hadn't loved her so much I would have just pushed my cock inside her and taken it. "Slowly baby, we'll do this slowly."

"Wait!" she called out as I slowed down my movements and kissed her back. I reached my hand around to cup her breast. "Have you ever done that with anyone else?"

Smiling, I shook my head and said, "No."

My body trembled with the look she gave me. "Good," she replied. "Don't stop, it feels good." Pushing her ass back for more, I pulled out and pushed in as I started working my finger in her ass.

Moaning, I tried like hell to hold off from losing control. "Fucking heaven."

"Can't take much more," Meagan cried out. Adjusting the position of my finger, I felt her body squeeze down on my cock, pulling out one of the most amazing orgasms of my life. I never knew I could come so hard and for long. When my dick finally stopped twitching, I pulled out and Meagan laid across the table, dragging in one long breath after another.

"Oh. My. God," I panted out as I tried to focus on my breathing.

"We . . . totally . . . have . . . to . . . Lysol . . . the table!"

Laughing, I kissed Meagan's shoulder and pulled her around to look at me.

"That was fucking amazing. I hope I didn't hurt you."

Her smile about blew me away. "No, it felt wonderful, and I might add, I liked your touch of dirty."

I all of a sudden felt the need to leave this place. As much fun as it was, it hit me where we were. Dancing for Meagan here was one thing but fucking her in a place where so many other women had touched me and I had touched them didn't feel so great. The guilt quickly swept over me and I tried like hell to push it away. "Let's get dressed and I'll clean up a bit and then I want to take you out to dinner."

Meagan sucked in her lip as she looked away. Placing my finger on her chin, I lifted her eyes back to mine. "Hey, is everything okay?"

Tears pooled in her eyes as she nodded her head. "I'm uh . . . I'm going to go get dressed."

Watching her walk away, I had the strangest feeling Meagan was feeling the same way I was. *The faster we got out of here the better.*

Chapter

TWENTY-SEVEN

Meagan

OH HOLY HELL. I just let my fiancé fuck me six ways to Sunday in a damn strip club. And I liked it. A lot! I'm going to be a mother and I liked getting my dirty on.

I'm going to hell. What kind of mother am I going to be?

Quickly getting dressed, I tried to get my emotions in check. The last thing I wanted to do was break down and tell Grayson about the baby in a stupid strip club! Ugh. The faster we got out of there, the better.

I sat in a chair while Grayson cleaned up. My mind was racing in a million different directions. *Why was I feeling this way?* I loved what had just happened between us, but I didn't love where we were. All I could think about was all the women who had put their hands on Grayson in this place.

Ugh. *Stop this, Meagan.*

I jumped when Grayson put his hand on my shoulder. Squatting down, Grayson looked into my eyes. "Baby, talk to me. You seem like you're lost in thought."

Pressing my lips together, I closed my eyes and shook my head. "I think just being here is starting to get to me."

"Do you regret what we did?"

Snapping my eyes back open, I shook my head. "No! I loved what happened between us. I loved you dancing for me . . . it was hot as hell. It's just, I don't like this place. My mind is wandering and I don't like where it's taking me if that makes any kind of sense."

Grayson took my hands in his and pulled me up. "Let's get out of here."

～❦～

My eyes opened to see Grayson picking me up and taking me out of his truck. I had fallen asleep almost as soon as we got back into the truck.

"I fell asleep," I whispered as I wrapped my arms around Grayson's neck as he carried me to our apartment.

His chest rumbled as he laughed. "I know. Hot sex wears my baby out."

Burying my face into his chest, I inhaled a deep breath. I'd always loved the way Grayson smelled. Lying in bed countless nights, I dreamed what it would be like to sleep wrapped up in his arms.

Once Grayson was in the apartment, he walked us to our room. Gently setting me down, he undressed me. Each time he removed a piece of clothing he kissed me softly. This simple act of tenderness had my eyes welling up with tears.

Oh lord. What happened to the days when I would just want him to fuck me senseless? Now I'm standing here like a baby about to cry.

"Do you have any idea how beautiful you are, Meg?"

My head dropped back as I felt tears build in my eyes. Dipping my hands into Grayson's hair, I pulled slightly while his lips moved across my hips as he pushed my panties down.

Was I dreaming? Was this really happening to me? I never in my wildest dreams thought I could be this in love with someone.

Bringing my head forward, I stared down at Grayson as he worshiped my body.

"Gray," I mumbled as I fought to the form words to speak. His eyes looked up to mine and he froze.

"Baby, why are you crying?"

Pressing my lips into a thin line, I fought to keep my sobs back as Grayson stood quickly. His hands cupped my face as he searched my face for answers. The love I felt for him was almost overwhelming as I fought to tell him how I felt.

"It's just . . . I've never . . . you . . . my heart . . . I can't even."

His mouth rose in a crooked smile as his blue eyes pierced mine. "Take a deep breath and blow it out."

I closed my eyes and did what he said. Inhaling a deep breath, I calmly blew out while opening my eyes again.

"For years I put on this show about not caring about finding love; then you came into my life and I found myself doing nothing but thinking of you every second of the day."

Grayson's smile grew bigger as he moved his thumbs softly across my skin. That simple action on his part meant more to me than he would ever know. The way he cared for me had my heart feeling as if it would burst from happiness.

"I pushed you away because I was afraid of how you made me feel. It was foreign for me to feel like that. I'd always been known as the one who just hooked up with a guy with no intentions of anything serious." With a slight laugh, I bit my lip. "Most of it was all an act on my part."

Grayson kissed my lips softly before pulling back and looking at me again. "The second time I saw you in Noah's house, I knew you were going to be so much more than just some guy I thought was good looking. I felt it in my heart. In the very being of my soul I felt it."

"Meg," Grayson whispered as he swallowed hard.

My hands came up and grabbed onto Grayson's arms. "I can't imagine my life without you and I'm so terrified you're going to get scared and run."

His eyes widened as he pulled his head back. "Scared? You could never scare me."

My stomach quivered as I gave a sideway glance and made a face. "I'm pretty sure I can."

Grayson laughed and pulled my lips to his where he kissed me hard and fast. "There is nothing you could ever do or say that would ever cause me to walk away from you."

Licking my lips nervously, I looked back into his eyes. "You don't miss your old life at all?"

He didn't even have to think about his answer. "No. I'm madly in love with my new life."

Oh God. Oh God. Oh God. I'm fixin' to spook him.

"Gray, I have to tell you something, and you have to promise me this isn't going to change anything."

His smile faded and was replaced by a concerned look. "O-okay."

"I . . . I um . . . well . . . I ah—"

"Jesus Christ, Meg, spit it out. You're freaking me out."

My stomach dipped as I fought to hold down whatever food was in my stomach. Just say it Meagan.

"I'm pregnant."

Grayson let out a low chuckle that was quickly replaced by his eyes widening and his expression going blank. He slowly shook his head and whispered, "What?"

Please don't make me say it again!

I stared at him as my stance became restless. Grayson's arms dropped to his side as he took a few steps away from me.

No. Please God don't do this to me. Please don't take him from me.

"Say something," I said as I wrapped my arms around my body.

His blinked rapidly as he whispered, "Give me a second."

Turning, he walked out of the bedroom and left me standing there, naked. This was not how I pictured the first time I told the man I loved that I was pregnant with his child. Glancing down, I saw one of Grayson's T-shirts on the chair. Reaching for it, I pulled it over my head. Grayson had brought my purse in and had dropped it to the floor so I grabbed it and searched for my cell phone.

When I heard the front door open and close, I dropped to the bed and cried.

Pulling up my contacts, I searched for Grace's number and hit call.

I was crying so hard that when she answered, I couldn't even talk between my sobs.

"G-g-grace," I fumbled out.

"Oh holy hell. I'm going to fucking kill him. What did he do?"

"I'm . . . I'm . . . oh, Grace! I'm pregnant and I just told Grayson and he . . . he . . . he . . ."

"He what? What, Meg? What!"

My body shook as I lost control. "He left."

I could hear Grace gasp from the other end of the phone. "I'm on the next flight out."

I shook my head. "No! Grace, no you're pregnant."

"Meagan Atwood, I'm coming there and we are going to kill him together and bury his worthless body so that no one will ever find him."

A small chuckle escaped my lips as I wiped my tears

away.

"He left, Grace."

"Oh, honey. Can I just say how excited I am that you're pregnant, but we'll talk about that later. I'm online right now and there is a flight that leaves at six a.m. I'm booking it."

Tears continued to roll down my cheeks as I shook my head. "Don't. I think I want to come home and see everyone."

"Yes! That's what you need. We need a girls' weekend. Come to me, Meg."

Nodding, I stood up and reached for my clothes. "I'm leaving our apartment now. I'll call you when I get to a hotel."

I sniffled loudly in her ear as Grace said, "Okay sweets, but are you sure you want to go to a hotel?"

Pressing my lips together, I felt another round of sobs coming. I needed to get off the phone before I lost it again. "Yes. I have to."

"Meg, sweetie, he may have just gotten spooked, you know? I mean if y'all weren't planning this, I'm sure it just caught him off guard."

Shrugging my shoulders, I whispered, "Yeah. Maybe. But he promised me he wouldn't ever leave me. I have to leave. I'll call you in a bit."

As I finished getting dressed, I walked out into the living room to look around. Grayson was gone. With not so much as a word to me, he just left.

I slowly walked to the door and opened it. My body felt numb as I headed down the elevators that went to the main lobby and smiled weakly at the doorman before stepping outside. A taxi pulled up right in time for me to walk straight to it. I didn't even care I was leaving my car behind. Nothing mattered right now.

Sliding in, I said, "Strater Hotel, please." Closing my eyes, tears rolled down my face while I silently cried.

Chapter

TWENTY-EIGHT

Grayson

I WAS AT a totally loss for words.

Pregnant.

Meagan was pregnant.

Fear instantly flowed through my veins and all I could think about was my own father. Would I be a failure like he had been?

Fuck.

My throat felt as if it was closing as I fought to drag in air. I needed fresh air.

Not even thinking, I grabbed my keys and headed out the front door. I needed a few moments to get my head on straight before I said anything to Meagan.

I found myself driving mindlessly before I ended up at a park. I parked my truck and got out and made my way over to the playground.

Pinching my eyebrows together, I looked around and

realized where I had gone. My heart slammed in my chest as a memory played in my mind.

"What do you mean you have to leave, Daddy?"

My father looked at me as he placed his hand on the side of my face. "I love you, Grayson and I've made some terrible mistakes in my life and I need to start over."

"Start over? What does that mean?"

His eyes looked down as he shook his head. "Grayson, I want you to do me a favor."

"Okay, Daddy! I'll do anything for you."

His eyes looked watery as he blew out a breath. "Someday, you're going to meet a girl who you will love very much and you both will have a big strong little boy just like how you're so strong now, buddy."

I stood up taller and nodded. "I am strong."

"Yeah, buddy, you are. Grayson, don't ever look back and use me as an example. Grayson, your mother is going to make sure you never end up like me. I promise."

"What's that mean, Daddy?" I asked confused.

A car horn went off and Daddy looked over his shoulder. Turning back to me, he stood and placed his hand on my head. "You be a good boy for your mommy and I'm so sorry, buddy. I know you're going to make her proud and me proud when you grow up to be a big strong man."

Turning, my father walked toward a girl who was standing waiting for him. They hugged and my father got in the car. Little did I know that would be the last time I ever saw him.

My eyes snapped open as I buried my face in my hands. "Stupid fucking idiot."

Running back to my truck, I pulled out my phone and called Meagan. I wasn't surprised when it went to voice mail.

Quickly finding Grace's number, I hit call and jumped

into my truck.

"Okay, motherfucker, you better have a damn good reason why you made my best friend cry so hard she could hardly talk."

I hit the steering wheel and cursed. "Fuck!"

"Yeah, you fucked up dickhead, asshole, motherfucking, manwhore; wrap your dick next time, jerk face!"

"Tell him how you really feel, Grace," Noah said as he took the phone from her.

"Gray, what's going on?" Noah asked.

Sighing, I shook my head. "I freaked, Noah. It was the last fucking thing I expected Meagan to say to me. All I could think of was my own good-for-nothing father. I needed a few minutes to think and clear my head."

"Dude, you walked out without saying a word to her. You freaked? Can you imagine how Meagan feels?"

"He's too busy being an asshole to care!" Grace shouted.

Rolling my eyes, I tried to keep calm as I pulled back into the garage of our apartment while Noah lectured me on the phone about how I wasn't anything like my father and I seriously needed to make this up to Meagan. Her car was still parked in her spot, so that was a good sign.

"She told Grace she was coming to Texas and—"

"What? What did you just say?"

My heart pounded in my chest while I took two steps at a time, trying to get to the apartment as fast as I could. There was no fucking way I was letting her run from me. I made a mistake and I would do whatever I had to do to make it up to her.

"Meagan said she was coming home to Tex—"

Throwing the door open, I called out Meagan's name as I ended the call with Noah. "Meg?"

I ran to the bedroom only to find it empty. Standing there for a few seconds, I quickly searched the rest of the apartment before stopping in the living room.

This time I called Noah's number to avoid another randomly strung set of curse words thrown my way.

"Did you really think I wouldn't answer?"

With a frustrated sigh, I tried to stay calm. "Grace, where is Meagan? She's gone. I mean, she left our place and she didn't take her car."

"Um . . . she said she was going to a hotel. Are you going after her?"

"What the fuck kind of question is that? Of course I am. I love her more than I love the fucking air I breathe, but I can't go after her if I don't know where in the hell she is."

"Okay well, just a word of advice, maybe kick that down a few notches and make it a bit more romantic. I mean, after all, she just told you she was carrying your child and you walked out on her."

My stomach dropped as excitement built in my body. *Meagan is carrying my child.*

A baby.

Holy hell.

The smile that spread across my face had to have been the biggest damn smile ever before Grace's words hit me again.

"That was the first and last time I'll ever walk away from her. I swear to God," I said as I quickly headed back to my truck.

There was silence on the phone as I heard Grace clear her throat. "Don't tell me that . . . tell her."

My jaw trembled at the idea of hurting Meagan. "The last thing I'd ever do is hurt her, Grace."

"I know," she whispered. "Just get your ass over to the Strater Hotel and make it up to her, Bennett. She called right before you did to say she was checking in."

I tried to smile, but all I could think of was getting to Meagan.

"Thanks, Grace. I owe you big time."

"Hell yes you do, stripper boy."

With a groan of frustration, I tossed my phone onto the passenger seat and drove as fast as I could to the Strater Hotel.

I pulled in so fast, the valet guy jumped out of my way. Pushing open my door, he came walking over. "Jesus, dude. You can't come pulling in like that, you . . ."

I flashed my badge and said, "Sorry, police business."

"Oh, right. Do you want us to park it?"

Glancing over my shoulder, I nodded and said, "Yes."

"Sir! What name should we put it under?"

"Bennett, Grayson Bennett."

My eyes scanned the lobby as I frantically looked for Meagan. Walking up to the registration counter, I flashed a smile to the redhead looking directly at me.

"May I help you, sir?"

"Yes," I said as I showed her my badge. "Do you have a Meagan Atwood who recently checked in?"

She nodded and said, "Yes, she is heading up to her room now."

"Would you mind giving me her room number?"

The girl frowned and looked to her left to what I was guessing was the manager. "Ahh . . . can you hold on for one second?"

With a grin, I motioned for her to do what she had to do. Walking over to the older gentleman, she said something that made him return with her.

"Excuse me, sir, do you mind if I ask if you are on the reservation with Ms. Atwood?"

Sliding my badge across the desk, my face turned serious. "Detective Bennett, and Ms. Atwood is being sought out for questioning. I got a tip she had checked in here. I'd like to make sure she doesn't try to slip out another door."

"Oh, I see." The manager turned to the redhead. "Go ahead and let him know her room number."

A part of me was pissed they were giving me the number just because I flashed a fucking badge. How did they know it was even real?

"We only had premium rooms left and she looked so sad; I felt bad for her. I only charged her for a regular room. She didn't even have luggage with her."

"No, she wouldn't have."

"Sixth floor, room six ten."

With a quick nod, I turned and made my way to the elevator.

It was luck I was riding up with a hotel employee. With another showing of my badge, I had him knocking on Meagan's door.

"Room service."

The door opened as Meagan said, "I didn't order room . . . service."

I stepped around the corner and patted the guy on the back and handed him a twenty. "Thanks, dude."

The poor son-of-a-bitch looked confused as hell as Meagan started to cry. I walked right into her room and shut the door behind me.

As I turned back to Meagan, I couldn't help but notice how her eyes seemed to light up as she searched my face. "As God as my witness, I swear to you I will never walk away from you again, Meg."

Dropping to my knees, I took a hold of her hips and pulled her to me as I buried my face in her stomach. In that moment I realized I not only loved her, but I loved our child I had only known about for an hour just as much. The feeling hit me so hard I had to fight to keep from crying.

"I love you so much. Both of you."

Chapter
TWENTY-NINE

Meagan

THE SECOND I saw Grayson standing at the door, I felt the wetness creep down my face again. If this was pregnancy, I was going to have to invest in Kleenex.

His face was buried in my stomach as he sucked in a shaky breath and said, "I love you. Both of you."

One hand covered my mouth to contain my sobs as the other laced through his hair.

"Gray," I whispered. "Damn you!"

His head shook slowly as he whispered, "I'm so sorry. I freaked. I'm so sorry."

Grace had been right. A part of me knew that was what happened, but it still hurt like hell for him to walk away from me. I dropped down in front of him as he cupped my face with his hands and captured my lips to his.

"I'm so sorry," he spoke softly.

"Gray, I need to know how you really feel because I'm

just as scared as you."

"Oh God, Meg. I swear to you, I will never leave you like that again. I love you and the idea of you carrying our child fills me with so much hope. You have to believe me."

His eyes were filled with fear as he pleaded with me to believe him. My hand came up to the side of his face as I gave him a small smile. "I do believe you, but tell me that was your one freak-out moment and it won't ever happen again cause I don't think I could do this without you. Plus, do you have any idea what my father is going to do to us when he finds out?"

Grayson laughed as his hand slipped behind my neck where he pulled me closer to him and kissed me like he hadn't seen me in days. It was full of passion, love, and it completely left me breathless. I knew I should have been pissed and screaming at him for what he did, but I also knew Grayson's past with his own father and how I had just delivered a bombshell.

"Let me make love to you, Meg."

Dropping my head so his lips could keep kissing me, I mumbled, "Like I would ever stop you."

Grayson stood and helped me up as he led me over to the king-size bed where he kissed me again. I was soon lost in a world where the man I loved worshiped my body and whispered how much he loved me while he took me to heaven and back.

Before rolling me over and pulling me to his side, Grayson kissed my stomach and talked to our child.

"I don't know you yet my sweet baby, but I swear to you, I will love and protect you and your mommy always."

And just like that, I fell even more in love with Grayson Bennett. His arms wrapped around my body as he pulled me against him. His heartbeat soon had my eyes closing as I let every worry and doubt drift away.

"How is Gray going to feel about you coming to Texas alone?"

I took a sip of coffee as I glanced up at the addresses on the buildings. The temperature yesterday was sixty-seven and today it was forty-three with a chance of snow tonight. I wasn't sure when I would get used to this insane weather. "He is totally fine with it. Besides, he knows how much I need to see my girls and I need a girls weekend in a desperate way. Plus, I need some warm Texas weather."

Grace chuckled. "So where are you going?"

"A meeting that this one mom put together to help educate the high school students about bullying."

Melissa had planned on going with me to the meeting with Susan Powell and the other moms, but she ended up having an emergency meeting with one of her clients.

I stopped in front of the building marked with the address Susan gave me. Narrowing my eyes, I looked around to make sure I was on the right road.

"Meg, are you even listening to me?"

"Um, yeah. Hey, Grace I'm here so I need to let you go. I'll call you after the meeting. I wouldn't think it would last more than an hour. At least that is what Susan said at any rate."

"Okay, good luck and I'll chat with you soon and we can make plans for our girls weekend!"

Walking up the steps, I nodded and said absentmindedly, "Sounds good. Talk to you later, Grace."

"Later!"

Grace hung up as I dropped my hand down to my side. "This makes no sense. This place looks empty."

Susan said the meeting was being held at one of the mom's office space, but this whole building looked empty.

Reaching for the door, I turned and pushed it open. The long hallway led to another door where light was barely peeking out from under it. "Hello? Susan? Is anyone here? It's Meagan Atwood, I'm here for the um . . . meeting."

A strange feeling washed over me as I stopped walking. Something was wrong. Nothing about this felt right.

I found myself having a hard time breathing as panic set in almost instantly. I pulled out my cell phone and sent Grayson a text.

Me: 77

Turning, I went to walk back out when I slammed into a hard body.

"I don't think so, sweetheart. I've been waiting patiently to make you mine."

My eyes widened as I opened my mouth to scream, only to feel an instant rush of pain in the back of my head. Before the room went totally black, I heard my cell phone ringing. *Gray, help me.*

❧

The pain in the back of my head was felt the moment I opened my eyes. It was so bad, I almost threw up when I slowly pushed myself into a sitting position.

Touching the back of it lightly, I gasped when I touched the open wound. "Son-of-a-bitch," I mumbled as I stood up and looked around slowly.

"Where in the hell am I?" I asked as I took in the one-room log cabin. There was a small kitchen set off in the opposite corner, a couch, and the queen-size bed I was on. A few end tables and other odd pieces of furniture were sprinkled throughout the room. It looked to be a hunter's cabin or maybe a vacation house. Something caught my eye as I walked to the window.

"Oh no. Oh God, where am I?"

Snow was lightly falling outside as it dusted the trees and ground. Any other time I would think the picture before me was breathtaking; right now all it did was scare the piss out of me.

Closing my eyes, I tried to get my thoughts together, the last thing I remembered was walking down the hall to meet—

My body shivered as the memory of what happened to me filled my head.

A door rattled and I jumped back at the sound. When the door opened and Susan walked in, I didn't know whether I should be glad or scared.

"Susan?"

She was carrying a tray with a few towels and a brown bottle on it. When she looked at me, her eyes were filled with sadness. "You better sit down, Meagan. That's a big cut on the back of your head and it took me forever to get it to stop bleeding."

My heart began pounding as I walked over to the bed and sat down. Swallowing hard, I placed my hands on either side of me and watched as she walked toward me.

"I'm going to clean it with some peroxide."

Not saying a word, I sat there as still as I could while Susan cleaned the wound on the back of my head. The pain was so bad, at one point I gagged.

"Are you okay?" she asked as she looked into my eyes.

"What happened? Where am I?"

Susan's eyes darted to the door. "I told him not to hurt you. I'm so sorry."

My jaw trembled. "Please tell me what's happening. I beg of you!"

Chewing on her lip, Susan finished cleaning up the wound and then started to clean up the mess. She stood up and looked at the door and then back at me. "I don't want him to hurt you. I really like you and I know about the baby."

I sucked in a breath as panic filled every ounce of my body.

"W-what?"

She looked away as she said, "I heard Grayson talking

to his mom on the phone as he walked by me earlier this morning. He told her about your morning sickness."

I stood up too quickly and got dizzy. My body swayed as Susan reached out to steady me. "Please, please let me out of here. I . . . I don't know what's going on, but if you let me go I swear I won't tell anyone about this."

A single tear rolled down her face as she took a few steps away from me. "He threatens my daughter if I don't help him. I can't help you, Meagan. I can only try to talk him out of it."

My eyes widened in fear. "Out of what?"

She opened her mouth to speak, only to quickly shut it. "I have to go. I'll be back with your dinner soon."

Rushing after her, she quickly shut and locked the door as I banged on it!

"No! Please don't go! Let me out! Please let me out!"

Turning, I leaned against the door and sank down to the floor. I pulled me knees into my chest and cried as I rocked back and forth.

"Gray . . . please find me. *Please*."

Chapter

THIRTY

Grayson

MY HANDS SHOOK as I held my cell phone in my hands and stared at it. I'd just hung up with Brad and Amanda. Having to tell them Meagan was missing was the hardest phone call I'd ever had to make.

I paced back and forth as I waited for some news. "Bennett, over here for a second, will you?"

Turning to where Derrick had called out my name, I quickly walked over to where he was standing along with two CSI officers. "Anything?"

"Nothing. The place has been wiped clean. But, we did find a small amount of blood on the floor in the hallway that we swabbed and will compare against Ms. Atwood."

Derrick thanked them and took me by the arm as we walked toward the car. "Tell me everything again."

Pushing my hand through my hair, I sighed in frustration. "I fucking told you already."

"Tell me again."

"She sent me our code text. I called her back within thirty seconds and it went to voicemail. I tried calling back three more times before I tracked where her phone was. It was in this building and then began moving."

"All right, so we know the tracking started here and moved up Highway 550. It stopped about twenty miles outside of Durango. We've got two state patrol officers currently trying to find the phone. My guess is the cell phone was tossed out the window."

It was the first time anyone had even hinted about Meagan being taken by someone.

"I called Melissa and she told me Meagan was going to a meeting with a group of moms about bullying. Supposedly her daughter went to the same school as Mitchell did."

"Name?"

"Susan Powell and she thinks the daughter's name is Kate."

Derrick nodded his head. "Let's get these names ran through the high schools and see if we can find a hit on either one of them."

I was about to say something else when all the air left my lungs. "It's right in front of us."

Derrick gave me a confused look.

"Joshua Black."

It didn't take long for us both to get into the car and race over to his office.

Stepping off the elevator, Derrick and I headed straight to Black's office. "Excuse me! Sir . . . um . . . you can't just go into his office! Sir!"

I pulled out my badge and showed Black's receptionist as I pushed the door to his office open. The same blonde I'd seen him with before jumped up and stumbled backwards as she covered her body with her shirt.

"Jesus Christ! You can't just come barging into my

office like that!"

Glancing over to the blonde, I motioned for her to leave. "Next time lock your door," Derrick said from behind me.

"Where is she?" I said as I walked up to Joshua and grabbed him. Derrick was right there, pulling me away from him.

"Easy, Gray. Take it easy."

Joshua smoothed out his suite and gave me a confused look. "Where is who?"

"Meagan! She's gone. What did you do to her?"

Narrowing his eyes, Joshua looked between Derrick and me. "What in the hell are you talking about?"

I slammed my hands on his desk and yelled out, "I don't have time for this, Black! Tell me what you know or so help me God I will give up everything just to beat it out of your ass!"

Swallowing hard, Joshua held up his hands. "Okay . . . okay . . . just take it easy because I'm really confused what in the hell it is you're talking about."

"Joshua? Is everything okay in here?"

I glanced over my shoulder to see Mr. Black standing there. "Yeah, everything is . . . um . . . it's fine. I've got it under control, Dad."

Shooting me a dirty look, Mr. Black took two steps back. "I'll be right out here if you need anything, son."

Joshua ran his hand through his hair and nodded.

When the door shut, I walked up and got in his face. "What did you have to do with the murders?"

His mouth dropped open. "W-what? Nothing!"

"Why were you so interested in them then?" Derrick asked as he walked around Black's office.

"Wait. Someone please just tell me what is going on. You mentioned Meagan, is she okay?"

My heart jumped to my throat as I fought to say the words. "She's missing."

Joshua's eyes widened in shock as he closed them and shook his head. "Oh God."

"I'm not going to lie and tell you that I wasn't planning on finding you sitting in your office playing around with your girlfriend."

Pulling his head back, he asked, "You think I had something to do with this?"

"I think you have a lot to do with a lot of things, Black."

With a shake of his head, Joshua walked around his desk and pushed a button on his phone. "Yes, Mr. Black."

"Lacy, get me Bob Freeman on the phone please."

Taking a quick peek over in Derrick's direction, I noticed him writing something down; I was guessing the name Joshua just used.

I was running out of time. The longer we stood around and played games, the more dangerous it was for Meagan. "Who is Bob Freeman?" I asked.

Joshua took in a deep breath and pushed it out. "Let me start from the beginning."

"I don't have fucking time for you to start from the beginning. My fiancée is missing and the longer we stand here the more of a chance that whoever took her his going to hurt her."

My cell phone rang as I pulled it out, praying to God it would be Meagan.

It was Meagan's parents. I hated doing it, but I sent them to voicemail. I needed more information before I talked to them.

"Listen, I understand, detective, but please let me talk."

Anger was beginning to mix with the fear and I knew that was a bad combination for me.

With my hand, I motioned for him to go on.

"Bob Freeman is a client of mine. He's been in and out of jail for the last two years for different reasons. Usually being hauled in for public intoxication. I started to get suspicious of him several months ago."

"What do you mean?" Derrick asked.

Joshua shrugged. "He made a few comments that bothered me. They were always about the girls who were found raped or murdered. I started trying to piece information together, get as much information on the cases as I could."

Pinching my eyes together, I asked, "Is that why you always asked us all those questions?"

Joshua nodded. "Yeah, I was trying to see if you guys had any leads, anything that might confirm my suspicion."

"Why didn't you just tell us about this Bob Freeman?" I asked with frustration lacing my voice.

"Well, this might come as a surprise to you, but my job is to defend people until proven guilty, plus he's still my client."

Derrick walked up next to Joshua's desk. "But if you thought this guy might have been connected, you could have given us some kind of clue."

His eyes fell to the floor and he nodded his head. "Hindsight, I see I was wrong." Looking up into my eyes, Joshua frowned. "Maybe I wanted to try to figure it out myself. A small piece of me trying to play—"

I lifted an eyebrow. "Detective?"

Joshua's eyes turned sad. "Yeah. I guess you could say that."

"Anyway, one day I saw him walking behind Meagan as she walked into a Starbucks. I didn't like the way it seemed like he was following her, so I walked into Starbucks and started talking to Meagan. I was hoping it would throw Bob off if he truly was following her."

I rolled my eyes and huffed. "Instead dude, you freaked Meagan out and caused more suspicion to be thrown on you!"

Derrick sighed. "So, all the following, and jack-assing around with Gray was because you wanted to play cop?"

Joshua sunk down in his seat.

"When was the last time you heard from this Bob?" I asked.

Joshua took a few seconds to think about it. "Oh hell, I don't know. He seems to be pulling himself out of the pits and turning his life around. He got a job, hooked back up with a previous girlfriend and I believe moved in with her."

Joshua's phone buzzed. "Yes?"

"Mr. Black, Mr. Freeman's boss said that he hasn't shown up for work the last week. I've tried calling his cell phone number and it goes right to voicemail."

Rubbing the back of his neck, Joshua said, "Call his parole officer and see when the last time was he checked in with him."

"Yes, sir."

"Mr. Black, was Mr. Freeman in town during all the murders?"

Joshua swallowed hard. "Ah . . . as far as I know . . . yes."

"Do you have any reason to believe he could be behind Meagan's disappearance?"

"Speaking as his lawyer, I would tell you no. Speaking as one guy to another, I think he had a thing for Meagan and to tell you the truth, the guy gave me the creeps. He talked about those girls as if he . . . knew them. So to answer your question, yes, I could see that happening."

"Do you know where he lives?"

Joshua turned and pulled open a cabinet and took out a file. "Yeah, I got his girlfriend Susan's address."

My heart stopped as I felt my knees shake. "What did you just say?" I asked slowly.

"Ah, I think I said I had Susan's address."

I turned and looked at Derrick as he pulled out his ringing cell phone.

Joshua pulled out a piece of paper and handed to me. "That's her and her daughter. I believe her name is, Kate."

I had to reach out and hold onto one of the chairs in front of me with one hand as I took the paper in the other.

Susan's address was written down on the paper and a black-and-white photo of her and a girl about sixteen was stapled to the paper.

"Holy fuck," I whispered.

Derrick hung up and hit me in the arm to snap me out of it. "We had a patrol officer head to Durango High. There is a Kate Freeman registered there, her mother is listed as Susan Powell. When she questioned Kate, she said the girl was scared to death. Mentioned something about her deadbeat father was back living with them and how he abused her mom. Her mother told her a week ago to leave and go stay with friends and she hasn't heard from the mom since."

I turned to Joshua. "Thanks, Mr. Black; you've been a huge help, but next time you have information like this, you better fucking come clean and let us know."

Joshua stood and nodded his head. "I hope Meagan is just out shopping somewhere and none of this is really happening."

With a somber look, I nodded and headed out the door.

Derrick was already on the phone with central giving them all of Susan Powell and Bob Freeman's information.

I climbed into the passenger seat of the car and pulled out my cell and called Brad back.

"Grayson! Please tell me you've found her. Please!"

Squeezing my eyes shut, I shook my head. "Not yet, sir, but I promise you I'm doing everything I can to find her."

"You don't think this is connected to those . . . to those other . . ."

My stomach felt sick as I pushed the door open. "No. I'm going to find her and bring her home safely; as God as my witness I will not let her down. I made a promise to protect her and I'll chase her to the ends of the Earth if I have to."

The silence over the phone was almost deafening. "Call us when you find something out."

I quietly said, "I will."

I hit End and turned to Derrick. "I've got an APB out on Susan Powell's car. Looks like she hasn't shown up for work in the last three days. No one has heard from her or seen her at her job."

"Her plates?"

"I've got Mandy running it through now. If she's been through any intersections we will find out soon."

My hands slammed against my face as I scrubbed them up and down. "Not soon enough."

"Derrick, if Black's suspicions are true, and this guy is our rapist murderer, he has Meagan. He has my girl."

"We'll find her."

I turned and looked out the window and I prayed I'd find her in time.

Chapter
THIRTY-ONE

Meagan

I STOOD AT the window and watched the snow silently fall to the ground. Susan had been back in once to bring me something to eat. I could see another light in the distance and wondered if that was where Susan was staying.

I'd thought about breaking a window and trying to run, but I had no jacket, no shoes and was only wearing a pair of dress pants and a dress shirt. I'd freeze to death before I made it a few miles.

Closing my eyes, I wondered where my cell phone had gone. Or my purse. I'd give anything to have something to put on my dry cracked lips.

The door wiggled and I turned to stare at it. When it opened and saw the same man I had seen in the hallway, I instantly walked away from him.

He walked slowly into the room and shut the door as he stared at me. "You're so much prettier than the others."

"The o-others?" I asked as I pinned myself up against the wall.

His eyes looked my body over. "Yeah. The other's. None of them were like you though. The moment I first saw you I knew I had to have you. Then you had to go off and start fucking around with that cop."

"Gray," I whispered.

The look in his eyes turned and anger quickly washed over his face. "Do not say his name. You're mine now and I'm going to take my time with you for a little while."

My body shook as I looked over his shoulder to see Susan standing there.

"She's pregnant."

The guy stopped dead in his tracks as I silently cursed her for telling him. How could she let slip that I was pregnant?

Balling up his fists, he walked faster and stopped right in front of me as my chest rose and fell with each breath I took. "You let him get you pregnant?"

Tears streamed down my face as I turned my head away from him. His cold fingers grabbed my face and forced me to look back at him. The smile that moved over his face made me so sick, bile moved up in my throat as a whimper escaped from my lips.

"I can fix that."

"No, please don't. I'll do whatever you want me to do, just please don't hurt my baby."

His head tilted as he looked at me. As quickly as he grabbed my face he let me go and took a step back. I could hear Susan let out a relieved sigh when it looked like he was going to turn and leave. I relaxed my body some so when he turned I wasn't expecting him to punch me in the stomach.

Screaming, I fell to the floor and wrapped my arms around my stomach as I heard Susan call out his name. "Bob! No!"

I lay on the floor and watched him grab Susan by the hair and yank her over to the bed as she kicked and screamed. Pushing her down, he quickly undid his pants as he pushed her dress up and ripped her panties off.

"No please, Bob don't do this! Don't do this!"

The pain in my stomach now matched the pain in my head as I cried. I made a vow that if this man did anything to hurt my child I was going to kill him.

Through my tears all I could see was him push Susan's legs apart as he slammed himself into her body while she screamed out. Closing my eyes, I slammed my hands over my ears to drown out her cries.

Before I knew it, I felt a sharp pain in my back followed by an excruciating pain in my head. Bob had kicked my back and then grabbed a handful of hair as he dragged me across the room. Susan was lying on the bed crying as he dropped down and held my chin with his hand.

"Next time it will be you, sweet girl. I've been wanting to feel you for a long time now." His hot breath on my neck caused me to jerk my head from his hand as he laughed.

I couldn't even feel my body anymore. I was either in too much pain, or too scared to feel anything. Susan turned and looked into my eyes. I could see her fear and it did something to me. It gave me a strange energy and willpower that for one moment I thought I had lost.

Pushing my body away from him, Bob let go of me and grabbed onto Susan's arm and pulled her off the bed and out the door.

I wasn't sure how long I sat on the floor just staring out the window. My tears had long since stopped and the only thing I knew to do now was pray that Grayson would find me or I found a way out of there before it was too late.

❧

The door opened and I flew out of the bed. It had been freezing in the cabin and I had used the pillowcases to put over my feet in an attempt to keep them warm. Susan walked in and set a tray of food on the bed.

"Are you okay?" I asked.

She looked stunned at my question as she said, "How could you even care how I am? I helped that monster bring you here."

I knew Susan had been filled with guilt, especially because she knew about the baby. I needed to think of how to use that to my advantage. Time was quickly running out. There was no way of knowing how long it would be before he came after me.

"He makes the girls watch."

Swallowing hard, I asked, "What did you say?"

Chewing on her lip, she said, "He makes them watch a few times as he fucks me. Then, once he gets tired of them crying, he fucks them over and over again until they pretty much pass out. Then he brings them back to Durango."

Oh. My. God. Does she not see what is wrong with this? How could she help this man?

"He kills them after he rapes them?"

Susan's eyes widened in horror. "Oh no! He told me he let's them go."

Dear God, this woman is delusional. "How . . . how many have there been, Susan?"

"Four, not including you."

My hand went to my mouth to keep myself from throwing up. There had been four rape/murders in Durango that Grayson and his partner had investigated.

My stomach was feeling sick and my body ached from where Bob had kicked and punched me. "Why are you telling me this?" I asked her.

She shrugged and said, "I like you. When you came and talked at my daughter's school I felt like I had connected to you. So when I had told Bob about you and he said he knew you, I knew it was all my fault."

"What was all your fault?"

Susan walked back to the door and looked back at me. "I'm not sure if I will be able to talk to you again. Bob will be coming back with the items he needs for when he takes you as his."

My stomach cramped as thoughts of what he was going to do to me raced through my mind.

Panic set in as Susan went to leave. I called out her name trying not to sound desperate. "Susan! Do you still have my purse?"

"Oh, he threw out your cell phone on the drive up to the mountains, so if that is what you think you'll find I'm sorry."

Fuck. Please don't have emptied my whole purse.

"No, I really need something for my lips. I'm pretty sure I have some lip moisturizer in my purse."

With a slight smile, she looked at me as my heartbeat drummed in my ears. Please don't catch on to what I'm doing. *Please.* It felt as if time stood still while Susan stared at me lost in thought. Each breath I took was forced to seem normal as I tried to make it appear as if I only needed this one simple thing.

"Can I have your purse after he brings you back to Durango?"

Holy shit. This lady is just as crazy as he is.

I smiled sweetly. "Of course you can."

Susan clapped and walked over to the side table and pulled it open. I was stunned to see her pull out my purse.

The room felt like it was going to spin as I watched her toss it onto the bed. "Bob already looked through it and said to keep it in here with you."

Fighting to keep myself from running over and grabbing it, I gave her another weak smile as I watched her turn and leave the room. The moment I heard her lock the door, I counted to sixty and then rushed over to get my purse. Dumping everything out, I frantically looked for the tube of lipstick. When I saw it, I cried out in relief.

"Please work," I whispered as I turned the tube until I heard it click. I thought Grayson was insane when he told me the lipstick tube was a tracker. Now I was praying to God it would be the one thing that saved me from this nightmare.

Throwing the lipstick back into my purse, I took out my ChapStick and ran it over my lips, sighing at the instant relief.

My eyes caught a glimpse of the bottled water, the two pieces of bread and the small container of peanut butter.

I hated peanut butter, but I needed my energy. Opening the water bottle, I drank half of it and then ate the two pieces of bread with the peanut butter. Once I was done with that, I finished the water. A light shined from outside as I jumped up and saw a truck driving up.

My body trembled as I prayed Bob didn't make his way to see me.

Chapter
THIRTY-TWO

Grayson

AS I STOOD before the grid map, I blew out a frustrated sigh. I stared at the pin that marked where they had found Meagan's cell phone. After it had been printed for fingers prints, it pulled up what just what we had all thought.

The prints of Bob Freeman.

After searching in this guy's file for a few hours last night, I finally found his mother and father's name. I sent it off to be cross-referenced with any property north of Durango that might be in their names.

My phone had been blowing up with messages and calls from my mother, Grace, Noah, Brad and Amanda, and even Melissa, trying to find out what was going on.

I hadn't slept in over twenty-four hours and the only thing I ate was a taco that Derrick insisted I eat.

I sat down and closed my eyes as I felt a heaviness come over me. Time was running out and if I didn't get a lead soon, I was going to lose my shit. Pulling up my mother's name, I sent her a quick text.

Me: Nothing yet. We're getting closer with a few new leads.

It didn't take long for her to text me back.

Mom: You'll find her, Gray. I know you will.

Closing my eyes, I knew it as well. There was no way in hell I was letting this asshole take Meagan away from me.

"Bennett, the idea you had to check on the property came back with a hit."

Jumping up, I pulled the paper out of Sergeant Winters hand. "What?"

"Carol and John Freeman own a camping facility about fifty miles north of here tucked pretty far back into the mountains. From the looks of the satellite, there are a few cabins on the property as well. It's been closed down the last few years, after they passed away. They have two kids, a boy and a girl."

Staring at the paper, I said, "Let me guess, the son's name is Bob."

"Robert, but close enough."

I grabbed my jacket and looked back at Derrick. "With the weather moving in, we can't fly in." Derrick followed me out the door.

I pointed to Sergeant Winters. "See how far the state police are from the location. We don't know if this guy is armed or not or what kind of situation we're walking into. Give them that address but no one makes a move without talking to me first," I barked out.

My phone buzzed and I almost didn't check it for fear it was Meagan's parents. It killed me every time I had to tell them we had nothing new.

As Derrick and I climbed into my truck, I looked at my phone with a shocked expression.

The tracker.

"Holy shit. She had it. She turned it on!" I shouted as I looked at Derrick with a perplexed look. *I cannot believe she had it and remembered to use it.* A sense of relief washed over me knowing that Meagan was still okay enough to have turned on the tracking device I gave her. Knowing this renewed my energy.

Derrick turned to me and asked, "What are you talking about?"

"I know where she is!"

"Listen, Gray, I know you think this new lead is going to be the key, but we need to stay focused; this is one lead and he might not be there."

Lifting my hands to get him to stop talking, I showed him my phone. "This is the same location as the address Winters just gave us."

"A tracking device?"

I turned the truck on and raced out of the parking lot. "I gave it to Meagan shortly after Black had been snooping around. She thought it was silly, but she tossed it in her purse. She must have remembered she had it and turned it on."

Derrick was on the phone and giving the exact location of the tracker as I raced up Highway 550, praying we would get to Meagan in time.

"I'm coming for you, baby," I whispered. "I'm coming."

❧

Derrick and I slowly moved in with the Colorado State Police moving in from the back and the side. The property was huge and mostly contained campground sites. The cabins looked to be toward the back of the property.

As we made our way, I stopped moving and grabbed onto Derrick's arm. "Why does this all feel too easy?" I asked in a hushed tone.

"What do you mean?"

Looking around confused, I turned back to Derrick. "We've been searching for months for anything on the guy who raped and killed those girls. Now, this Bob Freeman leaves his prints on Meagan's phone. It just seems like a silly move on his part."

Derrick nodded. "From what Black said, this Freeman's been obsessed with Meagan. He was probably so taken by the fact he finally had her he didn't think twice about grabbing her phone and tossing it out the window."

A hushed voice came through the headphone in my ear. "There are lights on in both cabins. There appears to be movement in one cabin."

We made our way through the tree line and got closer to the second cabin where the signal was coming from. Getting down, I looked through the binoculars. The car was the same make and model as the car registered to Susan Powell. There was an older truck parked near the cabin that was located further back. I could see the teams moving into place as Derrick and I started making our way toward the back cabin.

An uneasy feeling swept over my body. My phone buzzed in my pocket as I reached in and took it out, my heart dropped and my knees about gave out as I stopped moving.

"No. God please no. Don't do this to me."

Derrick grabbed my arm and gave me a quick shake. "Bennett! We need to move. Now!"

My eyes widened in horror as I said, "The signal stopped. The tracking signal stopped."

Screams from the cabin caused me to take off running as fast as I could.

Meagan needed me and I was not about to let her down.

Chapter
THIRTY-THREE

Meagan

AFTER TURNING THE tracker on, I moved to the window and prayed like hell it went through. Hearing Bob's truck pull up, I panicked. Before I had a chance to go back over to the bed and grab the purse, the door unlocked and Susan came tumbling in as she fell to the floor.

I ran over to her and asked if she was okay.

Pain radiated through my entire head as Bob grabbed a handful of hair and pulled me across the room and over to a pole that was in the middle of the room.

"Please, stop! Please just let me go!" I called out as he slapped me across my face and yelled for me to shut up.

"Because of you I got sloppy. I fucking got sloppy, you damn bitch. You better be worth the fuck, that's all I have to say."

I searched his face as a panicked look appeared on my face. "W-what?"

"Your fucking phone! I figured your damn boyfriend would track it, so I tossed it out the window on the way up here."

Hate filled my entire body as I squared my shoulders. "Well, if you threw it out the window how is that being sloppy? He can't track me here now."

Anger filled his eyes as he reached up and slapped me so hard it felt like my jaw came out of its socket. "I'm not stupid, you bitch. He can track down the fingerprints on there, which means soon he'll piece together where you are. So, it looks like we need to move up the time for our party."

Shaking my head, my eyes burned from the onslaught of tears. "Why are you doing this?" I asked between sobs.

His hand moved up my leg as I tried to pull as far away from him as I could. "Get undressed, Susan. Now!"

Oh God.

My eyes shot over to her quickly undressing before I looked back at Bob. He held up a pair of handcuffs in his hands and it was then I noticed he had on gloves. "Time for some fun, sweet girl." His hand moved over my shirt as his fingers brushed over my nipple, causing me to pull as far away as I could.

My head thrashed back and forth as I tried to push him away. Another slap and I was stunned enough for him to grab my arms and pull them behind the pole where he handcuffed me.

Bile moved up to the back of my throat as his hands cupped my breasts and he moaned.

"I can't wait to fuck you."

Using what energy I had left, I lifted my legs and began kicking him from me. "Stay away from me you asshole! Gray is going to *kill you*!" I screamed out as Bob stood up and laughed.

He grabbed onto my face as he moved his lips to my ear and whispered, "I don't think so. At least not before I

259

kill you."

My chin trembled as I fought to find my voice to scream. Bob walked over toward Susan and began touching all over her body as I looked away.

"Watch us!" he yelled out as I shook my head.

Something hit behind my head as I screamed out and turned to look at him. He was holding my purse in his hand. My heartbeat raced, nearly exploding out of my chest as my eyes landed on my purse and then down to the floor where a few things had fallen out. One of them being the tracker.

Bob dropped the purse and turned to go back to Susan.

"Let's give her a little preview of what she's going to get from me."

Susan began crying as she called out, "Bobby, she's pregnant, you can't do this to an innocent child."

He slapped her face and pushed her down onto the bed. Susan whimpered as I fought against the handcuffs.

"Stop! Leave her alone, you fucker!" I screamed out as Bob started laughing.

"Susan! Don't let him do this!"

"Shut up, bitch!"

The handcuffs started banging against the pole as I frantically began moving. Bob walked back over and my whole body went limp as he stepped on the lipstick tube.

"NO!" I screamed out as my eyes looked at the broken tracker lying on the floor. Looking back up at him, I knew I would fight with everything I had. He was not going to hurt my baby.

"I've had just about enough of you. It's time to give you the punishment you deserve."

With every ounce of anger inside of me, I began kicking and screaming. There was no way in hell this guy was going to even think of touching me.

"Shut up!" he shouted.

His hands tried to keep my legs from moving, but I

used everything I had in me to keep fighting. The look in his eyes was turning from angry to evil, and I knew I only had about thirty seconds to fight him off before he did something again to make me stop.

Bob lifted his hand in a fist as I closed my eyes and got ready for him to hit me. As long as he hit me in the face and not in the stomach, I had to protect my baby. The loud pop caused Susan to scream as I heard a crashing noise.

My eyes snapped open as I watched the pained expression on his face. Before I knew what was happening, Bob was on the floor with blood beginning to pool around his head and Grayson was cupping my face.

"Meagan . . . baby, look at me. Don't look at him. Look. At. Me."

I screamed out again as I looked down at Bob's lifeless body on the floor. I desperately tried to get as far away from him as I could when I felt someone's hands on me.

"He's gone, he's not going to hurt you. Meg, baby look at me."

My head jerked up and I was soon pinned with the bluest of blue eyes.

"Gray," I whispered as his lips pressed against mine.

Sobs rolled over my body as I fought to speak.

"You're here. You made it in time. You saved us!"

His lips were all over my face as I felt someone else releasing my hands from the handcuffs. The moment my arms fell free, I wrapped them around Grayson's neck and cried like I had never cried before.

"You're here," I whimpered out as I buried my face into his chest.

"Shh . . . it's okay, baby. You're safe now and I'm never letting you out of my sight again."

All the pain vanished as I let Grayson pick me up and carry me out of the cabin. I kept my eyes shut for fear of what I would see walking out.

"Please tell me this was all a nightmare."

Grayson held me close to him as he set me down inside of his truck. "We need to get you to the hospital, baby, to be checked out. Did he . . . did he . . . hurt you in any way?"

I shook my head. "It's just my head and my ribs hurt from where he hit and kicked me."

Sucking in a breath of air, I felt my hot tears run down my face.

"The baby," I whispered as everything began to spin and all the light slowly drifted away.

"Gray, our baby . . ."

❧

My entire body ached as I slowly opened my eyes. Looking around, I smiled.

Home.

With each painful movement, I sat up and looked around my old bedroom. Everything was the same as it was when I moved out.

Letting out a deep sigh, I swung my legs off the bed and stood. I could hear talking coming up through the opened windows in my room. Walking over to them, a warm feeling rolled over my body as I heard familiar voices.

I closed my eyes and thought back over the last few days. Grayson had been my knight in shining armor as he rushed into the cabin and literally saved me and the baby from the monster. After a quick stop by the hospital to make sure I was okay, he went straight to the airport to bring me home to Texas.

The whole ordeal pretty much knocked me out the whole flight to Texas and the drive to Fredericksburg. My body was exhausted and aching.

With my hand over my stomach while I walked to the

bathroom, I silently said a prayer of thanks that our baby was okay. I had two bruised ribs, which felt more like ten broken ones, a good size cut on the back of my head, and the side of my face looked like it had been used as a punching bag. Every time Grayson looked at my face; I could see the anger in his eyes. Thank goodness Melissa was so understanding in letting me take a few weeks off to recover.

After cleaning up, I changed and headed downstairs to the front porch.

"Thank you for bringing her home, Gray."

The rocking of the chairs was a soothing sound as I listened to Grace talking to Grayson. "It was a no-brainer for me, Grace. The last place I wanted her to be was somewhere she was not going to feel safe."

My heart felt as if it would burst. Grayson told the station he was taking a leave of absence and I knew how hard that had to have been for him. He was still so new and for him to just swoop in and fly me off to Texas was the most unselfish thing anyone had ever done for me.

"Good morning," my mother whispered as she leaned her chin on my shoulder. I smiled as I took her hand in mine.

"I love him so much, Mom."

Her hand gently squeezed mine. "He loves you so much too."

My body trembled at the idea of what could have happened. "Mom, I could have . . . what if he had . . ."

Turning me to face her, my mother shook her head and put her finger up to stop me from talking. "No. There are no what if's. The only thing that we have is our future and I have a grandbaby to start thinking about."

My heart felt as if it cracked a little as I thought about raising my child so far from my mother. Everything was so different now. The look on my parents' faces when Grayson and I told them last night I was pregnant. I was scared to death they would be upset with me, but it was the opposite. I'd never seen them both so happy and of course thankful that the baby was okay.

"Hey, how are you feeling, babe?"

Grayson had me wrapped up in his arms with a soft kiss on the forehead before I had too much time to think about the baby and Colorado.

"Better."

Grace walked up to me and as my eyes traveled down to her stomach. "Your baby bump!" I said as I placed my hands on her and started crying.

Letting out a giggle, Grace teared up and said, "Welcome to hormone hell! I cry at everything now."

I pulled my best friend into my arms and lost it. "Oh my God, I've missed you so much," I said as we held onto each other for dear life.

When we finally pulled back, Grace gave me a wink. "Do you feel up to going somewhere with me?"

"Yes!" I said without even thinking. Glancing over to Grayson, I asked, "Do you mind?"

The smile he gave me caused my stomach to drop and my heart to fall even more for him. "Of course not. As long as you're feeling up to it."

Lifting my eyebrow, I grinned as I said, "You'll be okay alone with my father?"

Grayson shrugged and said, "I saved your life, how can he possibly not like me now."

My mother chuckled as she made her way outside. "He'll be just fine, Meg. Go spend some time with Grace."

"Do I need to change?"

With a sneaky smile, Grace shook her head. "Nope. We can leave this second. You don't need anything."

I chewed on my lip at the idea of leaving Grayson. I knew I was safe, but I also knew I was that much more safe with him near me. He must have read the confusion on my face because he gently pulled me closer to him and kissed my lips softly. "I would never leave your side if I thought anything would happen to you."

"I know. I'm sorry, I guess I'm just trying to figure out how to process what happened and how I move on from here."

His hand came up and pushed a loose strand of hair behind my ear. "I'm almost positive you're going to be happy once you get there, babe."

"I have my phone, if Daddy bothers you, call me and I'll be there."

Grayson laughed as he kissed me once more and stepped out of the way while I followed Grace to her car.

Once we got into her car and started talking, everything seemed to just fall into place. It was as if I hadn't ever left Mason at all.

I hadn't been paying attention to where we were going until I realized we were pulling up to the Mathews' main gate. "What are we doing here?"

"You'll see," Grace said.

"Have you talked to Libby? I really want to see the baby. I bet he is so big now."

Grace giggled. "Almost six months old, the little bugger."

My stomach fluttered knowing I was carrying a baby. I'd watched three of my friends already have kids and I never in my wildest dreams would have thought I'd have wanted it as bad as I did.

Driving down the familiar driveway, I asked Grace a million questions about being pregnant. When she pulled up and put her car in park, I turned and grinned so big I was sure my cheeks would cramp.

"Grams and Gramps."

"The best place on Earth!"

"Hell yeah it is," I softly spoke as I took in the familiar white ranch house.

The screen door opened as I got out of the car. My

hand came over my mouth as I watched my girls all pile out onto the porch. Alex was holding Bayli's hand as she walked along her side. "Oh my God! Bayli is walking!"

Grace laughed and wrapped her arm around mine. Libby was standing there holding Trey in her arms as Mireya jumped all around calling out my name.

Lauren stood there with a smile on her face that caused me to smile even bigger. She looked beautiful with her blonde hair all pulled up and piled on top of her head. "Lauren looks amazing!"

"Yeah, she really does," Grace said as we started walking toward the porch. That's when I saw my sister.

"Taylor," I whispered.

With tears streaming down her face, Taylor ran down the stairs and into my arms.

I wanted to cry out in pain, but I couldn't. I wrapped my sister up in my arms as we both stood there and cried.

When we finally pulled apart, Taylor wiped her tears away. "I've missed you so much, Meg."

My heart felt so at peace as I looked at my beautiful little sister standing before me. "I've missed you more, Tay."

Then I came face to face with the bluest of blue eyes.

"Grams," was all I could say as she took my hand in hers.

"Welcome home my sweet girl."

Tears fell freely as I scanned over the scene. I never in a million years would have imagined missing these girls as much as I had. Bending down, I called out for Mireya. When her little arms wrapped around my neck, I felt a complete peace move through my body.

Home.

I was home.

Chapter
THIRTY-FOUR

Grayson

ALMOST TWO WEEKS had passed since I brought Meagan back to Texas. In those two weeks we had done everything from attend barn parties, celebrated belated birthdays we missed, shopped for baby clothes, and I had learned to do more to a cow than I ever wanted to know in my lifetime.

I stood and looked out over the Texas hill country as I took in a deep cleansing breath.

"Feels good don't it?"

Glancing over my shoulder, I smiled as I watched my future father-in-law walk up.

"I thought the air in Colorado was amazing. But something about this place . . . I can't put it into words."

"Texas air has something in it. Something that reaches down and grabs ahold of you tightly and never lets go."

I nodded as I looked back out over the countryside.

"Is there a reason you asked me to meet you on some

random piece of land off of Highway 1871?"

With a deep breath through my nose, I slowly blew it out as I nodded my head. "Walk with me for a minute, Brad."

Brad followed me as we walked up the short hill and came to a stop at the top.

"Holy shit, look at that view of the Llano River."

With a smile, I took in the rolling hills. It was beautiful and the more I stood there, the more I knew I was doing the right thing for my family.

"It looks like a picture," I said as I turned to Brad. "I need your advice."

His eyes met mine as he let a small smile play across his lips. "Okay."

"I know everything that happened to Meagan has been a shock to her and she feels safe here. I also know, I've never seen her so happy like she has been these last two weeks. With the baby coming, I'm starting to think Meagan is having second thoughts about living so far away."

Brad's eyes lit up and I had to give him credit, he tried really hard to hold back his excitement. Trying to look serious, he nodded and said, "I'm not going to lie to you, Gray, knowing y'all are having a baby and living so far away is going to be really hard for us. I also know, if the tables were turned, it would be hard for your mother if you both lived here."

I had already talked to my mother last night for two hours about the possibility of moving to Texas. She agreed, it would be much easier for her and James to travel to see us than it would be for us to travel to Texas.

"That's true," I said in a thoughtful voice. "But, the person I care the most about is who I want to make happy."

"Meagan," Brad said as tears built in his eyes. Looking away, he blinked rapidly.

"Would she be happy here, Brad? Ever since I've met her, she's only talked about leaving Texas, not buying a hundred acres of land. I'm not a cowboy and I'm not looking into getting into cattle and all that shit."

Brad laughed and shook his head. "Somehow that doesn't surprise me, Gray."

"I was thinking though, with all the land, we might be able to start a camp for kids who have been bullied or who are from underprivileged homes. I know you don't care for my previous job, but I made a lot of money and invested it well. I have enough money to purchase this land and build a house on it out right. Once we get settled, we could start looking into the camp."

Brad stood there and stared at me as I moved from foot to foot. I couldn't tell what he was thinking, and I started to wonder if I shouldn't have brought up my old job.

"You're serious, aren't you?"

My eyes widened in surprise. "Yes. I mean I know I have to talk to Meagan about all of this and I know how much she loves her job, but I also see how full of life her eyes have been since we've been here. Grace checked into a few jobs around the area for Meagan. She's made it clear she wants to keep working after the baby and hell, she can even start her own company if she wants. I'll support her in whatever she wants to do."

Brad took a step toward me as I took a step back. He took another step as I took another back. We did this about five times before he finally snarled his lip and asked, "Why do you keep backing away from me?"

"I don't know. I'm kind of picturing you doing something to hurt me for some reason."

With a raised brow, he asked, "Like what?"

"I don't know. To be honest, you scare me."

Brad smiled a triumphant smile. "I simply wanted to give you a slap on the shoulder, Gray. Your mother should be very proud of the man she raised. I know I'm proud of you son. My heart is overwhelmed to know that my daughter has a man who loves her so much that he has made her happiness his number one concern."

Tears built in my eyes as I stared at him. "That . . . that means more to me than you will ever know, sir."

Brad walked up and pulled me into a quick hug as he slapped the living shit out of my back before he pushed me away.

"All right, enough of that shit. Now how are you planning on running this idea by Meagan?"

I grinned and said, "Well, after being around everyone as much as I have been, I figured out that my go-to guy on all things romance was either Gunner or Josh. So I hit them both up for an idea."

Brad shook his head as he mumbled, "Stupid romantic bastards. What did they say?"

"Picnic, right here in this spot."

Brad rolled his eyes. "That would be a solid plan. Keep her eyes closed so she doesn't know where you're taking her."

"Yes, sir. Josh said the same thing."

Brad frowned. "Of course he did. Make sure you have it all set up ahead of time, so you'll need to talk to the realtor."

"Oh, Gunner already arranged all that for me. He was the one who told me about this piece of property. He already talked to the agent and got it all squared away."

Brad shook his head. "Good ole, Gunner." Shaking his head again, he let out a chuckle as if thinking of a memory. "Well if you buy it, this would make a great place to get married."

My eyes lit up as an idea hit me. Placing my hands on Brad's shoulders, I gave him a quick shake. "That's a great idea! I need to get it planned right away!"

I took off jogging back toward my truck as Brad called out, "What idea did I give you? Is it better than Gunner and Josh's?"

～⚬～

"You want to do what?" Lauren asked me as she stood outside Alex and Grace's flower shop.

Alex held up her hands and began waving them. "Wait. Gray, are you hearing yourself? Because you're talking so fast that I'm not even sure I understand what you're saying."

"A wedding. I want to plan a wedding for tonight."

Grace laughed. "Tonight?"

"Yes. Tonight."

"As in today tonight?" Lauren said as everyone looked over at her.

"Um . . . yes?" I said as I stole a peek over to Colt who smiled and gave me a let-it-go look.

"You don't even have a marriage license," Grace said.

With a chuckle, I looked at Grace. "I don't want to do a real wedding, I want to reaffirm my love for Meagan and I want her whole family there. How about that?"

Libby did a little jump as she said, "We can totally do this! We can totally put this together. It will be like a pre wedding! Alex, Grace, all you need to do is make a bouquet for Meagan." Libby turned to Lauren. "Lauren, all you need to do is find Meg a beautiful white dress and your closet is full of beautiful clothes."

Lauren smiled and called out, "Oh my glitter! I have the perfect dress in mind!"

"Once she gets back from spending the morning with Taylor, I'll do her hair and tell her you planned a romantic dinner for two and doing her hair gives me an excuse for having some one-on-one girl time with her."

Smiling, I looked around the small group. I'd never met a group of people like them. There wasn't anything they wouldn't do for each other and I was amazed at how they opened their hearts up to me.

Noah walked up and gripped my shoulder. "Welcome

to the family, Gray."

Blowing out a deep breath, I shook my head and said, "Damn I've missed you, Noah."

Noah pushed my shoulder back and laughed. "Falling in love has made you a pussy. Come on, let's get this all taken care of so we can go out and celebrate the good news."

Chapter
THIRTY-FIVE

Meagan

I SAT IN a chair in the middle of Libby's living room as she pulled my hair up and began messing with my make-up.

"Lib, it's just dinner in Fredericksburg. It's not like I'm getting married."

"Why would you say that?" Libby asked as she walked around and stood in front of me with a shocked look on her face.

Narrowing my eyes, I tiled my head and gave Libby a look. "What's going on?"

"What do you mean?" she asked as she dabbed at my lipstick and fixed a curl hanging down.

"Something is going on. Taylor was acting weird today, Gray was acting weird, and now you're acting weird."

Libby let out a nervous laugh. "You're paranoid, Meg."

Dropping my shoulders, I thought about it. *Was I being paranoid? Probably.*

"Have you enjoyed being home the last few weeks?"

Happiness bubbled up inside of me, but was quickly replaced with dread. For all those years I'd repeated over and over I didn't want to live in Texas. I didn't want to live in Fredericksburg or Mason. The last two weeks all I had been thinking about was living here. Being close to my friends and family. Every time I thought about the baby, I had to fight back the urge to cry.

Gray was so happy with his job and he was a detective. There was no way he could move to small-town Texas and even come close to that. Then there was his mother. No way would he ever even think of leaving her even though James had asked her to marry him.

"What's wrong, Meg? You look lost in thought and a million miles away."

I pressed my lips together and forced a fake smile. "Nothing. I guess I'm feeling a bit queasy."

"Oh yes, the morning sickness that lasts all day."

The sound of a car pulling up had my stomach twisting, but in a good way. "Gray," I whispered. I'd only seen him once today and that was this morning before I left to spend the morning with Taylor. We'd talked a few times on the phone and I could tell something was weighing on his mind. I had planned on talking to him about my conflicting feelings about living in Colorado tonight at dinner.

Libby rubbed my shoulders and said, "You're all done. Wait until your baby daddy sees you."

The door opened and Luke and Grayson walked in laughing about something. My body warmed at the sight. Grayson fit into our little group like he'd been there his whole life. It was another reason I was struggling with going back to Colorado. Sure, I had Melissa there, but really no friends. Not like my friends here.

Grayson's eyes met mine as his smile turned to a look of pure fascination. "Meg, you look beautiful."

I glanced down at the off-white dress Lauren had

insisted I wear along with my cowboy boots.

My hair was pulled up and pinned to perfection, according to Libby.

With a shy grin, I kicked at nothing on the floor and sunk my teeth into my lip as Grayson made his way over to me. His hand came up to my face where he softly brushed his thumb across my skin.

"Holy shit. Is Meg blushing? Seriously, am I seeing this with my own eyes? Meagan Atwood has been bitten by the love bug and it makes her blush."

My eyes shot behind Grayson as I pinned Luke with a pissed off stare. "Fuck off, Luke."

With a wink, Luke gave me a head pop. "And there she is, always buried deep down inside waiting to come out."

Grayson laughed as he slid his arm around my waist and led me to the door. "We need to get going."

Peeking over to Libby, I gave her a thumbs-up as we headed out the door while Libby yelled out, "Don't mess up her hair! I can only imagine the kind of sex you two have!"

Grayson opened the door to our rental car and shook his head. "Why does everyone think we have hot sex?"

With a shrug, I gave him a sexy grin. "Because I tell them about our sex."

"Oh. So you think we have hot sex?"

"Let's just say, staying with my parents the last two weeks has really caused me to have a build up and I'm pretty sure I'm going to need a release soon. Very soon. And all I can think about is our hot sex."

"My god," Grayson whispered as he shut the door, pulled out his phone and typed away. When he got in, I looked at him and asked, "Who were you texting?"

"Noah. I asked him to book us a room in Fredericksburg for tonight."

I chuckled at first then shook my head. "No way. My parents will know what we're doing."

Grayson drove down the driveway and laughed. "Um, Meg, we're engaged to be married and we're having a baby. I think the idea of us having sex is pretty solid now."

Wringing my hands together, I cleared my throat. It was now or never. "Gray, I was wondering if we might talk about something."

His hand came across and grabbed mine as butterflies danced about in my stomach. "Of course we can."

Damn it all to hell. How do I say this? Where do I start? What if Grayson wants one thing and I want something else? After all, I'm changing the way the game is played in the middle of the damn game.

Shit. Shit. Shit.

I tried to work it all out in my head as Grayson continued to drive. I wasn't sure how long he had driven for before I realized he was not heading toward Fredericksburg.

"Ah . . . where are you going?"

"I want to show you something, but what was it you wanted to talk about? You got super quiet."

"Well . . . these last two weeks home have been pretty amazing. I mean, I know all the stress of what happened and everything. But I um . . ."

"You've been enjoying being home with everyone."

Swallowing hard, I nodded my head. "I have enjoyed it. Have you?"

His smile was so big I couldn't help but smile back. "I've really enjoyed myself. But then I've always loved coming to visit here in Texas."

Ugh. He said visit.

Shit. Shit. Shit.

I dropped my head back against the seat and wondered how in the hell I could sit here and ask him to give up his career to move to the middle of fucking Texas!

My eyes opened when I felt him turning and driving down a gravel driveway.

"Where are we going?"

Grayson stopped the car and handed me a handkerchief. "Turn away from me, baby, and let me put this on. Where we are going is a surprise."

My stomach jumped. Surprise?

"What kind of surprise?"

With a low rumble coming from his chest, Grayson leaned his lips close to my ear and said, "One I have a feeling you're going to love."

I still needed to talk to him about the confusion I was feeling, but it could wait. I was dying to see what he was going to show me.

We drove for a good five minutes before the car parked and Grayson said, "Hold on and I'll come around and get you."

The excitement in Grayson's voice had me feeling giddy as I held onto his hand as he led me to wherever we were going.

With a giggle, I asked, "Are we there yet?"

"Almost."

Coming to a stop, I waited patiently for Grayson to take off the blindfold so I could see where we were. The only thing I knew for sure was we were outside.

"Ready?"

With a nod of my head, I laughed and said, "Yes! I want to see where we are."

He was standing behind me as he placed one hand on my hip while pulling the blindfold off with the other. It took a few seconds for my eyes to adjust but when they did, I took in a breath of air. "Oh my, Grayson that is a beautiful view."

"Yes it is."

I slowly shook my head as tears built in my eyes. It was in that moment that it really hit me. I loved Texas. I wanted to be in Texas, near my family and friends. But I wanted Grayson more than anything and Colorado was his home.

"Meagan?" Grayson whispered against my neck.

"Yeah?" I managed to say without letting out the sobs I was desperately holding back.

"Turn around."

I didn't want to pull my eyes from the view. The Llano River meandered below us as a slight wind blew my curls around. The blue sky touching the green valley was almost more beautiful than the snow-covered Rocky Mountains.

"Meg?" Grayson said as he put pressure on my hip for me to turn.

When I turned around, I saw everyone standing behind Grayson. My jaw trembled as I looked at the people I loved so much. My father and mother stood up front with huge smiles on their faces. Grams and Gramps were even there standing next to Gunner and Ellie.

My head slowly shook as I looked back to Grayson. "I don't understand."

Taking my hand in his, Grayson's eyes teared up. "Meg, I found us the perfect place to get married."

My eyes widened. We hadn't really talked about where we would get married.

"Oh . . . I think it would be a perfect place to get married too," I said.

Grayson cleared his throat as his blue eyes pierced mine and held me for the longest time. "I also think it would be the perfect place to raise our family."

I frantically nodded my head as I cried and said, "I think so . . . wait. What?"

"Can't you just imagine a house sitting right here, overlooking that view?"

Tears streamed down my face as I silently cursed my stupid hormones.

"A house?"

"And I was thinking, with all the land we could have a camp for kids who are bullied or come from underprivileged homes."

My eyes searched everyone's faces behind Grayson and all I saw were smiles and tears. My mother was crying like a baby and my father looked happy as a clam.

"A camp?" I asked as I sobbed. "Wait. What . . . are . . . you saying?"

"I'm saying that if you want to make this our home, I want that too."

My body shook as I tried to contain all the emotions I was feeling. "But . . . but what about your job? Gray, you worked so hard and . . . and . . . I won't let you give that up!"

His hands cupped my face as he kissed my tears away. "I love you, Meagan Atwood. Haven't you figured it out yet, the only place I need to be is by your side."

My lips trembled. "Your mom? What about your mom? You've always depended on each other and you'll be thousands of miles away from each other."

The feel of his thumbs gently moving over my skin caused my body to erupt in tingles. "She has James now and lets not forget Rick and Sandy . . . the she-devil herself. Besides, she can come visit and stay with us anytime she wants."

I couldn't help but giggle as my eyes searched his face. He was completely serious.

"You'd really move to Texas just for me?"

A sexy crooked smile slowly appeared on his face as my knees wobbled. "No, I'd move to Texas for us. For our happiness, our future, and our family."

"I never, in my wildest imagination, thought I could ever love you more, but you keep doing these things that make me fall deeper in love with you."

Wiggling his eyebrows, Grayson dropped his hands and pulled me closer to him. "Then I hope you fall deeper tonight."

My face grew red as I playfully hit him on the chest.

Grayson's face grew serious. "Meg, if this is what you

want, then I'm behind you one hundred percent and we can figure it all out as we go."

I nervously chewed on my lip before Grayson pulled my lip from my teeth and gently kissed my lips. When he pulled back, I asked, "Can we afford this? I mean, Gray, it's so much land and we have to build a house. Neither of us will have jobs!"

"Your job is to take care of my son growing in your belly. My job is to do all the worrying and get it all figured out."

My body felt like it was humming when Grayson mentioned having a son. "What if it's a girl?"

His eyes sparkled as he glanced down to my stomach and back up at me. "I guess if it's a girl, I need to start preparing now because I'm almost positive she'll have me wrapped around her finger."

Throwing myself against him, Grayson wrapped his arms around me. I buried my face into his neck as I heard everyone shouting out and clapping.

Grayson spun me around a few times before setting me back down. I'd never tell him the action caused me to lose my breath from the pain in my ribs. I'd never say anything to ruin this perfect moment.

Everyone walked up and began congratulating us. Taylor grabbed my arm and pulled me off to the side as she wiped her tears away.

"You'll never know how happy I am to know my sister is home again. I've missed you so much, Meg!"

Her reaction caught me off guard and I was sure there was something more behind it, but now was not the time or place to ask her.

"Me too, Tay. I love you so much and I've missed you."

Taylor hugged me and I couldn't help but notice how she held onto me a little tighter and longer than usual.

When she stepped back, my parents walked up to me next. After a gentle hug from both of them, my mother tried desperately to not start crying again but failed.

After getting hugs and kisses from everyone, Grams walked up to me and handed me a small box.

"Should I open it now?" I asked as I looked into her beautiful blue eyes.

"Yes!"

Feeling the excitement bubble up inside of me, I opened the box and gasped. My fingers ran along the wooden plaque as I felt my tears falling yet again. *Holy hell this pregnancy is going to do me in with the crying!*

"It's kind of a little tradition Garrett started when Drew and Ellie built their house. Now it's your turn."

My finger moved along each word as it spelled out *Welcome Home.*

Home.

Lifting my eyes I looked between Grams and Gramps and smiled so big I was sure my cheeks would cramp up. "I love this so much."

Grayson gave Grams a kiss and hug and shook Gramps' hand as I hugged and kissed them both.

"Thank you so much, this means so much to us," Grayson said as I experienced the most amazing moment of peace I had ever experienced in my entire life.

For the first time ever, I truly felt like I was home.

Chapter

THIRTY-SIX

Grayson

AS I STOOD over the bed, I watched the love of my life sleeping so peacefully. Her brown hair was lying across the pillow and her kiss-swollen lips were begging for more attention.

I'd kept her up almost all night making love to her and I knew she was exhausted. I also knew her ribs had to be killing her. When I saw the pain on her face, I knew I was being selfish. I gave her one last orgasm and let her sleep the rest of the night.

After we left the land, everyone headed into Fredericksburg and celebrated until late. It was probably one of the best nights of my life.

I set the two cups of coffee down on the side table and picked up one of the orange muffins and moved it around Meagan's nose. When she stirred, she lifted her eyebrows and moaned.

"Mmm . . . oh God. I know what that is!"

Her eyes snapped open as she instantly zeroed in on the muffin. Her eyes danced with happiness as she sat up and pulled the sheet up to cover her bare breasts.

"A little birdie told me these were your favorite."

Meagan licked her lips as I put the muffin up to her mouth. Taking a bite, she closed her eyes and moaned, causing my dick to jump.

Laughing, I asked, "Is it that good?"

Her eyes about rolled to the back of her head as she nodded. "Oh God. I'd dare say it was better than an orgasm."

My brow lifted. "Is that so? A muffin is better than an orgasm?"

Meagan pointed to the muffin. "This one is."

Challenge accepted.

I slowly pulled the sheet down and away from Meagan's beautiful body. She flashed me a sexy grin, knowing full on what I was doing. The bruising on the side of her face was nearly gone. Thank God. Every time I saw it, I wanted to hurt someone.

"Whatcha doing?" she purred.

"You just keep eating your fabulous orange muffin and don't pay any attention to me."

With a giggle, Meagan slid down onto the bed as I pushed her legs apart and placed light kisses up her leg. Once I got to her inner thigh, she let out a contented sigh. Peeking up, I asked, "Was that for me or the muffin?"

Her lips parted open as she gave me the sexiest fucking smile I'd ever seen. "That's still to be determined," she said as she took another bite of the damn muffin.

My lips moved closer to her pussy as I ran my tongue along the edge of her lips. Meagan's body trembled as she gasped when I quickly swiped her clit.

Glancing up her way, I couldn't help but grin as I watched her abusing the fuck out of her lip with her eyes closed. "How's that muffin?"

"It's good. Oh *so* good."

She held the half-eaten muffin in her hand as she lifted her hips some, silently pleading for more.

My finger moved around her mound before I slowly pushed it inside of her warmth.

"Gray!" she whispered as her fingers laced through my hair and pushed my face closer to her need.

Running my tongue along her lips, I sucked one into my mouth and gently bit down as Meagan's hips jerked up.

"You're driving me crazy."

Smiling, I pushed another finger in as I played with her clit.

Soft whimpers slipped from her mouth as she tried to cause more friction with her hips while I blew softly on her clit.

Another lick across her clit and small bite on her soft lips, and I was ready to go in for the kill.

Dirty talk.

Meagan's weakness.

"Mmm, baby. I love eating you for breakfast. You taste so fucking good." Meagan dropped her muffin and took both hands and grabbed onto my hair.

"Grayson . . . goddamn it . . . give it to me!"

My fingers pulled out as I buried my face between her legs and gave her what she wanted. I could feel her body vibrating as her orgasm began to build.

"Yes, yes, yes! Don't. Stop."

My finger moved to her ass. I made a circle pattern and pushed slightly against it.

"Oh God!" Meagan cried out. "More. Gray, I want more!"

Now I was losing control as I sucked and licked her faster.

Meagan's body lifted off the bed as she cried out my

name over and over.

When she begged me to stop, I pulled away and sat back against my feet as I watched her chest heave up and down while she tried to regain her normal breathing pattern.

My eyes caught sight of the orange muffin lying next to her on the bed. Dropping back down, I kissed all over her stomach as her hands pushed through my hair. Moving up, I gave each nipple attention before I moved up to her mouth. Stopping, I smiled when she smiled up at me.

"So. Much. Better. Than. The. Muffin," she whispered between heavy breaths. I kissed her nose as I reached for the half-eaten muffin and pushed it into my mouth and began chewing.

Holy fucking shit. Damn that thing is good.

Meagan wore a grin from ear to ear as she watched me eat the muffin. With a moan, I rolled my eyes and said, "Almost as good as an orgasm but not quite there."

Laughing, she hit my chest as I fell over and pulled her on top of me. "You about ready?" I asked as her eyes glassed over.

"Yes. Are you nervous?"

I shook my head. "Nope. I'm excited though."

"Me too!" Meagan said as she jumped up and headed into the bathroom.

"I think we have time for a little more fun, if you're . . ." Glancing down to my dick, she licked her lips and purred, "Up for it."

Moving as fast as I possibly could, I joined Meagan in the shower where she successfully proved that the orange muffin was for sure a far second to an orgasm.

❦

Meagan sat on the end of the table and swung her legs as she nervously twisted her hands together.

"Wow. Did you know during labor and delivery, it's not that uncommon for the cord to get stretched or compressed, which could lead to a brief drop in the fetal heart rate?"

Meagan stared at me with a blank expression. Shrugging, I turned back to what I was reading. "Wow, induced labors are twice as likely to end in a C-section."

Meagan sighed as I kept on. "Only one in ten women's water actually breaks before labor begins."

"That's great, but what are you reading?"

"Facts about childbirth," I said to Meagan as if she should know.

"Holy shit! The heaviest baby ever born weighed twenty-two pounds!" I said with a laugh.

"You can stop reading now," Meagan said.

"Your sense of taste and smell will get sharper, but your feet are also gonna get bigger." Glancing back at her, I pouted. "Sorry, baby."

"Gray. Stop."

"Only five percent of—"

"Grayson!"

Spinning around, I looked at Meagan and boy did she look pissed. "You want me to stop reading?"

Giving me a look like I was stupid, she nodded and said, "Yes. Please!"

I wasn't sure what to do with my nervous energy. What if something was wrong with the baby? What if when that motherfucker punched Meagan in the stomach, he did damage?

Meagan was now chewing on her thumbnail and swinging her legs harder. Walking up to her, I pulled her hand from her mouth and kissed her lightly on the lips. "It's all going to be okay, baby. I promise."

"What if . . . what if when Bob . . ." Her voice cut off as she sucked in a deep breath.

"No. Don't even think that way. You heard what the

doctors said, the baby was very protected and everything seemed to be normal."

"Seemed to be are the keywords there."

The knock on the door caused us both to turn and look.

A fairly younger woman walked in holding a laptop.

"Meagan Atwood?"

"Um, yep that's me."

She turned and looked at me with a genuine smile. This must be another nurse.

"Mr. Atwood?"

With a nervous chuckle, I said, "No. Mr. Bennett, fiancé."

With a wink, she nodded and made a note on the laptop.

Looking back up, she glanced between the two of us and smiled bigger. "Let me tell you a little about me before we get started. My name is Hope Johnson. My father retired recently and I've taken over his practice. He still does consulting work for the office, but pretty much he spends his days fishing."

Meagan laughed. "He delivered every one of my best friends pretty much!"

Dr. Johnson smiled. "I hear that a lot. He was an amazing doctor and an even more amazing father."

"Wait, *you're* the doctor?" I asked.

Dr. Johnson smiled. "I sure am."

"How old are you?" I asked as Meagan pinched my arm.

Dr. Johnson chuckled. "I'm thirty-two. And I have two children of my own. My husband is a chemical engineer and we both met at the University of Texas."

She lifted her brow as if waiting for me to respond. "Wow. And you've done this before?"

"Grayson!" Meagan said.

Laughing, Dr. Johnson said, "Yes, Mr. Bennett. I've

done this lots of times."

I pulled in a deep breath and blew it out. "Sorry. I guess I'm just nervous."

Giving me a reassuring smile, she clapped her hands together and looked at Meagan. "So, now I understand that y'all currently live in Colorado, but you're moving to Texas. Have you seen a doctor there yet?"

"No," Meagan said as she reached for my hand. "I made an appointment but some things . . . well . . . they got in the way."

Dr. Johnson held up her hands and flashed a toothy grin. "No worries at all. It looks by the date of your last period, you're about ten weeks along. That would put your due date at November twelfth. That's not a firm day; it's what I like to call a best guess."

"Of course," Meagan said as she squeezed my hand.

Dr. Johnson stood and walked toward the door. Before opening it, she asked, "So, would the two of you like to see your baby?"

Chapter
THIRTY-SEVEN

Meagan

"EXACTLY HOW LONG has he carried that picture in his hand?" Taylor asked.

With a grin, I said, "Ever since the doctor handed it to him. Then when Dad held it, I thought Gray was going to start stomping his feet to get it back."

Taylor chuckled. "It is kind of sweet though how excited he is."

Lifting my eyebrows, I let out a huff. "It was a much better reaction compared to when I first told him I was pregnant."

"Oh no!" Taylor said as she started laughing harder. "Do I want to know?"

"No. You really don't."

As I rocked in the chair, I watched Grayson, my father, and Josh attempt to put together a swing set. Shaking my head, I looked at Taylor. "You don't think they're jinxing anything by putting that up do you?"

Taylor continued to watch the guys as they argued about what step was next.

"Nah, I don't think so. Besides, I've never been so entertained in my life! Plus, it doesn't hurt your future husband is hotter than hell with a body to die for. Or the fact that he took his shirt off."

Sinking my teeth down into my lip, I turned to look at Grayson. He was hot as hell; there was no doubt about that. No matter where we went, he snapped heads. And his body. Oh lord, his body. He ran every day no matter what and worked out four times a week, and his stamina was insane. I swear he could fuck me for hours and not break into a sweat.

"Dear lord, please stop thinking about whatever it is you're thinking about. Oh God. I'm gonna gag!"

Taylor made a gagging sound as she leaned over in the chair and attempted not to get sick.

"What is wrong with you?"

"You! You and your sick love and awesome sex life. Blah!"

Remembering yesterday and what Taylor had said to me on top of the hill, I turned a bit more and faced her.

"So, tell me what's going on in your life. You're almost finished with school. Are you excited about your trip this summer?"

Taylor gave me a weak smile. "I guess so."

"Talk to me Taylor, please don't hold anything in. I see it all over your face that you need to talk to someone."

Pulling in a deep breath, she pushed it out and smiled. "Do you remember when I ran into the guy from college in Durango?"

"Yes! The one you had the crush on."

"Right. Well, I'm so confused because one minute he acts like he is interested in me and then it's like I don't even exist. I saw him at a party the other night and he flat out ignored me while he drank with his buddies and ended up leaving with some girl. I didn't think it would bother me as much as it did."

"Ugh. He's one of those."

Taylor turned to me. "Those?"

"Manwhore. You see, Tay, there are a group of guys who just want to do nothing but have fun and fuck everything that walks in front of them. But at the same time, they've got their eye on the one girl who they know would never just put out. That's the girl they want to end up with."

"You think Jase is that way?"

I shrugged my shoulders. "I don't know. I mean just because he left with a girl, doesn't mean he had sex with her."

"Why does he ignore me when we're both out and at places? I mean not all places, mostly parties and when he's drinking."

My heart hurt for my sister. I was so glad I had Grayson and the games with guys were over.

"Maybe he's afraid he'll do something he regrets."

Taylor looked straight ahead as her face turned ten shades of red.

"What is it? Why are you blushing so hard?" I asked as I hit her on the arm.

Taylor looked over toward the guys and then around her shoulder to check where our mother was. "I ran into Jase one time when I was out running. He asked me to coffee, and we sat there for three hours and just talked. It was one of the best afternoons of my life."

Smiling, I reached for her hand. I could see it all over her face, she liked this guy. "Then what happened?"

Taylor looked away. "I um . . . I asked him if he wanted to come back to my place and catch a movie."

"And?" I asked with bated breath.

"He did and before I knew it we were all over each

other and he had his hand down my pants and I was . . ."

"Ew! No! Stop . . . leave out those kind of details please!"

Taylor chewed on her lip as she giggled. Rolling my eyes, I motioned for her to keep talking.

"Okay so anyway, one thing led to another and all of a sudden he stopped."

"He stopped what? Feeling on you?"

Taylor's eyes teared up. "Yes. I mean, it was getting pretty serious, and I was the one who said we needed to slow things down and he totally agreed with me but I didn't think he would just stop all together. I mean, Meg, he said such sweet things to me."

My heart hurt for my sister. I wanted her to find someone who would be her everything and she would be his. "Like?"

"Like how much he liked me and he didn't mean to lose control like that and he would never push me into something I wasn't ready for. But I think I messed up because now he doesn't want me at all."

My mouth dropped open. "You didn't mess up."

Scrunching up her face, Taylor nodded. "I did. I dropped the V word."

Peeking back out to make sure the guys were still busy, I turned back to Taylor. "What did he do?"

Taylor lifted her shoulders and gave me a confused look. "He smiled."

My head jerked back as I looked at her shocked. "Like what kind of smile?"

"I don't know, Meg. He just smiled and said that made everything so much better for when it was the right time."

"Huh. So he liked the fact that you were a virgin, which I'm still shocked that you are, but that's good Taylor. You're saving yourself for that one guy."

Taylor smirked. "Thanks I guess."

"Okay, so let me think about this. He got hot and heavy

with you and then stopped when you said you needed to go slow. Then you told him your cherry is intact. Clearly he wanted your first time to be something a little more special than on the couch in your apartment."

Rolling her eyes, Taylor hit my leg. "Ugh! Meagan!"

Laughing, I shook my head to clear my thoughts. "He hasn't talked to you since then?"

"Well, he's talked to me, and has even asked me out a few times. Then all of a sudden, he just stopped paying any attention to me at all. It's like I don't even exist anymore."

Pinching my eyebrows together, I stared at my sister. "Then fuck 'em, Tay. Don't ever let anyone treat you like that. Ever. If he can't even see what is in front of his face, then the hell with him."

"I thought so too, but then, a few weeks ago, he walked up to me and asked me how I was doing."

"Did you tell him to fuck off?"

Taylor smiled weakly. "I wanted to. I did give him the cold shoulder. He walked with me for a bit and told me he was sorry he just up and stopped talking to me."

"Was there a reason?"

"He said he felt like an asshole but that he thought it was best if he left me alone. I guess he said he ended up getting drunk at a party one night and woke up with a girl in his bed and he felt guilty as hell and that he didn't want to hurt me. I told him I wasn't under the impression we were dating, so why should he feel guilty. I feel like he just wants a girl with experience and I'm not her."

My heart broke for my sister. Reaching over, I took her hand in mine. "Taylor, that was actually a sweet thing for him to do, he just went about doing it in a totally messed up asshole kind of way. Guys are like that. They think they are doing right by you and all they are doing is being stupid jerks."

Taylor chuckled and nodded her head. "Maybe. It's

just, he makes me feel so different when I'm around him. Like he literally lights up my entire world, Meg. I've never met another guy who has done that." A tear fell from her eyes as it rolled slowly down her cheek. "But I think it's pretty clear, he's not interested in me. Even if he was, do you really think he'd wake up in bed with some girl he had sex with the night before if he liked me?"

I wanted to punch this Jase guy so hard in the face he'd lose a few teeth.

Pushing a piece of her brown hair behind her ear, I shook my head. "Tay, if a guy doesn't make you feel like you are the center of his world, he's not worth having. He should make you feel like a princess and nothing less."

"Does Gray make you feel that way?"

Pressing my lips together, I smiled and nodded my head. "Yes."

Expelling a breath, Taylor shook her head. "Well, maybe it's time I started not playing it so safe. I had this stupid silly idea I was going to save myself for that one special guy. Just think of all the sex I've lost out on!"

I shuddered and said, "Change of subject! Fast!" My face turned serious as I took my sister's hands in mine. "Taylor, don't do it. You'll know when it's right. Don't have sex just to get back at this guy."

Her lips pressed into a hard line as she nodded her head. "I won't. I promise. But he is going to Europe this summer."

"Really?" I asked as I lifted my eyebrows. "That should be interesting."

Taylor attempted to smile, but I saw how conflicted she was. "Tay, if it's meant to be, it will happen. In the mean time, don't wait around for this guy."

She nodded her head and looked back out at the guys. "So . . . how long before Dad and Josh start arguing about whose way is better?"

With a chuckle, I said, "Thirty minutes top."

We spent the next hour laughing and talking about our future as we watched our father and Josh nearly get into a fist fight about which way the slide went on.

Yep. This was the life I wanted. The life I needed.

～❦～

"Meagan? Is everything okay?"

Spinning around, I smiled when I saw Ashley. Grayson's mother had been so supportive of our decision to move to Texas and the guilt was beginning to eat away at me.

"Hey," I whispered as I tried to find my voice. I wasn't sure if it was the pregnancy or a combination of everything that had happened to me over the last two months that was making me so emotional.

With a wave of my hand and a terrible fake laugh, I said, "I'm fine."

Ashley walked out to the edge of her deck and stared straight ahead at the snowcapped mountains. "It's so hard to believe it's June. Where has the time gone?"

I slowly shook my head, but didn't answer. When we came back to Colorado, I'd given Melissa my notice. Grayson did the same. Melissa had asked for a months' notice to be able to find someone and then for me sit with the new person and go over each case I had, to which I agreed. Grayson's boss was stunned he was leaving, but put in an excellent recommendation for him with a friend of his who worked for the Texas Department of Public Safety. Grayson had flown back to Texas and interviewed for two days. He passed their tests with flying colors and so far had been offered two jobs. He was going to make his decision today, and I was on pins and needles to see which job he would accept.

I was offered a position with the high school in Mason, but they didn't need anyone until the next school year.

It worked out perfect. I'd be able to have the baby and spend time at home before I headed back to work.

"Are you upset that we're moving? I feel like I'm taking your son away from you and to be honest, it's tearing me up inside."

Ashley's face dropped. Taking my hands in hers, she gave me the warmest smile. "Meagan, I'm not upset at all. Gray called me from Texas about a week after he took you there and told me what he wanted to do. Sweetheart, I can come visit you any time."

"But what about the baby?"

Her eyes turned sad for one moment before she squeezed my hands. "Oh, James and I plan on coming and staying with you after the baby is born, and I know we can come anytime to see you. Meagan, my sweet, sweet girl." Placing her hand on the side of my face, I could practically feel her love. "You make my son so happy and that is all that matters to me. I don't care if that takes him to Alaska and beyond. As long as he is happy." She looked down and cleared her throat before looking back up into my eyes. "Gray told me what happened when he first found out you were pregnant. It still bothers him so much."

I shook my head. "No, it shouldn't. It wasn't like we had planned this pregnancy." My hand went to my stomach automatically. I was four months pregnant and barely had a tiny bump.

Her eyes turned soft as she glanced down to my hand. "I know, but I can only imagine the fear that was in him. I know it hurt him so much when his father left him. But also know that because of that, Gray is going to be the best father ever."

Nodding my head, I softly said, "I agree."

Ashley chortled and wiped her tears away. "Goodness. Let's stop all this silly emotional stuff and get back in there. This is your last night in Colorado and I want to celebrate!"

"Agreed! I'm going to get drunk on apple juice!"

Ashley laced her arm around mine as we made our way back into the house. The rest of the evening was spent playing games, laughing, and looking at baby pictures of Grayson. It ended with lots of hugs and kisses.

By the time we got back to our apartment, we were both exhausted. The only thing left in the apartment was our suitcases and the bed. Grayson and I had donated everything to a battered women's shelter. Derrick was coming by tomorrow to get the bed and bring it to the shelter.

After taking a shower, I stared at myself in the mirror. My stomach fluttered when I saw the baby bump that seemed to have popped out somewhere during the day.

"Gray! Come quick!"

Grayson ran so fast into the bathroom he almost bit it and fell. "What? What's wrong?"

Giving him a grin, I stood sideways and ran my hand over the little bump. "Look!"

Grayson literally gasped out loud like a girl, which caused me to laugh. Heat surged through my body as Grayson dropped to his knees in front of me.

"Our baby," he whispered as his hands moved across the small bump.

Oh. My. Stars.

This man is so utterly romantic and he doesn't even know it!

"Hey, little peanut. You decided to make your presence known, huh?"

Grayson's eyes lifted to mine. "Can you feel her moving yet?"

I swallowed hard. He said . . . her. He said her! He said her!

My heart dropped as I shook my head. "Not yet. My mom said it will feel almost like a little rumble of gas or feel like butterflies."

Glancing back down to my stomach, Grayson started

kissing all over my stomach. Before I knew what was happening, I was lying in bed and softly calling out his name as I lost myself to his lovemaking.

Grayson whispered my name as he poured himself into me. "Thank you, Meg. Thank you for loving me."

My fingers moved lightly across his skin as I let this moment settle into my heart. "Grayson," was all I could say as my emotions took ahold of my throat.

Before he rolled off of me, he looked into my eyes. "I made a decision about the job."

My happy feeling quickly vanished. I loved that Grayson loved being a cop, but after my whole kidnapping incident and the baby, I now lived in constant fear something would happen to him.

Trying to keep my voice neutral sounding, I asked, "What did you decide?"

When he leaned down and whispered it in my ear, a single tear slowly made its way down my cheek while I wrapped my arms tightly around him.

Chapter
THIRTY-EIGHT

Grayson
Late October

STANDING IN FRONT of the house, I rubbed the back of my neck to relieve the tension.

"Looks good," Noah said from beside me.

My eyes traveled over the two-story house as I agreed by simply nodding my head. I wasn't sure how we did it, but we got the house built and finished in time.

Letting out a sigh, I said, "If I wasn't so tired, I'd jump up and down for joy."

Leaning down, I opened up the cooler and reached in for a beer and a soda. Handing it to Noah, I laughed. "Here, drink this and you'll feel better."

Noah grabbed the soda and damn near drank it in one gulp.

"Is little Hope keeping you up still?"

Noah's eyes lit up. Any mention of his almost

three-month-old daughter, Hope Alaina, and he was fly-ing high. Grace had given birth to Hope on August second with everyone waiting patiently in the waiting room. This little family was growing bigger by the day.

"She was sleeping through the night, but the last two she's been waking up in the middle of the night. Grace is so busy with Homecoming mums that I've let her sleep and I've gotten up with Hope."

With a crooked smile, I shook my head. "That must be such hell for you."

Noah laughed. "Dude, I cannot wait for you to experi-ence this. I can't even put fatherhood into words. I'd never be able to describe how amazing it is."

"Thinking more?"

Noah tipped the soda back and finished it off. Dropping the empty can into the bag, he shook his head. "I don't think so. Grace and I talked about it; we kind of like having just the three of us. Besides, she has so many cousins, it's unreal!"

Throwing my head back, I laughed. "She sure does."

We stared at the house for another few minutes be-fore I blew out a breath and started making my way to the front door.

"Meagan is going to love it, Gray," Noah said as we walked into the foyer. Straight ahead was a staircase that winded up to the second floor. To the left was a for-mal living room, and to the right was my office. I'd tak-en a job with the Texas Department of Public Safety as a training coordinator at their tactical training center in Fredericksburg. My job was to train all incoming recruits both mentally and physically. Each recruit school lasted about twenty-six weeks. I loved my new job. And, Meagan had peace of mind I wasn't in any danger to get shot at every single day when I walked out the door.

Walking down the hall, we went into the formal din-ing room that opened right up into the massive kitchen.

The open floor plan had the breakfast area on the other side of the kitchen with a huge family room that would be perfect for having family over. The massive sandstone fireplace was the main focal point of the room.

The master bedroom was downstairs, along with a huge master bath. I had decided to add a fireplace that could be seen in both the bedroom as well as the bathroom. Meagan had loved the idea. Upstairs were three bedrooms, a playroom, and a media room I threw in at the last minute above the garage. Meagan hadn't really been able to see the house that much since she had been put on bed rest shortly after Grace had Hope. She hadn't seen it at all the last month. When she started having early contractions, the doctor thought it best for her to take it easy the rest of the pregnancy.

Noah walked out onto the massive deck that overlooked the hill country. The Llano River flowed peacefully through the canyon. "You tell Meg about the media room yet?"

"Nope."

Shaking his head, Noah sighed. "She is going to be so pissed at you."

I let out a chuckle as I blew out a sigh of relief. "I'm just so glad it was all done before Meg's due date. Although I have to say, I am going to miss our little rental house." A memory quickly popped into my mind as Noah and I stood there looking out over the hill country.

"I kind of like this little house," Meagan said with a crinkled nose.

Hitting play, I replied, "It's cute."

Meagan dropped down onto the sofa and said, "Don't get me wrong, I want our house and I'm so glad we started it when we did. I just pray it gets finished by mid-October."

I nodded. "Yep, me too."

We had rented a little three-bedroom house in

301

Fredericksburg and all Meagan ever said was how much she loved how cozy it felt.

Reaching over, Meagan grabbed some popcorn and went to put it in my mouth when she cried out.

"Oh. My. God."

Pausing the movie, I sighed and then shoved popcorn in my mouth. "Hurry up and go to the bathroom . . . again . . . so we can get the movie started. I need to be in at work early tomorrow."

Meagan squealed in delight.

She grabbed my hand and put it on her belly "The baby! She moved!"

"What?" I shouted as I jumped up and popcorn went flying everywhere.

I placed both hands on her belly and started talking to the baby. "Hey sweet girl, kick for Daddy. Please kick for Daddy."

We both jumped when the baby kicked. "Oh my God! I felt her! I felt her!"

Meagan giggled and pushed on the side of her stomach to see if she would do it again.

Nothing.

"Talk to her again. I think she likes your voice," Meagan said softly.

"Sweet baby girl, move for Daddy."

Another hard kick caused my eyes to fill with tears. "She's moving for me."

Glancing up, Meagan was smiling so big as we spent the next five minutes feeling our child kick.

When she finally stopped the show, I looked into Meagan's eyes with a stunned expression. "We're going to have a baby. She's moving around in there." I pointed to her belly and said, "Our baby is in there. Growing! Kicking! Hearing my voice!"

"I know!" Meagan replied as she covered her mouth to hold back her laughter.

"I know a way to make her move," I said as I took her hands and led her to our bedroom.

"What are you doing?"

"Sex! Noah said it makes the baby move more."

Meagan stopped walking and dropped her mouth open. "So you're going to use me for sex so you can feel the baby move?"

I gave her a look like she had just said the stupidest thing in the world. "Well yeah. It's like win-win for me."

Giving me a sexy smirk, Meagan replied, "If I wasn't so damn horny all the time I'd tell you to get lost."

I got lost in not one orgasm, but three. And each time, our daughter jumped all over the place. Much to my delight, I felt our child moving around as I made love to my wife.

My cell phone rang in my pocket as I pulled it out. "It's Taylor. She came home for the weekend and has been spoiling the hell out of Meagan."

Noah laughed as he started down the back steps.

"Hey, Tay, what does my beautiful fiancée want now?"

Meagan and I had decided to get married at the house once everything was completed. It only made sense, especially when she ended up being on bed rest. Plus we wouldn't be able to take the honeymoon I wanted to take her on until my first round of recruit school was over.

"Where are you, Gray?"

"At the house. Noah and I were just walking through before moving day tomorrow. I'm sure Meg wants to get into our own place."

"Yeah well, moving day is gonna have to wait."

My heart sunk. "Why? What's wrong?"

"Meagan is in labor."

We knew there was a risk of her going into labor early, and honestly I was surprised she made it as long as she did. Her due date was still two weeks away.

"We're on the way to the hospital."

"What? You can't wait for me to get there?"

Taylor said something to her mother before she came back on the phone. "Um, you're an hour away, Gray. Her contractions are coming fast."

"How long as she been having them?"

"She said for the last few hours but she wasn't sure at first if it was false labor or not."

Fuck!

Taking off running toward my truck, I yelled out to Noah. "Noah! She's in labor! I'm on my way, Taylor. I'll meet you guys at the hospital!"

"Wait, Meg wants to talk to you."

I heard a bunch of noises before I heard her beautiful voice come across the phone. "Hey," was all she said.

"Hey, baby. You doing okay?"

"Well . . . it's time I guess, so yeah. I'm doing good."

Throwing my truck into drive, I hit the gas and peeled out down the driveway.

"Don't be scared, baby. I'm on my way."

"Are you spooked?"

With a smile, I shook my head. "If haven't been yet, I doubt I'm going to anytime soon."

I could hear Amanda barking orders about helping Meagan walk to the car.

Her voice cracked as she said, "I'm huge, Gray. I look like a whale."

"No. I don't think I've ever seen you look so beautiful. I may have to keep you pregnant all the time because you look so beautiful."

"The hell with that. I'm done. This is it. If you want more kids, you're going to have to find a willing woman to carry them and birth them. This girl is done! And the hard part hasn't even started yet."

Noah let out a chuckle as he listed to Meagan over the truck speakers. "Meg, I'm on my way. I swear to you, it's all going to be okay."

"O-okay. Hey, Gray?"

"Yeah?"

"Mom won't stop so, will you run and pick me up some orange muffins on your way to the hospital?"

Pressing my lips together to keep from laughing, I simply said, "Sure I will."

"K. Got. To. Go. Contraction . . . oh . . . hee hee hee hee—"

"Meg? Taylor? Taylor! Shit, the line went dead."

Pressing down on the gas, I raced to Fredericksburg as fast as I could.

❧

I jumped back into my truck and quickly pulled out and headed to the hospital. "I seriously cannot believe you stopped to get orange muffins when your wife is in labor! What in the hell is wrong with you?"

Widening my eyes, I gave Noah a dazed look. "Have you ever had those damn things? They are amazing!"

Noah shook his head as he stared at me for a few seconds as we headed to the hospital.

"Just pull up and I'll park."

"Right! Good thinking."

Coming to a stop in front of the hospital, I jumped out of the truck, only to have Noah call out my name.

"Gray! Shit dude, it's still in drive!"

The truck was rolling forward and headed toward another car. "Shit!" Jumping in, I threw it into Park. "Did you call Grace?"

Noah looked at me like I was insane. "Did I act this way when Grace went into labor? Please tell me I didn't cause I really want to punch you in the face right now."

Giving him a dirty look, I shot him the finger and said, "Fuck you."

Racing in through the doors, I jogged up to the front desk to the sweet little old ladies who volunteer. My heart was racing and all I wanted to do was get to Meagan.

"Where is the fire, darlin'?"

With a polite smile, I looked between both women. "My wife. She's gone into labor. It's the third floor right?"

"For babies?"

My head pulled back as I looked at them with a baffled look on my face. "No, I'm not looking for the babies. I need to get to Labor and Delivery."

Shit. Why was I standing here talking to them? We did the tour! I took the tour. The Labor and Delivery was on the second floor.

Taking off, I ran past a few people and headed to the elevators. "Excuse me, oh, sorry! Coming through!"

Hitting the Up button, I stood there and willed the damn thing to move faster.

"You know, I broke my leg trying to get to my wife when she was in labor."

My eyes looked over to an older man standing next me. He had a cane and looked straight ahead as he spoke. "Boy howdy was my wife mad at me. You know how hard it is to take care of a new baby when you've got yourself a broken leg?"

My stomach was in knots as I turned to him. "No sir, I can't even imagine."

His eyes met mine. "It's hard, son. Very hard. So stop acting like the world is ending and get to her in one piece. You ain't gonna be any use to her with a broken leg."

I couldn't help but smile. Nodding, I said, "Yes, sir. No more running."

When the elevator door opened, the old man walked in first after I motioned for him to. Hitting the second floor first, he then hit the fourth.

We rode in silence before it dinged for my floor, before getting off the elevator, he took a hold of my arm.

"Be sure to have flowers for her. And make sure you tell her how beautiful she is. There is nothing more magical than the woman you love birthin' your baby."

My heart warmed as I looked into the eyes of the older man. "I'll be sure to do just that. Thank you, sir, for the tips."

He beamed back at me as he nodded and let go of my arm. "Enjoy it. Your life is about to change."

The doors shut and I stood there for a few moments letting his words settle in. I'd never felt so happy in my entire life as I turned and made my way to my new life.

Chapter
THIRTY-NINE

Meagan

THE MOMENT HE walked into the room, the energy changed. With a smile so breathtaking, I would have fallen to my knees had I been standing up. "Hey," I barely said as tears flowed freely from my eyes.

Quickly wiping them away, I let out a frustrated cry and shook my head. "I'm so damn sick of crying!"

Sobs shook my body as Grayson quickly kissed me. "You look beautiful."

My lower lip jetted out in a pout as I said, "I don't feel it. I don't think I can do this."

Cupping my face in his hands, Grayson looked into my eyes. "Listen to me. You are the strongest person I know. You've been through hell with this pregnancy, Meg. Hell, this whole year!"

My hands covered his. "No! This has been the best year of my life. Look at us. We have a house and our world is about to be forever altered." Lifting a brow, I asked, "You're not spooked?"

Grayson chuckled. "Not in the least bit."

My heart felt as if it was going to burst.

"Come on, Meagan. One more push and you're done!"

Exhaustion swept over my body as I leaned into Grayson. "I can't do this. I'm so tired."

Grayson kissed my forehead and held onto my hand. "Baby, one more push, do it for me."

Looking at him, I shot him a dirty look. "Do it for you? Do it . . . for you? You got me in this position in the first place! You do it if you think it's so easy . . . oh God another contraction!"

"Push now, Meagan. One good push sweetie and you're done," Dr. Johnson said.

Leaning forward, I pulled every ounce of energy I had to push again. The sounds of crying filled the air as I collapsed back against the bed.

Grayson's face was covered in tears. Turning to me, he cupped my face and kissed me so passionately, I couldn't help but let out a little whimper.

"You did it! And you looked beautiful the whole time."

I let out a chuckle as I watched the nurses moving about. Grayson's eyes followed mine as he took everything in. "Holy crap. I think God's paying me back for my previous profession."

Laughing, I shook my head at Grayson. "I think so, stripper boy!"

Two nurses walked up on either side of me as they placed a baby in each of my arms. Grayson leaned over and kissed the baby in my right arm first.

"Welcome to the world, my precious Arabella Marie Bennett."

Pulling back, he kissed the baby in my left arm. "Welcome to the world, my sweet Charlotte Christine Bennett."

His eyes lifted as they captured mine. "Are you happy?" I asked.

Nothing but loved filled his eyes as he slowly shook his head.

"I've never been so happy in my entire life." Glancing down to our two baby girls, Grayson's chin trembled as he fought to hold back his tears. "I promise you, I will forever love and protect you, and I will *never* leave my three beautiful girls."

I was quickly brought back to the moment our lives were forever changed.

Dr. Johnson placed the warm gel on my stomach and smiled. "Let's take a look at your baby shall we?"

I was bubbling over with excitement as Grayson squeezed my hand as I glanced at my mother and Ashley standing behind Grayson. Ashley and James had flown in to meet my parents and she was thrilled when we asked her and my mother to come today.

Turning, I stared back at the monitor as I heard a heartbeat. Then another heartbeat. Then I saw one little heart beating super fast. Then another little heart beating super fast.

"Is that?" Grayson asked as he leaned closer.

My eyes widened as I let out a gasp.

Dr. Johnson giggled. "I thought I heard two heartbeats." Turning to look at us, she flashed a huge smile. "Looks like y'all need to buy two of everything."

Ashley, my mother, Grayson and I all said at once. "Twins?"

My mother and Ashley instantly started crying as they hugged each other. I peeked back as I watched Grayson while he stared at the monitor. I couldn't believe the smile on his face. His blue eyes turned to look into mine.

"Tell me what you're thinking."

Grayson chuckled as he bent over and kissed my lips.

Pulling back slightly, he said, "I'm thinking I'm so glad I let Gunner talk us into three bedrooms upstairs instead of two!"

"Some crazy couple of years, huh?" I said as Grayson placed his hand on the side of my face.

With a wink and a crooked smile that left me breathless, he rubbed his thumb across my lips. "I have a feeling it's only gonna get crazier."

EPILOGUE

Taylor

WALKING OUT OF the hospital, my phone buzzed. Glancing down at it, I saw it was Jase.

I wasn't sure if I should be excited or angry he was calling me. At least I knew that meant he was thinking about me. Everything changed between us when we were in Europe last summer. Jase made his choice and now we both had to live with it.

By the time I got to my car, my phone notified me of a text.

> *Jase: Hey! I just got back from Montana. How is your sister?*

I dropped my head back against the seat and let out a frustrated sigh. I was tired of playing games. I'd officially had enough.

Pulling up his name, I hit Jase's number.

"Taylor," he said, almost sounding relieved.

"I can't do this. Not anymore."

The silence that loomed between us killed me.

"Taylor, I'm so sorry I . . ."

"Just stop. If you don't want me, Jase, then that's fine,

I get it. But this whole thing with you pretending to be my best friend is not working anymore. I told you I loved you in Europe and you made your decision. I'm not a damn toy you can push and pull whenever you feel like it. So you don't have some hot, blonde bitch on your arm right now . . . well too bad. I'm not playing second anymore."

"You were never second, Taylor. Ever! That's the problem."

Tears threatened to build in my eyes, but I quickly pushed them away.

"Stop talking in riddles, Jase. Now is not a good time to talk. I have a date I need to go home and get ready for."

"A date? With who?"

A smirk appeared across my face. I could almost hear the panic in his voice and I loved it. I also hated myself for feeling that way.

"My sister had her twins," I spattered out to change the subject I had brought up.

"She did!" Excitement filled his voice and for one moment, I wanted to pretend everything was okay. I wanted to pretend Jase really meant it last summer when he whispered in my ear that he loved me. I wanted to pretend he didn't walk away from me the morning after I gave myself to him in Paris. I wanted to pretend the girl I saw him with that afternoon never existed.

My stomach twisted as the pain of that day returned and punched me right in the chest.

"I um . . . I have to go."

"Taylor?"

My eyes squeezed shut because I knew what was coming. "Yeah?"

"I love you."

Slamming my hand over my mouth, I held my sobs in.

"I have to go, Jase."

Hitting End, I dropped my phone into my lap and let myself cry until I didn't have the energy to cry anymore.

꧁

Look for Taylor and Jase's story April 2016

Loving You will finish out both the Love Wanted in Texas Series and the Broken Series. It will be a bittersweet end to both series, but a journey I can't wait to share with y'all.

PLAYLIST

Danielle Bradbery ~ "Friend Zone"
Meagan and Grayson spending the day
together as friends only

Tori Kelly ~ "First Heartbreak"
Meagan telling Grayson she has feelings
for him and how that scares her

Major Lazer & Ellie Goulding ~ "Powerful"
Grayson dancing for Meagan at the benefit

Hunter Hayes ~ "Invisible"
Meagan telling Grayson about Claire
bullying her in college

Beyoncé ~ " Dance For You"
Meagan dancing for Grayson

Rascal Flatts ~ "Fall Here"
Grayson and Meagan admitting their
feelings for one another

Rascal Flatts ~ "Why"
Meagan finding out what happened to Mitchell

Carrie Underwood ~ "Heartbeat"
Grayson and Meagan talking about moving to Texas

Luke Bryan ~ "Fast"
Grayson and Noah at the new house

Thomas Rhett ~ "Die A Happy Man"
Grayson when the twins are born

Colbie Caillat ~"Never Getting Over You"
Epilogue

THANK YOU

THANK YOU TO everyone who plays a part in helping me do what I do to get each book out. Without your help, I'm not sure what I would do!

Thank you to Nichole and Christine with Perfectly Publishable. The both of you make me smile, put up with my constant changing schedule, not to mention my numerous moments of . . ."Wait, what am I supposed to be doing?" The two of you are the best.

Thank you to Lauren Abramo with Dystel & Goderich for working tirelessly to get the Love Wanted in Texas Series sold to a UK publisher!

Thank you to Kristin Mayer for being such an amazing friend. I'd be lost without you. Love you Special K.

Thank you to Laura, Nikki, and Ana for helping with beta reading. You're the best!

Darrin and Lauren. Thank you for putting up with my crazy schedule, my mad personalities that change depending on where I'm at in the writing process, and the endless amount of nights I don't have dinner cooked. You both mean so much to me and I love y'all to the moon and back.

LOVE READING ROMANCE?

Fall in love with
piatkus

Entice

Temptation at your fingertips

An irresistible eBook-first list from
the pioneers of romantic fiction at
www.piatkusentice.co.uk

To receive the latest news,
reviews & competitions direct to your inbox,
sign up to our romance newsletter at
www.piatkusbooks.net/newsletters

Do you love fiction with a supernatural twist?

Want the chance to hear news about your favourite
authors (and the chance to win free books)?

Keri Arthur
Kristen Callihan
P.C. Cast
Christine Feehan
Jacquelyn Frank
Larissa Ione
Darynda Jones
Sherrilyn Kenyon
Jayne Ann Krentz and Jayne Castle
Lucy March
Martin Millar
Tim O'Rourke
Lindsey Piper
Christopher Rice
J.R. Ward
Laura Wright

Then visit the Piatkus website and blog
www.piatkus.co.uk | www.piatkusbooks.net

And follow us on Facebook and Twitter
www.facebook.com/piatkusfiction | www.twitter.com/piatkusbooks

piatkus

Do you love historical fiction?

Want the chance to hear news about your favourite authors (and the chance to win free books)?

Mary Balogh

Charlotte Betts

Jessica Blair

Frances Brody

Gaelen Foley

Elizabeth Hoyt

Eloisa James

Lisa Kleypas

Stephanie Laurens

Claire Lorrimer

Sarah MacLean

Amanda Quick

Julia Quinn

Then visit the Piatkus website and blog
www.piatkus.co.uk | www.piatkusbooks.net

And follow us on Facebook and Twitter
www.facebook.com/piatkusfiction | www.twitter.com/piatkusbooks

piatkus